MARY
ROBERTS RINEHART
THE TOP SUSPENSE WRITER
OF ALL TIME
PRESENTS
A SPINE-TINGLING STORY
OF MURDER AND MYSTERY IN

the yellow
room

the yellow room

room A DELL MYSTERY
BY MARY ROBERTS RINEHART

Published by
DELL PUBLISHING CO., INC.
750 Third Avenue, New York 17, N.Y.

© Copyright, 1945, by Mary Roberts Rinehart

© Copyright, 1945, by The Curtis Publishing Co., Inc.

Dell ® TM 681510, Dell Publishing Co., Inc.

Reprinted by arrangement with
Holt, Rinehart & Winston, Inc., New York, N.Y.

Previous Dell Edition #D179

New Dell Edition
First printing—October, 1962

Printed in U.S.A.

ONE

As she sat in the train that June morning Carol Spencer did not look like a young woman facing anything unusual. She looked merely like an attractive and highly finished product of New York City, who was about to park her mother with her elder sister in Newport for a week or two, and who after said parking would then proceed to Maine, there to open a house which she had never wanted to see again.

Now she was trying to relax. Mrs. Spencer in the next chair was lying back with her eyes closed, as though exhausted. As she had done nothing but get herself into a taxi and out again, Carol felt not unnaturally resentful. Her own arms were still aching from carrying the bags and her brother Greg's golf clubs, which her mother had insisted on bringing.

"I wonder if I ought to take some digitalis," Mrs. Spencer said, without opening her eyes. "I feel rather faint."

"Not unless you have it with you," Carol said. "The other bags are piled at the end of the car, with about a ton of others."

Mrs. Spencer decided that a glass of water would answer, and Carol brought a paper cup of it, trying not to spill it as the car swayed. She did not return the cup. She crumpled it up and put it on the window sill. Her mother raised a pair of finely arched eyebrows in disapproval, and lay back again without comment. Carol eyed her, the handsome profile, the fretful mouth, the carefully tailored clothes, and the leather jewel case in her lap. Since George Spencer's death she had become a peevish semi-invalid, and Carol at twenty-four, her hopes killed by the war, found herself in the position of the unmarried daughter, left more or less to wither on the maternal stem. And now this idiotic idea of reopening the house at Bayside—

She stirred uneasily. She did not want to go back. What she wanted was to join the Wacs or the Waves or be a Nurse's Aide.

She was young and strong. She could be useful somewhere. But the mere mention of such activity was enough to bring on what her mother called a heart attack. So here she was, with the newspapers in her lap still filled with the invasion a week before, and Greg's golf clubs digging into her legs. She kicked them away impatiently.

She had not come without protest, of course.

"Why Maine?" she had said. "Greg would much rather be in New York, or with Elinor at Newport. He'll want to be near Virginia. After all, he's engaged to her."

But Mrs. Spencer had set her chin, which was a determined one.

"Virginia can easily come up to Maine," she said. "After that jungle heat Greg needs bracing air. I do think you should be willing to do what you can after what he's been through."

Carol had agreed, although when she called Elinor in Newport her sister had said it was crazy.

"It's completely idiotic," she said. "That huge place and only three servants! Do show some sense, Carol."

"You don't have to live with Mother."

"No, thank God," said Elinor, and rang off after her abrupt fashion without saying good-bye. Elinor was like that.

Carol thought it over, as the train rumbled on. Of course she wanted to do what she could for Greg. After all, he deserved it. At thirty-four—he had been flying his own plane for years—he had become a captain and an ace in the South Pacific. Now he was home on a thirty-day furlough, and was about to be decorated by the President himself. But she was still edgy after the scene at Grand Central, the crowds of people, the masses of uniformed men, the noise and confusion, and the lack of porters.

Her mind, escaping the war, ranged over what had been done and what there was to do. The three servants, all they had left and all women, were finishing the Park Avenue apartment, sprinkling the carpets with moth flakes and covering the lamp shades against the city soot. Carol herself had worked feverishly. With no men to be had she had taken down the heavy hangings and done the meticulous packing away which had always preceded the summer hegira, and as if Mrs. Spencer had read her mind she opened her eyes and spoke.

"Did you ship the motor rugs?" she demanded.

"Yes. They're all right."

"And my furs went to storage?"

"You know they did, mother. I gave you the receipt."

"What about Gregory's clothes?"

"He'll be in uniform, you know. He had left some slacks and sweaters at Crestview. I saw them last year."

The conversation lapsed. Mrs. Spencer dozed, her mouth slightly open, and Carol fought again the uneasiness she had felt ever since the plan had been broached. It had of course to do with Colonel Richardson. Even after more than a year he had never accepted Don's death. It was not normal, of course. All last summer he had come up the hill to see her and to sit watching her with anxious eyes.

"Don will have my cottage some day, Carol. You'll find it very comfortable. I've put in a new oil burner."

She put the thought away and began going over what was to be done. This was Thursday, June fifteenth, 1944. She was to stay at Elinor's in Newport until Sunday. Then, leaving her mother there for a few days, she would meet the three servants in Boston on Sunday and take the night train to Maine. Nothing would be ready, of course. The plan had been too sudden. She had wired Lucy Norton, the caretaker's wife, to drive over and open the house for them. But the place was large. Unless Lucy could get help— She knew that was improbable and abandoned the idea. The grounds too would be hopeless. Only George Smith remained of the gardeners, and as they had not meant to open the house he would hardly have had time to cut the grass.

The usual problems buzzed through her head. George had always refused to care for the coal furnace, or carry coal to the enormous kitchen range. Maybe Maggie would do this herself. She had been with them as cook for twenty years, and she was strong and willing. But the other two were young. She wondered if she could take them to the movies in the village now and then, and so keep them. Only there would be little or no gasoline.

She sighed.

The train went on. It was crowded, and it was hot. A boiling June sun shone through the windows, setting men to mopping their faces and giving to all the passengers a look of resignation that was almost despair. The only cheerful people were the men in uniform, roaming through the car on mysterious errands of their own and eying Carol as they did so.

She tried not to think about them and what they were facing. She went back determinedly to Bayside and the situation there. The heat had started early, so at least a part of the summer colony would have arrived. There had been no time to announce their coming, so she would have a day or two at least. But Colonel Richardson would know. He lived at the bottom of their hill, and he was always in his garden or sitting patiently on his porch watching for the postman.

She felt a little sick when she remembered that. All last summer, and the colonel saying: "When Don comes back." Or: "Don likes the peonies, so I'm keeping them." Puttering around his garden with a determined smile and haggard eyes, and Carol's heart aching for him, rather than for Don. For most of the pain had gone now, although she still wore Don's ring. They had been engaged since she was eighteen and he was twenty, but he had no money, so they had simply waited. Now he was gone. He had crashed in the South Pacific. There was no question about that. The other men of his squadron had seen his fighter go down, and his death had been officially recognized.

Mrs. Spencer opened her eyes.

"I left the Lowestoft tea set at Crestview, didn't I?" she inquired.

"Yes, mother. You were afraid to have it shipped. It's in the pantry."

This promising to reopen a long discussion of what had or had not been left in Maine the year before, Carol took refuge in the women's lavatory. There she lit a cigarette and surveyed herself in the mirror. What she saw was an attractive face, rather smudged at the moment, a pair of candid gray eyes, heavily lashed, and a wide humorous mouth which had somehow lost its gaiety.

"Watch out, my girl," she said to it. "You're beginning to

look like the family spinster."

She took off her gloves and used her lipstick. She had broken two fingernails getting ready to move, and she eyed them
resentfully. Elinor would spot them at once, she thought.
Elinor who was the family beauty, Elinor who had married
what was wealth even in these days of heavy taxes, and Elinor
who had definitely refused to look after her mother so that
Carol could go into some sort of war work.

"One of us would end in a padded cell," had been Elinor's
sharp comment. "And Howard would simply go and live at his
club. You know Howard."

Yes, Carol reflected, she knew Howard, big and pompous
and proud, of his money, of his houses at Palm Beach and
Newport, his lodge in South Carolina for quail shooting, his
vast apartment in New York, his dinner parties, his name in the
Social Register, and of course of his wife. Carol had often
wondered whether he loved Elinor, or whether he merely dis-
played her, as another evidence of his success.

She powdered her damp face and felt more able to face her
sister and her entourage. But although the Hilliard limousine
met them at Providence, Elinor was not in it. Nor was she
at the house when they finally reached it. There were no longer
three men in the hall, but the elderly butler was still there. He
seemed puzzled.

"I'm sorry," he explained. "Mrs. Hilliard expected to be
here. She took her own car and went out some time ago. She—
I think she had a long-distance call. Probably from Captain
Spencer."

"I can see no reason why that should take her out of her
house," said Mrs. Spencer coldly. "Very well, Caswell. We
will go to our rooms."

Carol followed her mother. The house always chilled her.
It was on too large a scale. And she was puzzled about Elinor,
too. Whatever her failings, she kept her appointments. It was
part of her social creed. Mrs. Spencer, however, was merely
exasperated.

"I have learned not to expect much from my children," she
said, "but when I come here so seldom—"

"She'll turn up, mother," Carol said pacifically. "She always does, you know."

But it was a long time before Elinor, so to speak, turned up. She was even in the house almost an hour before they saw her at all. Carol, standing at the window, saw her drive in in the gay foreign car she affected, and smiled at her mother.

"She's here," she said. "Brace yourself, darling."

Only Elinor did not come. Mrs. Spencer's reproaches died on her lips. Her air of dignified injury began to weaken. And when at last the prodigal did appear there was obviously something wrong. Not that she did not give an excellent performance.

"Sorry, my dears," she said in her light voice. "Some awful man here about the blackout. Have you had lunch?"

"We had trays up here," her mother said, the injury returning. "I do think, Elinor—"

But Elinor was not listening. She glanced around the luxurious apartment, a boudoir and two bedrooms, and jerking off her hat, ran a hand over her shining blond hair. Carol, watching her and still puzzled, wondered how she had kept her beauty. Thirty-two, she thought, and she doesn't look as old as I do. Or does she? Certainly Elinor was looking tired and harassed, and perhaps—if such a thing were possible—rather frightened.

"I hope you will be comfortable," she was saying. "It's the most awful rotten luck, but I have to go to New York tomorrow. In this heat too. Isn't it dreadful?"

Mrs. Spencer stared at her.

"I do think, Elinor—" she began again.

"I know, my dear," Elinor said. "It's sickening. But I have to go. We're giving a dinner next week, and my dress has to be fitted on Saturday. I had to have one. I'm in rags."

Carol smiled faintly. Elinor in rags, with a dressing room lined with closets filled with exquisite clothes, was not even a figure of speech.

"Where will you stay?" she asked. "Your apartment's closed, isn't it? I thought Howard was at his club."

"I'll find some place," Elinor said, still airily. "Maybe the Colony Club. Howard's not coming out this weekend. He's playing golf on Saturday at Piping Rock."

Mrs. Spencer had lapsed into indignant silence. Elinor did not look at her. She was really not looking at anyone.

"I have a shocking headache," she said, putting her hand with its huge square-cut diamond to her head. "Do you mind if I lie down for a while? Do what you like, of course."

"Just what would you propose," Carol said, amused. "I can curl up with a book, but what about mother?"

Once more, however, she realized that her words had not penetrated Elinor's mind. Behind her lovely face something was happening. It was as if her speech was following a pattern, already cut and prepared when she entered the room.

"Dinner's at eight," she said abruptly. "I'll see you then."

"I do think——" Mrs. Spencer began again. But Elinor had already gone, the door closing behind her. In spite of her bewilderment Carol laughed. Then, feeling repentant, she went over and kissed her mother's cheek.

"Well, we're here," she said cheerfully. "Don't bother about Elinor. Maybe she has something on her mind."

Mrs. Spencer caught her arm almost wildly.

"Carol, do you think Howard is being unfaithful?"

"He may have a pretty lady somewhere," Carol said. "But Elinor wouldn't mind, of course, unless it got out."

This picture of modern marriage proving too much for her, Mrs. Spencer closed her eyes.

"I think I'll have some digitalis," she said faintly.

Elinor left the next day, looking as though she had not slept, and piling her car with the numberless bags without which she never moved. She had not appeared at dinner the night before, sending word she still had a headache, and as she left shortly after lunch her mother's grievance continued.

Elinor's plan, it appeared, was to drive herself to Providence, leave her car there and take a train to New York.

"That leaves the limousine for you," she explained. "You can use it all you like. Howard laid in plenty of gas."

Mrs. Spencer said nothing resentfully, but Elinor did not notice. She talked on feverishly during lunch: Greg's citation, the probability of his marriage to Virginia Demarest before he went back, the dress for which she was to be fitted. And—— which was unlike her——she smoked fairly steadily through the meal. Carol was uneasy, and when Elinor went upstairs for her coat and hat, she followed her.

Elinor was at the safe in her bedroom. She started somewhat.

"Money for the trip," she said lightly. "What's the matter with you, Carol? You look ghastly."

"I thought you did," Carol said bluntly.

"Nonsense. I'm all right. See here, Carol, why not stay here for a while? Greg won't go to Maine. He has other things on his mind, and it only reminds you of things you'd better forget."

"I can manage," Carol said rather dryly. "I can't change the plans now. It's too late."

"Let the servants go up alone. Lucy Norton will be there, won't she?" There seemed a certain insistence in Elinor's voice.

"I'm leaving Sunday," she said. "It's too late to change."

She watched Elinor at her dressing table, laden with the gold toilet things, the jars and perfume bottles which were as much a part of her as her carefully darkened eyebrows. She was running a brush over the eyebrows now, but the line was not too even.

Elinor's hands were shaking.

TWO

THE TRIP TO BOSTON was a nightmare. The train was jammed with a Sunday crowd, and stopped frequently with a jerk that almost broke her neck. It was still hot and her mind was filled with the events of the past three days.

Any attempt to locate Greg in Washington had met with failure, and Mrs. Spencer had taken refuge in her bedroom and a dignified silence. Then on Sunday she had openly rebelled.

"I think I'll go with you, Carol," she said. "I might as well. If all Elinor provides me with is a place to sleep and food to eat, I see no reason for staying."

It had taken Carol a half hour to persuade her to stay. June was often cold in Maine, and the house would be damp anyhow, she said. Also the girls would have all they could do. Her mother would certainly be uncomfortable. Better to wait a few days. At least she was well housed and well fed where she was.

And that crisis was barely over when she had a visit from Virginia Demarest. Virginia was a tall slim redheaded girl, very pretty and very young, and just now very indignant.

"I wish you'd tell me where Greg is," she said. "Or don't you know either? I haven't heard from him since he left San Francisco for Washington the first of the week."

She lit a cigarette and threw the match away almost violently.

"We only know he's in this country, Virginia. We are opening Crestview for him. Not my idea," Carol added hastily, seeing Virginia's face. "Mother thinks he needs to be cool after where he's been. He's somewhere in Washington probably. He was to get his medal or whatever it is this week. Of course he's busy."

"There are telephones in Washington," Virginia said stormily. "All the phones in the country seem to have been sent there.

Also I presume they still sell three-cent stamps. What does Elinor say?"

"She's in New York. She hasn't heard either."

Virginia eyed her.

"She and Greg are a pretty close corporation, aren't they?"

Carol smiled.

"I came along later," she said. "Rather as an unpleasant surprise, I gather. Yes, they're fond of each other."

Virginia was not listening. She was looking at a photograph of Greg, tall and handsome in his flying clothes and helmet. Her truculence had gone now. She put out her cigarette and glanced rather helplessly at Carol.

"There's something wrong," she said. "Something's happened to him. Ever since he left after his last leave his letters have been different. I suppose men can fall out of love as well as in."

"That's ridiculous," Carol said, with spirit. "If ever I saw a man who had gone overboard completely it was Greg. Of course his letters are different. They had to be read by a censor. You know that."

But Virginia was not convinced.

"They have girls out there," she said. "Nurses, Wacs, all sorts. He may have found someone he likes. He's no child. He's thirty-four, and he's been around. You know him."

Carol knew him, she admitted to herself. She had always adored him, his good looks, his debonair manners, even the lightness with which he threw off his occasional lapses. It had been she, years ago, who had slipped to him the headache tablets or even the Scotch which braced him the morning after so that he could face the family. And she had understood him better than Elinor.

"You'd better grow up soon," she had told him one morning, standing long-legged and gawky by his bed. He grinned at her.

"Why?" he inquired. "God, what awful mess is this?" He took it, grimacing. "It's fun to be young, Carol. Or it was last night."

She roused herself when she reached Boston. She managed to get to the North Station in a taxi which threatened to break down at any moment, and she found there three tired and discouraged women servants who had had no dinner and were standing by the bags they had carried themselves. Only Maggie, the cook, gave her a thin smile.

"Well, we've got this far, Miss Carol," she said. "And if you know where we can get a cup of coffee—"

She got them fed after some difficulty, sitting with them at the table and trying to swallow a dry cheese sandwich. They cheered considerably after the food.

There were no porters to be had. They lugged their bags to the train and got aboard. It had taken on the aspects of adventure to the two younger girls, especially since Carol was with them. But when she tried to enter her drawing room the door was locked, and the porter said it was already occupied. It was useless to protest. If two tickets had been sold for the same room, you could blame the war and anyone who protested was unpatriotic.

She smoked a cigarette in the women's room before she crawled resignedly into her lower berth. She supposed everything was all right. Elinor would be at home by this time, and Virginia would have heard from Gregory. But her depression continued. Partly of course it was the thought of men fighting and dying all over the world. Partly it was the belonging to what her friends called the "new poor" and having a mother who refused to change her standard of living. And partly it was an odd sense of apprehension, compounded partly of her dislike for returning to Crestview, where before the war Don Richardson had courted her so gaily and won her so easily. To escape she tried to plan about the house. Lucy had had too short notice to have done much, but at least she would be there, small, brisk and efficient. In that hopeful mood she finally went to sleep, and it persisted even when at six the next morning they got out onto a chilly station platform and looked for the taxi Lucy was to send.

There was no taxi there, only a sleepy station agent who regarded the summer people as unavoidable nuisances and disappeared as soon as the train moved on. There was a small restaurant not far away, and after a wait they got some coffee. But no taxi arrived, and at last Carol managed to locate one for the ten-mile drive.

It was cold. The girls shivered in their summer coats, and Carol herself felt discouraged. She did her best to keep up their morale, pointing out the fresh green of the trees and when they reached it the beauty of the sea.

"Look," she said. "There's a seal. They're usually gone by this time. I suppose with no motorboats around—"

"It's awfully lonely," said Freda. Freda was the house maid, young and rather timid. "I feel all cut off from everything."

"You feel cool too, don't you?" said Maggie briskly. "After the fuss you made about the heat. Just feel that air! Ain't it something?"

There was of course plenty of air, all of it icy, and Freda shivered.

"I'll be glad to get into a warm house," she said. "Where are we? At the North Pole?"

Nora, the parlormaid-waitress, had kept quiet. She was not much of a talker at any time, but she looked blue around the lips and Carol felt uneasy. If the girls didn't stay—

"Mrs. Norton will have breakfast ready," she said. "The house will be warm, too. And the lilacs ought to be lovely still. They come out late here."

No one said anything. The taxi had passed Colonel Richardson's cottage and turning in at the drive was winding its way up the hill to the house. Carol began to have a feeling of home-coming as the familiar road unwound. They passed the garage and the old stable, unused for years; not, she remembered, since Gregory had kept a saddle mare there and she her pony. She took off her hat and let the air blow through her dark hair.

"Look, there are some lilacs," she said, hoping for a cheerful response. No one said anything. They made the last turn and before them lay the house, big and massive and white. It faced out over the harbor, but the entrance was at the rear, with the service wing to the left and what had been her father's study to the right. She saw the two younger women eying it.

"It looks big," Nora said, doubt in her voice.

"It's not as large as it looks," Carol said briskly. "It's built around an open court. I wonder what has happened to Lucy?"

Except that the winter storm doors and windows had been

removed, the house looked strangely unoccupied. The front door was closed, and no small brisk figure rushed to greet them. They got out and Carol paid off the taxi, but there was still no sign of movement in the house. Also to her amazement she found the door locked, and while the women stood disconsolately among their bags and the car departed with a swish of gravel she got out her keys. The door opened, she stepped inside, to be greeted only by freezing air and a vague, rather unpleasant odor.

The women followed her in, looking sulky.

"I can't imagine what has happened," she said. "Mrs. Norton must be sick. If you get a fire started in the kitchen, Maggie, I'll telephone and find out."

She put her hat and bag on the console table in the hall. It was impossible to take off her coat, and except for Maggie, starting toward her kitchen, nobody had moved. The two girls stood as if poised for flight.

"What's the smell?" Freda said. "It's like something's been burned."

"Leave the door open," Carol said impatiently. "Mrs. Norton has been here. She may have scorched something. Go on back with Maggie."

She went along the passage around the patio to the library. The old study was untouched, and the covers were still on the hall chairs at the foot of the wide staircase at the side of the house. But the covering was off the shallow pool in the patio, and the shutters off the French doors and windows opening on it. To her relief she found that at least an attempt had been made to make the library livable. The rug was down, the dust covers were gone, some of the photographs and ornaments were in place, and a log fire had been laid, ready for lighting.

She put a match to it and straightened, feeling somewhat better as the dry logs caught. But the odor—whatever it was—had penetrated even here. She opened the French door onto the terrace and stood there looking out. The air was fresh, and the view had always rested her. The islands were green jewels in the blue water, and a mile or so away she could see the town of Bayside, small and prim among its trees. She drew a long breath and turned to the telephone.

It was not there. She gazed in dismay at the desk where it had stood. The silver cigarette box was there as always. The little Battersea patch case was in its place, as was the desk pad and the old Sheffield inkstand with the candles to melt the wax and the snuffers to extinguish them. But the telephone was gone.

Something else was there, however, which made her stop and stare. On the ash tray lay a partially smoked cigarette, and there was lipstick on it.

Lucy Norton neither smoked nor used lipstick, and Carol looked down at it incredulously. Then she smiled. Of course someone had dropped in. Marcia Dalton perhaps, or Louise Stimson. Almost any of the women of the summer colony, climbing the hill and coming in to rest, could have left it. Nevertheless, her feeling of uneasiness returned. She moved swiftly through the adjoining living room and dining room to the pantry and kitchen. Maggie had taken an apron from her suitcase and was tying it around her ample waist. The two girls were standing like a coroner's jury, reserving decision.

"I'm afraid some of the telephones have been taken out," she said with assumed brightness. "Is the one in the kitchen hall still there, Maggie?"

Maggie opened a door and glanced back.

"It's gone," she said. "Looks like they've taken them all."

"Good heavens," Carol said. "What on earth will we do?"

"Folks lived a long time without them," Maggie said philosophically. "I guess we'll manage. What do you think that smell is, Miss Carol? There's nothing been burned here."

It was not bad in the kitchen, although it was noticeable. Not unexpectedly, Freda, the youngest of the three, broke first.

"I'm not staying," she said hysterically. "I didn't plan to be sent to the end of the world, and frozen too. And that smell makes me sick. I'm giving you notice this minute, Miss Spencer."

Carol fought off the nightmare sensation that was beginning to paralyze her.

"Now look, Freda," she said reasonably, her face a little set, "you can't leave. Not right away, anyhow. I can't call a taxi. The cars in the garage have no gasoline and no batteries.

They're jacked up anyhow. There's not even a train until to-night."

Maggie took hold then.

"Don't be a little fool, Freda," she said. "I expect Mrs. Norton's ordered the groceries. You take off your hat and coat, and I'll make hot coffee. We'll all feel better then."

A hasty inspection of the supply closet revealed no groceries, however. There was an empty coffee can and the heel of a loaf of bread. In the refrigerator were a couple of eggs, a partly used jar of marmalade, and a few slices of bacon on a plate. Maggie's face was grim. She looked up at the eight-day kitchen clock, which was still going.

"If that lazy George Smith's here we can send him into town," she said. "Go out and see if you can find him, Nora. He's the gardener—or he says he is."

She ordered Freda to the cellar for coal, and under protest Freda went. Carol sat down on a kitchen chair while Maggie looked at her with concern.

"You're too young to have all this wished on you," she said, with the familiarity of her twenty years of service. "Don't take it too hard. Somebody's sick at Lucy's, most likely. I don't know why your mother got this idea anyhow. Mr. Greg won't come. He's got only thirty days and probably he'll want to get married. It's a pity," she added grimly, "that you and Mr. Don didn't get married before he left."

Because Carol was tired and worried, tears came into her eyes. She brushed them away impatiently.

"That's all over, Maggie," she said. "We have to carry on."

Then Freda came back, gingerly carrying a pail partly filled with coal, and Maggie started to light a fire. The odor—whatever it was—was not strong here, but when Maggie poured a little kerosene onto the coals and dropped a match into it, Carol realized the odor was much the same. Perhaps Lucy had started the furnace fire that way.

Nora came back, shivering, from the grounds. "I don't see anybody," she reported. "The grass has been cut here and there, but there's nobody out there."

She huddled by the stove, and Carol got up abruptly.

"Something's happened to Lucy," she said. "Take over, Maggie, and get started. I'll go down to the village and find out what's wrong. I'll order some groceries too. The Miller market will be open now."

"One of the girls can do it," Maggie objected.

But Carol refused. She was worried about Lucy. Also she knew what was needed, and how to find it. And—although she did not say it—she wanted to get out of the house. Always before when she came it had been warm and welcoming, but that day it was different. It felt, she thought shiveringly, like a tomb.

THREE

She was still shivering as she got her bag from the entrance hall. She did not put on her hat. She left the front door open to let in more air, and stood outside looking about her.

There was no sign that George Smith had done much. Branches from the great pines littered the turnaround of the drive, and where the hill rose abruptly behind it the tool house appeared to be closed and locked. But the day was brilliantly bright, a bed of peonies by the grass terrace at the side of the house was beginning to show radiant pink and white blossoms, and a robin was sitting back on its tail and pulling vigorously at a worm. It was familiar and friendly, and she started briskly down the hill.

This was a mistake. She had not changed her shoes, and walking was not easy. The gravel had been raked into the center of the drive to avoid washing away in the winter rains and thaws, and the hard base underneath was rough. It was no use going to the garage, she knew. The cars had been put up for the winter. At the entrance gates, however, she hesitated. She could, she knew, telephone from the Richardson cottage, but she did not yet feel able to cope with the colonel and with his talk of Don. And the Ward place, separated from Crestview by a narrow dirt lane, was as far up the hill as Crestview itself.

In the end she decided to walk the mile to the market. It was easier going on the streets, and besides she had always liked the town. Its white houses, neat and orderly, its strong sense of self-respect, its New England dignity, all appealed to her. It looked friendly, too, in the morning sun, and her anxieties seemed foolish and slightly ridiculous.

It was still early. Here and there, it being Monday, washing was already hanging out in the yards, but she saw no one she knew until she limped into the market. Fortunately it was open, and behind the counter Harry Miller was putting on a fresh white coat.

He looked rather odd when he saw her.

"How are you, Miss Carol?" he said, as they shook hands. "I heard you were coming. Early, aren't you, this morning?"

She smiled as she pulled up a stool and sat down.

"I had to walk," she explained. "No car, no telephone, no groceries, and no sense. I forgot to change my shoes."

"Sounds like a lot of misery," said Harry, eying her.

"It was. It is. Harry, do you know anything about Lucy Norton? She's not there, and even George Smith isn't around. I don't understand it."

Harry hesitated.

"Well," he said, "I guess you've run into a bit of hard luck, Miss Carol. Take George now. He's in the hospital. Had his appendix out last Thursday. Doing all right though. Kind of proud of it by this time."

"I'm sorry. He wasn't much good, but he was somebody. I'll go to see him as soon as I get things fixed a bit. What about Lucy?"

Harry still hesitated. He had always liked Carol. She was just folks like the rest, not like some he could mention. And that morning she was looking young and wind-blown and rather plaintive.

"About your telephone," he said evasively. "I guess your mother didn't pay any attention to the notice. You had to pay all winter even to keep one, and then you were lucky if you did."

"I suppose Mother got one," Carol said. "We didn't expect to come, of course. What about Lucy Norton? Is she sick too?"

"Well, I suppose I'd better tell you," he said, not too comfortably. "Lucy's had an accident. She fell down the big staircase at your place and broke her leg. In the middle of the night, too. She might be lying there still if that William who takes down the winter stuff hadn't come along. Seems like he wanted to borrow some coffee and the kitchen wing was locked. He went around to the front door and found it open. And found Lucy there. She's at the hospital too. Doing all right, I hear."

Carol looked startled.

"What on earth was Lucy doing on the stairs in the middle of the night? She always sleeps in the service wing."

He grinned.

"Well, that's a funny thing, Miss Carol. She says somebody was chasing her."

Carol stared at him.

"Chasing her? It doesn't sound like Lucy."

"Does sound foolish, doesn't it?" he said. "She's a sensible woman too, like you say. But that's what she claims. I only know what they're saying around here. Seems like she says it was cold that night, and she'd got up to get a blanket from some closet or other. The light company hadn't got around to turning on the electric current, so she took a candle. She got to the closet all right, but just as she was ready to open the door she says somebody reached out and knocked the candle out of her hand. Knocked her down too, and practically ran over her."

"It sounds fantastic."

"Doesn't it? They're calling it Lucy's ghost around here. Anyhow she was so scared that she picked herself up and made for the stairs. It was black dark, you see, so she fell right down them. It's a mercy she was found at all. Old William saw the front door wide open and went in, and Lucy Norton was at the foot of the stairs, about crazy with one thing and another. He got Dr. Harrison there and they took her to the hospital. She's in a plaster cast now," he added, almost with gusto.

Carol stared at him.

"It wasn't a ghost if it opened the front door," she said. "If the whole town knows about it, my maids will hear it sooner or later." She remembered Freda with a sense of helplessness. "It was a tramp, of course. Who else could it be? Unless she dreamed the whole business."

"Well, she sure enough broke her leg."

The market was still empty. She was aware that Harry was watching her with a mixture of curiosity and the deference he reserved for his summer people. She rallied herself.

"I'm terribly sorry," she said. "We're all fond of her. I'll see her as soon as I can. But a tramp—!"

"Anything missing from the place?" he inquired.

"I haven't really looked. I don't think so. We never leave much."

He cleared his throat.

"Might as well tell you," he said. "There was a light in that upper corner room of yours late that night. The one that looks this way. I was driving home, and I saw it myself. Looked like a candle, only Lucy says she wasn't in there."

"In the yellow room? Are you sure?"

"Sure as I'm standing here. About half past twelve it was."

She gave her order finally, and went out with her head whirling. But there was no time to see Lucy Norton then, or George either. She went to the office of the telephone company, only to find that there was less than no hope. As usual, she was told there was a war on and, in effect, what was she, a patriot or not? She was able to have the electric current turned on, and at the service station to find someone to put her small car in running order.

It seemed to her that everyone she saw looked at her with more than normal interest. Lucy's story had evidently spread and probably grown.

This was verified when she met the village chief of police at the corner. His name was Floyd, a big man with a sagging belt which carried the automatic he invariably wore as a badge of office, and with small shrewd deep-set eyes. He grinned as he shook hands with her.

"Glad you're back," he said. "We'd heard you weren't coming."

"Mother thought Gregory would like it."

"Bit quiet for him, I'd think. Unless Lucy Norton's ghost gets after him."

He laughed, his big body shaking. She had known him all her life, and the very fact that he could laugh was a relief. She found herself smiling.

"If there was anyone it may have been a tramp. Harry Miller says William found the front door of the house open."

He laughed again.

"No tramps around here, Miss Carol. Ten miles from a railroad! What would they be doing here? They'd starve to death."

She left him still grinning, and went on her way. She ordered coal, she bought some candy at the drugstore as a peace offering for the two recalcitrant girls, and at last she got a local taxi, picked up part of her order at the market, and drove home. She did not go to the house at once, however. She sent the taxi on with the groceries, and herself got out at the garage and unlocked the doors. The cars were there, mounted on blocks, her small car, her mother's limousine, and Gregory's old abandoned roadster. They looked strange under their dust sheets, but nothing had been disturbed.

She left the door open for the men from the service station, and went back to the drive, to find there what she had dreaded for so long.

Colonel Richardson was waiting for her. He was standing in the roadway, his tall figure erect, the wind blowing his heavy white hair. A veteran of two wars, he was colonel to every one, and—except for his obsession about his son—universally beloved. With his smile Carol's apprehensions left her.

"Hello," he said genially. "Come and greet an old man. I didn't know you were coming so soon."

She went over and kissed him, and he patted her shoulder.

"Look as though you could stand some good Maine air," he said, surveying her. "I only heard about Lucy Norton yesterday. Too bad. She's a fine woman. How are you getting along?"

"We'll manage. No telephone of course, and no cars or lights yet. Otherwise we're all right. How are you?"

"Fine. I find the waiting hard, of course, but I have to remember that I am not alone in that. Can I do anything now?"

She told him she could get along, and watched him going down the drive, swinging the stick he always carried, but with his back straight and his head held high. She looked after him, distressed for them both, that he should believe and she could not, that to him Don was still a living force and to her he was becoming only a memory. She was deeply depressed when she got back to the house.

She found Maggie at the stove, with a kettle boiling and her face smeared with soot.

"I got the furnace started," she said cheerfully. "Otherwise those fools of girls would still be hugging this fire. And I started Freda at your room. Soon as she's made the bed—"

Carol dumped her groceries on the table.

"Lucy Norton's broken her leg, Maggie. She's in the hospital."

Maggie turned, her face shocked.

"The poor thing! How did it happen?"

"Here in this house." Carol sat down and kicked off her pumps. "She fell down the stairs. There's a silly story going around that she found someone upstairs and tried to get away."

"When was all this?" Maggie, practical as ever, was opening the new pound of coffee.

"Last Friday night or early Saturday morning. The lights were off, of course." She looked at her feet. They were hurting, and she picked up one and began to rub it thoughtfully. "George is there too. He's had his appendix out."

"For God's sake!" said Maggie, her poise finally forsaking her. "Something scared *him* too?"

There was no time to answer.

There was a wild scream from somewhere upstairs, and a minute later Freda half ran, half fell down the back staircase, and promptly fainted on the kitchen floor.

Later Carol was to remember that faint of Freda's as the beginning of the nightmare, to see herself bending over the girl, whose small face was ashy gray and the palm of one hand oddly blackened, of trying to prevent Nora from dousing her with a pan of water from the sink, and of catching Maggie's eye as she straightened.

"Something's scared her too," said Maggie ominously. "Too much scaring around here, to my way of thinking."

Nora was still clutching the pan.

"Maybe she saw a mouse," she said. "She's deathly afraid of mice."

"We'd better leave her flat," Carol said. "Go up and get her a blanket, Nora. The floor's cold. You'll find them in the linen closet."

She bent over and felt the girl's pulse. It was rapid but strong, and a little color was coming back into her face. Carol herself felt rather dizzy. She stepped into her pumps and looked at Maggie.

"What's that on her hand?"

Maggie bent over and looked.

"Seems like soot," she said. "Maybe she was lighting your fire. I'd better go and look. The place could burn up while we're standing here."

She did not go, however. Freda was stirring. She opened pale-blue eyes and looked around her uncertainly.

"What happened?" she said. "I must have fainted or something."

"If you didn't you gave a good imitation of it," said Maggie dryly. "You scared the insides out of us. Better lie still for a while. You're all right."

Freda was far from all right. With returning consciousness came memory, and without warning she burst into loud hysterical crying.

"I want to go home," she said between wails. "I never did want to come here."

"Shut up," Maggie said grimly. "Noise isn't going to help you. What scared you?"

Freda did not answer, and it was a part of the nightmare that Nora chose that moment to return. She came rather quietly down the back stairs and stopped, bracing herself against the frame of the kitchen door as if she needed support. There was no color in her face, but her voice was steady.

"There's somebody dead in the linen closet," she said, and shivered. "There's been a fire there too."

FOUR

SHE DID NOT SAY any more. She made for the door which led outside from the service hall, and they could hear her retching there. Carol made a move toward the stairs, but Maggie was ahead of her.

"They're both hysterical," she said. "Probably saw a blanket on the floor. Better let me go up, Miss Carol. You don't look so good yourself. You stay with Freda."

Freda was still crying, but she was sitting up now and fumbling for a handkerchief. Carol gave her one from her bag and she dried her eyes.

"I guess I flopped," she said. "So would you, if you seen what I did." She shuddered uncontrollably. "I opened the door where you said the linen closet was, and—"

She did not finish. Maggie came in, and one look at her face was enough.

"I guess you'll have to get the police," she said. "There's somebody there. Better not go up. I opened the windows in the hall, but I didn't touch anything else."

She went to the sink and washed her hands. Then she sat down abruptly, and began nervously pleating her apron.

"I don't feel so good," she said. "They're right about the fire. We'll never use them sheets and things again."

The nightmare feeling closed down on Carol. It had been growing since their arrival, with Lucy not there, and Harry Miller's story, and now this! She felt young and incapable, and the house itself had become horrible. She found she was shaking.

"Could you see who it was?" she asked.

Maggie shook her head.

"I told you. There's been a fire." She got up heavily and went to the stove. "I'd better make some coffee," she said, her voice flat. "It's a help. You'd better have a cup before you start for the village. Maybe you can get Colonel Richardson to drive you in. He's near."

"I ought to go up myself."

"You stay where you are," Maggie said forcefully. "Freda, you go up and lie down. Nothing's going to hurt you. Whatever it is it's over, and your room ain't near it."

Nora had come back by that time, but neither girl would go upstairs again. They looked shocked and helpless, but they looked, too, like a defiant combination against Maggie's common sense. Carol looked at them with what amounted to despair.

"I'm sorry, girls," she said. "Whatever has happened it has nothing to do with us. Mrs. Norton has broken her leg. She's in the hospital, and probably some tramp came in while the house was empty."

Nora was the first to recover.

"And burned himself to death!" she said, her voice high and shrill.

"That's for the police to find out."

"I'm staying for no police."

Maggie turned from the stove.

"That's where you're wrong, my girl," she said coldly. "You'll stay here as long as the police want you. Don't get any ideas about running away, either of you. You found the body, and here you're staying till they let you go."

It was a subdued pair of young women that Carol took upstairs. The service wing was cut off from the main house by a heavy door, and after she had seen them to their rooms she opened it. From this angle she could see the door of the linen closet. It was next to that of the elevator which had been installed for her mother some years before, and it was standing open, its white paint blackened and blistered.

She stood still, almost unable to move. Soon she would have to get help, but first she must see for herself. The odor was very strong. It was a combination of scorched linen, burned paint, kerosene, and something else she did not care to identify.

The morning sun was flooding the closet. The house was

built entirely around the patio, with a passage running around
it on the second floor and the bedroom doors and that of the
elevator and closet opening from it. The windows were open,
and she was grateful for the air. She moved forward slowly,
past Greg's old room, past the blue guest room and past the
elevator door. Then she was at the closet, staring in.

The women had been right. There was a body inside, but
it was not that of a tramp. It was that of a woman.

She did not go back to the kitchen. She went on rather
blindly to the main staircase and huddled there on the top
step. She was still wearing the black dress and fur-collared coat
in which she had arrived, and she pulled the coat around her
as if she were cold. She was not thinking yet. Her mind was
too chaotic for that. She knew there were things she should do,
but she was not ready to do them. Maggie found her there,
her eyes wide and staring and her face chalk-white.

"I warned you," she said. "Maybe I'd better go for the police.
It's nobody you know, is it?"

Carol looked up blankly.

"How can anyone tell?" Her voice was bleak, and Maggie
was frightened.

"Now look, Miss Carol," she said, "it's not that bad. Maybe
you couldn't recognize her, but she's—not really burned up.
And the house is cold. If it's only been there since Saturday—"

Carol roused herself

"Saturday? Why Saturday?"

"Because Lucy Norton was here Friday night," Maggie
explained patiently. "You don't suppose this went on while
she was in the house, do you?"

"It might have. I didn't tell you all the story. She says somebody reached out of the linen closet and knocked her down.
That's how she got hurt. She was running down the stairs in
the dark."

Carol got up slowly, holding to the stair rail, and Maggie
caught her arm to steady her.

"I'd better get Floyd," she said. "Maybe I can telephone
from Colonel Richardson's." And when Maggie protested, "I
need the air," she said flatly, "I'm all right now. Let go of me.
I'm only glad Mother isn't here."

Maggie nodded, and Carol went down the stairs. The sunlight on the white walls of the house made the patio dazzling, and she blinked in the glare. The blue pool needed paint, she thought distractedly, and some of the tiles had been cracked by the winter ice. It had been idiotic to build a house entirely around an open court. In winter any heavy snow had to be shoveled into a wheelbarrow and dumped on the drive, and when there was a rapid thaw the drainpipe in the pool was not adequate. More than once the plumber had had to come, have the current turned on, run a hose through the entry hall and pump the water out onto the drive.

She pulled herself together. All this was pure escapism, and she could not escape. There was a dead girl or woman upstairs, and she would have to notify the police. She was more normal when she left the house again, although her feet still bothered her. She had a pair of sandals in her bag upstairs, but she could not go back for them. Perhaps Colonel Richardson would telephone, or drive her into town. But as she stumbled down the drive once more, it was to see the Richardson garage doors open and the Colonel's car gone. This was the time, she remembered, when he drove his man, his only servant, into town to market, and the house would be closed and locked.

She stood still, shivering in the cold air. She could go up to the Wards' and get help there, but once again the long steep drive was more than she could face. She decided to walk, and some twenty minutes later she opened the door of the police station and went in.

Floyd was relaxing. He had taken off the belt and automatic, which lay on his desk, and was resting in a chair, with another drawn up for his legs. He looked up in astonishment when he saw her, and got to his feet.

"Anything wrong?" he inquired. "Here, maybe you'd better sit down."

She did not sit, however. She stood just inside the door, holding the knob as if to support her.

"There's somebody dead in the linen closet at Crestview," she said, her voice flat. "I thought maybe you'd better come up."

He looked astounded.

"Dead? Are you sure?"

"Yes. I think somebody tried to burn her. The house too, I suppose. Only the door was shut and the fire didn't spread."

"For God's sake," Floyd said softly. "So Lucy Norton wasn't crazy, after all."

He buckled on his heavy gun, his face set.

"My car's in the alley," he said. "I'll call Jim Mason. He's got the night job, so he's at home. I'd better call the doctor too. He's the coroner." He reached for the telephone and stopped, his hand on the receiver.

"You're sure of all this, are you?" he said. "Not mistaking something else for a body?"

"I saw it myself."

She sat down then and kicked off her shoes, and the next thing she knew Floyd was holding a glass of whisky to her lips and telling her to get it down somehow.

"I'm not the fainting sort," she protested. "I'm just tired."

"You gave a damn good imitation of passing out," he said gruffly. "Take the rest of this."

And she was still half strangled when he put her into his car.

The whisky helped. She felt less cold, and things were out of her hands now. The law was beside her, looking stern and capable. She was no longer alone. And the chief was a shrewd man. He asked genially about the family, her mother, and especially about Gregory.

"All mighty proud of him here," he said. "Hear he's being decorated by the President."

"He came home for that. They sent him. You know Greg. He didn't want to leave his men, or his plane."

She was looking better, he thought. He had always liked her. Had a rotten time, too, he considered, with that mother of hers and her hoity-toity sister. Then she'd been engaged to Don Richardson, and Don was dead, although his old man wouldn't believe it.

He turned into the drive and put his car into second gear. The engine promptly began to knock, and he apologized.

"Car's all right," he explained. "It's this rotten gas we're getting. Hello, there's the Dane fellow. Maybe we'd better get him."

He stopped the car. A man in slacks and a yellow sweater had been slowly climbing the drive and limping slightly as he did so. He stopped when he heard the car behind him and turned, a tall figure with a lean, rather saturnine face and an aggressive jaw.

"Hello, major," said the chief. "Kind of early for a walk, isn't it?"

Dane grinned.

"My daily dozen," he explained. "When I can run up this hill I'll be ready to go back. Anyhow I saw smoke in this direction, and after the stories going round I thought I'd look into it."

The chief remembered his manners.

"Miss Spencer, meet Major Jerry Dane," he said. "The major had some trouble with the krauts a while ago in Italy, and he's here getting over it." He looked at the man again. "Miss Spencer's had some trouble too," he added. "Maybe you'd like to come along. She says there's a dead body in the house up here."

The major looked interested rather than astonished.

"A body?" he said. "Whose is it?"

He glanced at Carol.

"I have no idea," she said coldly. "If you want to discuss it I'll go on, if you don't mind."

"If it's dead there's no great hurry, is there?"

He was deliberately baiting her, and she felt her color rise. He saw it and grinned, showing excellent teeth in a sunburned face.

"Sorry," he said. "I'll hang onto the running board. Get going, Floyd. Let's see this corpse."

It was obvious that he did not believe her, and none of them spoke as the car climbed the rest of the hill. Carol promptly forgot Dane and braced herself for what was to come. And Dane himself simply lit a cigarette and from his precarious hold on the running board eyed her quizzically. Plenty of spunk, he thought, if what she said was true. Only —a body in the house! Whose body? Good God, he had walked up this hill daily for two weeks, and except for the

Norton woman's accident the place had been merely an ostentatious survival of an era that was finished. In a way it had annoyed him, sitting smug on its hill while the rest of the world blazed and died.

He was relieved when Carol let them go upstairs alone, and he saw now why the house had looked so huge. The court around which it was built might be a lovely thing when it had been put in order, but was now neglected and ugly. But once upstairs he forgot the house. He was accustomed to death, as a man in his particular job knew death. But not the death of a woman. And what lay on the closet floor had been a woman.

It lay relaxed and face up, with the hands and arms close to the body, and the legs neatly outstretched toward the door. When Floyd tried to step inside Dane held him back.

"Better wait," he said. "Let's see what we can first. She wasn't burned to death, of course. Look at the way she's lying. If she'd been burned—"

"I don't get it," Floyd said thickly. "Why kill her and then try to burn her?"

"That's a very nice question." Dane looked about him. "When was the Norton woman hurt?"

"Friday night. Saturday morning, maybe."

Dane began whistling softly to himself.

"No fingerprint people around, I suppose?" he asked, after a pause.

"Why would we be needing a fingerprint outfit?" the chief demanded belligerently. "We haven't had a crime here since one of the waiters at the hotel stole a watch, and that's twelve years ago."

Dane went back to his whistling, but his eyes were busy. The doorknobs were no good. Whoever had found the body had smeared them badly, both outside and in, and a thick layer of soot lay along the shelves and over the piles of neatly stacked scorched linen.

"Ever see her before?" he asked finally.

"How can I tell? Even her own mother— There's no local girl missing. That's all I know."

"How about a camera? There ought to be some pictures

before she's moved."

Floyd's patience was rapidly going.

"Listen, son," he said. "There's a war on. I haven't seen a roll of film for the last year. And I don't own a camera anyhow. What do you think this is? The FBI in Washington?"

Dane did not reply. The doctor's car had chugged up the hill and now he was coming up the stairs, with Jim Mason, Floyd's assistant, at his heels. He stopped outside the closet and stared in.

"Good Godamighty!" he said. "How did that happen?"

"Maybe you can tell us," Dane said with his slightly sardonic smile. "I wouldn't touch anything but the body, doctor. Not that I think there's anything there. Just the usual procedure."

Floyd gave him a cold stare.

"We'll attend to that, Dane," he said. "Go ahead, doc. The major here says she was dead before the fire. How about it?"

The doctor went inside the closet and stooped over the body. He was there a couple of minutes before he backed out. He looked rather white.

"Hit on the head," he said. "Bad frontal fracture. Probably dead two or three days. No way to tell. Certainly dead before the fire."

"Then why any fire at all?" Floyd persisted.

The doctor was lighting a cigarette by the open window.

"How do I know?" he said irritably. "Maybe somebody didn't like her. Maybe somebody didn't want her recognized. Or maybe it was just a fire-bug. Remember the Elks' Club?" He sucked at his cigarette. "Better get her out of here," he said. "I want to look her over."

Dane left them then. He went downstairs, to find Carol in the library. She was curled up in a big chair by the fire, looking young and stricken. There was a tray with coffee on a small table beside her, but she had not touched it. His quick eyes took in the room before he spoke.

"I'm sorry to bother you," he said, "but have you got a camera in the house?"

"A camera?"

"They want to take her away, but I think there should be a picture or two first."

"My brother's camera is here. There are no films in it."

He shrugged his lean shoulders.

"Well, I suppose that's that," he said. "None in the town either, I understand. No telephone, I suppose?"

"No. They're all gone. Who is it up there, major? I mean—in the closet. Does anyone know her?"

He shook his head.

"Not yet. We'll find out later, of course. They don't think she's one of the local people. That's as far as they go."

She shivered, and he went to the tray and poured a cup of coffee. Her hand shook as she took it, but she tried to smile.

"The cook's cure for everything," she said. "I've been having it ever since I came. I have practically a coffee jag. Not to mention Floyd's whisky." She glanced up at him, standing beside her. Aside from his slight limp he appeared to be a strong, well-muscled man in his early thirties, and his face as he looked down at her was now friendly and smiling.

"Don't take this too hard," he said. "It has happened in this house, but it has nothing to do with you. A little paint and a little time, and you can forget it, Miss Spencer."

"I'll never forget it. Do you think it was this—this woman who scared Lucy Norton the night she fell?"

"Might be," he said lightly, and turned to go.

But she did not want him to go. She could not be alone again. Not then, with only the servants in the house and that horror upstairs.

"Would you like some coffee?" she asked, almost desperately.

"Is it strong?"

"It would float an egg."

"I'll be back for some in a minute."

He was longer than a minute. Mason had disappeared when he went back. He left Floyd and Dr. Harrison in the hall and went into the closet. There he stooped for some time over the body, touching nothing but inspecting everything. When he came out again his face was set.

"She was a young woman," he said. "And I don't think she

was killed here. That's not certain, of course, but it doesn't look like it. The autopsy will tell a good bit more, probably. She wasn't wearing much when it happened. Apparently she'd slipped a fur jacket over not much else. Any girl around here have a silver fox coat?"

The chief snorted.

"A few, but mostly we leave them to the summer people. I'll ask around, of course. Taking a lot of interest, aren't you, Dane? Sure you didn't know her yourself?"

"Don't be a fool, Floyd. You brought me here. Why don't you get busy and look around for her clothes? If she didn't belong here she didn't arrive in what she's got on."

"I'll find them, all right."

But Dane was aware as he went down the stairs again that the chief's eyes, hard and suspicious, were following him.

FIVE

HE FOUND CAROL as he had left her. An extra cup and a pot of fresh coffee were waiting for him, and he sat down for the first time.

He nodded approval over the coffee.

"First real stuff I've had since I got here," he said. "Maybe I'd better explain myself. I know the Burtons well, and when I needed to fix up this leg before I went to France they offered me their house just along the hill from here. But of course you know it. And I've got a good man to look after me. He nurses me like a baby, but he can't make coffee."

He talked on quietly, about Alex, the man he had referred to, and who had lost an eye in Italy, about the war and his anxiety to get back into it.

"I've missed the invasion," he said with suppressed bitterness, "but there's still plenty to do. I want like hell to get back. I will too, if Alex and two hands like hams can fix me up."

He was lighting a cigarette for her when the screaming of a siren announced the arrival of the ambulance, and he was still talking against the sounds as the stretcher was carried down the stairs and out of the house and the other cars started their motors.

But she rebelled at last.

"I'm not a child, Major Dane," she said. "I'm twenty-four years old, and I'm perfectly strong. I want to talk about this murder. It is murder, isn't it?"

"Don't you think you'd better forget it? What's the use of discussing it? It's over."

"Over!" she said indignantly. "It has only started, and you know it. I suppose you've heard Lucy Norton's story. Everybody seems to know it. It was that closet she went to to get an extra blanket, and it was someone in that closet who rushed out and knocked her down. That's right, isn't it?"

"That's the story. I haven't seen Mrs. Norton."

"Do you think it was this—was this woman?"

He hesitated, but she had asked for it, he thought grimly.

"I think it unlikely, Miss Spencer. It is more likely to have been whoever killed her."

"Then it was murder?"

"It was murder. Yes. I don't need to tell you that a fire was set, after the crime. She wasn't burned to death."

"I don't understand it. The fire, I mean. When we came in this morning we all smelled something. If the house had burned it might have killed Lucy too. It's—horrible."

"That's one curious thing," he said thoughtfully. "Between Alex and myself I suppose we've heard every variation of the Norton story. She has not apparently mentioned any fire, or even smoke. I wonder—" He did not finish. "There may not have been much. By shutting the door the oxygen was cut off. Still, if you noticed it after two or three days she should have. It's curious. I've been around here every day. I watched the winter shutters being taken down, and on Friday morning I knew someone was working in the house. Mrs. Norton, of course. As a matter of fact—"

"Don't start and stop like that. What was a matter of fact?"

He smiled.

"Probably a mistake. I made a regular round, you see; up the drive, back to the house and over the grounds to that fountain of yours. From there I take the path through the woods to the Burtons'. That takes me past the kitchen. On Friday morning I thought I heard Mrs. Norton talking to someone."

"You didn't see anyone?"

"No. Nobody."

"It might have been William. He was taking down the shutters."

"Very likely. I just remembered it. It's probably not important. Mrs. Norton was late, wasn't she? I mean in opening the house."

"She got here only Friday morning. You see, we hadn't intended to come at all. Then my brother Gregory received thirty days' leave—he's been flying in the Pacific—and Mother thought he'd like to be cool." She smiled faintly. "He won't, you know. He will want New York and Newport. His fiancée is in Newport now."

He was thoughtful. The fire had burned down, and he got up and put a log on it.

"Let's reconstruct this thing," he said. "Just what would Mrs. Norton do when she got here Friday morning? She was alone, I suppose. That's the story as I get it."

"Yes. She couldn't get any help, and George Smith wasn't here. He'd had his appendix out. I suppose she'd light the furnace first. She'd probably light the stove in the kitchen too. After that—well, I think she came in here, so I would have a place to sit. I haven't been up in my room, but with so little time she probably did something there."

"Such as?"

"She would make the bed, I imagine. Or at least get out the sheets to air them. Oh, I see what you mean."

"Exactly," he said soberly. "The linen closet was probably all right then, on Friday morning."

Nora came in for the tray just then. She looked better, but she was still pale, and Dane smiled at her.

"Thanks for the coffee," he said. "And do you know if Miss Spencer's room is ready for her? She looks tired."

"The bed's made up, Freda says. That's about all, sir."

"So you see," he said when she had gone. "The linen closet *was* all right on Friday. Maybe someone was in the house talking to Mrs. Norton, maybe not. But there was no murder until that night."

He took his cup and wandered about the room. The tissue paper had been taken off a jumble of vases, a plaster cast of one of her father's mares when people still kept horses, a Russian ikon, a Buddha or two, and the photograph of Elinor in her finery when she made her debut. But there was another photograph there, one of Gregory Spencer in uniform, and he stopped before it.

"Your brother, I suppose?"

"Yes. Can you see what I mean when I say he'd prefer New York?"

Dane inspected it carefully. A playboy, he thought, until war had sobered him. Or had it?

"Fine-looking chap," he said. "No wonder you're proud of him."

Carol did not answer. She was looking around the room, apparently puzzled.

"That's queer," she said. "I don't see my father's picture. It's always here. Mother wouldn't ship it to New York last fall, for fear something would happen to it. I wrapped it up myself and left it on top of that bookcase."

She got up and moved anxiously about the room. When she reached the desk she stopped.

"I've just remembered something else too," she said. "This morning I found a cigarette here, in this ash tray. It had lipstick on it. Lucy doesn't smoke, and as for lipstick—"

The stairs had made Dane's leg ache. His limp was more noticeable as he went to the desk.

"Any idea where it is now?"

"I suppose Nora threw it out."

"If that's true," he said, "the lipstick, I mean, it throws my first idea into the discard. What I thought was that, as the house was supposed still to be empty, anyone wanting to dispose of a body could bring it here, set fire to the house, and then escape. That whoever did it possibly had no idea Mrs. Norton was here. But if the dead woman was here, and smoking in this room—"

He left soon after. She went out to the terrace with him, and for a moment they stood together, looking down at the shore line and the roofs of the houses buried in foliage below.

"It looks peaceful," she said. "It's hard to believe that anyone here could do a thing like murder."

"There's murder all over the world," he said dryly. "Why think people like you are immune?"

She felt rebuffed as she went back into the house. It was obvious that Dane did not like what he called people like her. It had been in his face when he looked at Greg's picture. And she could not tell him that she loathed her own uselessness. Why should she? she thought resentfully. Just because he had been wounded in Italy did not give him the right to criticize those who could not fight.

In the library she resumed her search for her father's picture. It was not there, although she looked behind the books. It was not in the study either. When she went upstairs to continue the search she saw that the door of the linen closet had been sealed with strips of adhesive tape and blobs of red wax. They looked like blood, making her shiver. But the picture was not in her mother's room either, and at last she gave up and went downstairs again, to find an angry Maggie waiting for her.

"Did you tell that man he could look at my garbage can?" she demanded. "The tall one with the limp."

"You'll have to expect things like that, Maggie," she said wearily. "We've had a murder, you know."

"And what's happened to your mother's china tea set?" Maggie inquired, her arms akimbo. "It ain't here, and she sure thought a lot of it. If you're asking me, we've had a burglary as well as a murder."

"Who on earth would steal a tea set?"

"It was valuable, wasn't it?"

Carol felt completely confused as she went back to the library. There were things she would have to do. She would have to call Elinor at Newport and ask her to break the news to her mother as carefully as she could. But she dreaded doing it. She could see Elinor's lifted eyebrows and her angry reaction, as though she—Carol—was responsible. And of course she would have to see Lucy. If the girl had been in the house long enough to smoke a cigarette, Lucy must know about her.

She might even have admitted her. Only Joe Norton, the caretaker, had keys to the house, and Lucy would have used his, as she always did. Joe had the keys, so he could come in during the winter. So far as she remembered there were only two sets of keys.

But the real question was the identity of the body, and here she felt helpless. She would have to see Lucy as soon as possible, she thought. It would be only an hour or two before she had her car, and Lucy must know something. Only it was queer she had not said anything. According to Harry Miller, Lucy's story was merely that someone had come out of the closet and knocked her down.

She was starting for the garage to see what progress had been made when Freda stopped her.

The drive was empty. By this time the village certainly knew what had happened, but no crowd of thrill-seekers had gathered. The town, self-respecting as ever, was evidently going about its business as usual. Down at the garage someone was hammering, and the morning chill had gone. The sun was warm and heartening.

She had taken only a step or two when Freda called her. The girl still looked pale, but she was no longer hysterical. Carol stopped.

"What is it, Freda?"

"If you'll excuse me, miss," she said. "Maggie thought I'd better tell you. Somebody has been sleeping in the yellow room. There's sheets on the bed, and two or three blankets. The bathroom's been used too. The tub's still dirty."

Quite evidently she was enjoying the sensation she was making. For it was a sensation. Carol looked incredulous.

"I don't believe it," she said. "Mrs. Norton would never sleep there."

"No, ma'am," said Freda smugly. "She was using a room in our wing. Maybe you'd better come and look."

She followed Carol up the stairs, to find the other two women in the upper hall. The yellow room was at the front of the house, so she did not pass the closet to reach it, but she was acutely conscious of it behind her, its seared door and ruined contents. She was still certain Freda had made a mistake. The last person to use it the summer before had been Virginia, and some oversight—

But she knew as she reached the door that there had been no mistake.

The yellow room looked out over the bay, and had been one of her pet rooms. Its walls were yellow, its furniture painted gray, and the hangings and chair covers were a delicate mulberry. She saw none of that now, however. Freda had been right. The bed had been made up and slept in, there was powder on the glass top of the toilet table, and while the ash trays were empty there were cigarette ashes here and there on the floor. A candle on the table beside the bed had burned itself out. Only a shapeless blob of wax remained.

Maggie was the first to speak.

"Looks like she was sleeping here," she said. "She had her nerve, if you ask me."

Carol turned to Freda.

"You haven't touched anything in here, have you?" she asked.

"No, miss. I just opened the door and saw it. Then I looked at the bathroom. It's like I said."

Carol stepped inside the room. The nightmare feeling was returning, and there was something wrong. It was a minute before she realized what it was. There was no clothing in sight, and when she glanced in the closets they were empty.

"She must have had clothes," she said. "She wasn't wearing any. At least not a dress," she added. "They think she was wearing a kimono or something of the sort. There ought to be a bag too, and a hat. Unless the police took them."

"Plenty of girls don't wear hats nowadays." This was Freda, beginning to enjoy herself.

Carol turned to them.

"There mustn't be any talk about this," she said. "I'll tell the police, but nobody else is to know. Do please be careful. It may be very important."

She locked the door behind her and took the key. No use worrying about fingerprints, she thought. Freda's would be on the doorknob, and almost anywhere else. She waited until they had started down the stairs and then went into her own room. The bed had been made up with sheets from the servants' linen closet, and was turned down ready for use. Her dressing case had been unpacked, and Freda had placed on the toilet table the photograph of Don in his flying helmet which she always carried with her.

She did not look at it, beyond seeing that it was there. After all, one remembered the dead. One could not go on loving them. What concerned her now was a mystery which only Lucy Norton could solve, and she could not see Lucy until her car was ready.

She bathed and dressed, changing her traveling clothes for a knitted suit, but she did not go downstairs right away. She went to the window and stood there, looking out at the bay. The tide was low, and the sea gulls were busy hunting for clams, the white ones the adults, the gray ones of this spring's hatching. Even here back from the water she could hear them squawking. Over to the left, beyond the fountain her grandmother had sent from Italy, and hidden by the trees, was the Burton house. For a minute she was tempted to go there, to see Major Dane and tell him about the yellow room. But his final words had drawn a definite line between them. She decided against it. It would have to be the police.

When she went downstairs, however, it was to hear a male voice in the hall, and to find that the press had already discovered her. The press itself was in the shape of a rather engaging youth, who gave her a nice smile and looked apologetic.

"Name's Starr," he said. "Just happened on this. Came over from the big town to get a story on the new fish cannery here, and found this. I'm sure sorry about it, Miss Spencer. You're pretty young to run into murder."

"I'm old enough not to give any interviews to the press," Carol said sharply.

"I'm not asking for an interview. I was just thinking. You and this other girl. Only she got the raw deal. She's dead."

"How do you know she was only a girl, Mr. Starr?"

"Saw the body," he said, and reached into his pocket for some folded yellow paper. "Age approximately twenty to twenty-five," he read. "Bleached blonde. Possibly married, as wedding ring on finger. Feet small. Bedroom slippers originally blue. Silver fox jacket, no maker's name. Clothing under body not burned. Looks like red silk negligee. Underwear handmade." He looked at her. "Make any sense to you?"

Carol shook her head.

"Doesn't sound like anyone you know?"

"It sounds like everyone I know."

He stood looking over his notes.

"Where's her dress?" he said. "She didn't come here in a thin silk negligee, did she?"

"I don't know anything about it," Carol said. "I suppose the police looked over the house. If she left any clothes, they would know it."

He thought that over. He looked young and rather shocked, for all his businesslike manner.

"Well, look," he said. "She's in a wrapper and she's got a fur coat on. So she's cold. So she looks around for a blanket. So she goes to the closet, and maybe she's smoking. So she faints—maybe something scares her—and that starts the fire. How about it?"

"Is that what they think in the town? The police and the doctor?"

"Hell, no. That's my own idea. Just thought of it, in fact. Anyhow, it's out. The doc says she's got a fractured skull. Sure you don't know who it is?"

"I haven't really seen her. All I saw was somebody lying there."

"You didn't miss anything," he said gruffly.

He put the paper back in his pocket and picked up a rather battered hat.

"No interview," he assured her. "Just a bit of local color. You know, big house, summer people, first murder in town's history. The doc says it was probably kerosene. Maybe gasoline. Any about the place?"

"Gasoline?" she said with some bitterness. "We were out of it before we left last year. Even the matches were left in a closed jar, for fear of field mice."

He departed finally, saying that he left his car at the gate, and promising not to quote her on anything. She rather liked him, engaging grin and all.

SIX

Back at the house Dane was met by a glum and scowling Alex. Even the black patch over the socket from which he had lost an eye looked peevish.

"What you been doing to that leg, sir?" he demanded.

"Nothing that a rest can't help. How about lunch?"

Alex refused to be conciliated.

"Maybe you don't want to go back to your job," he said, forgetting the "sir." "Just a smell of murder and you forget there's a war."

"Oh, go to hell," Dane said wearily. "Get me a drink and something to eat. How do you know there's a murder?"

"I buy our food in the town," Alex said, still sulky.

"Know any details?"

"Cracked on the head. Killer tried to burn the body." He added the "sir" here, and Dane grinned.

"Go on," he said. "Get me a highball, and don't be too stingy with the whisky."

He limped out to the porch and sat down. Alex was right, of course. He had a big job to go back to, and the stairs at Crestview hadn't helped his leg any. He put it up on a chair and fell into thought. He was still absorbed when Alex brought the Scotch. He roused, however.

"Sit down, Alex, and pour yourself a drink. I want to talk to you. We've got a case on our hands, and I'm damned if I know what it is. Except it's murder."

Alex fixed his drink and sat down, his one eye showing complete disapproval.

"If you'll excuse me, sir," he said, "I don't think it's any business of yours. Unless it's a spy case."

"No. I'm pretty sure it has nothing to do with the war. No spies. No escaped PW. Somebody wanted a girl out of the way, that's all. As far as they can tell, she wasn't local. Nobody is missing from around here. Now, how did she get into that house next door? And why? The family wasn't there. Only the Norton woman, and you know her story."

Alex stirred.

"I still don't see why you want to look into it, sir."

"I suppose it's because it's something to do. God knows I've been bored for months, hospitals, doctors, nurses and— What do you know about the Norton woman? Any family?"

"Only herself and Joe. That's her husband."

"No wealthy connections? Anyone likely to visit her dressed up in an expensive fur jacket? That sort of thing?"

Alex thought it more than improbable, and Dane shifted to the Spencers. Where Alex got his information he never knew. Perhaps it was because of his long job on the police force before the war. But Alex knew quite a bit: Carol's engagement to Don Richardson and the colonel's defiant refusal to believe in his son's death; Greg's fine record in the war in spite of his reputation as a souse, to use Alex's own words; and even Elinor's marriage to Hilliard, with all that it entailed.

Dane was thoughtful when he finished.

"So we wash out the Nortons," he said. "And apparently we wash out the village too. That seems to put it up to the family, doesn't it?"

Dane ate his lunch on the porch, as absent-mindedly as he regarded now and then the view of the bay below him. He was puzzled. Jim Mason had taken a hasty survey of the bedrooms at Crestview and reported no clothing anywhere. But if the girl had been staying in the house her clothes should have been there. That left two alternatives: she had not been staying in the house, or she had, in which case there had been probably three days to dispose of what she had worn.

When Alex came back for his tray he had lit his pipe, the cigarette he had found in Maggie's garbage can on the table in front of him.

"Suppose," he said, "you wanted to get rid of a girl's clothes, and had plenty of time to do it. How would you go about it?"

Alex pondered.

"How about burning them? Plenty of furnaces around."

Dane shook his head.

"No good. Too much stuff in women's clothes that won't burn, zippers, hooks and eyes, God knows what. Nails from shoes, too. You ought to know that."

"Well, if it was me," Alex said, "and I had plenty of time I'd ship them somewhere. Hard to trace that way. I remember once—"

"I see. It's worth thinking about. You might check on that today. See if the express people sent something of the sort from any of the families around here the last of the week or today. The office is closed Saturday and today's truck doesn't leave until four o'clock. Try to get a look at what they have." He got up. "I'm going to the hospital. I'll drop you off in town."

While Alex cleaned up, Dane surveyed the possibilities. The nearest was Rockhill, the Ward property. But the Wards were elderly and lived largely in retirement, and Colonel Richardson, on the road below, was in the same category. The Dalton place was beyond the Richardson cottage facing the water, and with the Burton property, where he himself was staying, he had about completed the circuit.

None of them, he thought wryly, was likely to be involved in a cold-blooded crime. And the mystery was increased by the disappearance of the clothing. If she had been staying at Crestview, why in the name of all that was sensible hide it, since it had evidently been the intention to burn the house?

He climbed stiffly into the car when Alex brought it around, and that gentleman regarded him with a disapproving eye.

"You ought to be in bed, sir," he said. "What's the use my working on that leg if you don't take care of it?"

"I'll rest it later. I won't be long at the hospital."

Nor was he. Lucy Norton, according to the office there, was not so well and was allowed no visitors. If he suspected Floyd's large hand in this he said nothing. And Alex, picked up in the village, simply reported no soap.

"Nothing going out," he said. "Ladies in the town packed a barrel early last week for Greece. Nothing since."

Dane had been right about Floyd. By noon that day he had already traced the girl's arrival Friday morning, and after lunch he called a meeting of four men in his office: Dr. Harrison, Jim Mason, a lieutenant from the State Police, and Floyd himself. On the desk lay a bundle of partially burned clothing, and Floyd indicated it with a stubby finger.

"Well, there it is," he said. "No marks, no anything. You gentlemen got any ideas?"

Nobody apparently had, and leaning back in his chair Floyd told what he had learned of her movements after her arrival.

"One thing's sure," he said. "She set out for Crestview and she got there. She wasn't followed. She was the only passenger on the bus that got in at six-thirty that morning. So whoever killed her was around here somewhere already."

There were no dissenting voices, and he got up.

"I'm going to the hospital," he said. "Lucy Norton knows something, and she's going to talk or I'll know why."

But Lucy in her hospital bed, her leg in a cast and her hands clenched under the bedclothes, could apparently tell only of the hand that had extinguished her candle, and that some-one had rushed past her and knocked her down. Her shock when she was told of the body in the closet was genuine to the point of terror.

"A body?" she said weakly. "I don't believe you. You mean somebody at Crestview was found dead?"

"That's what I'm telling you. A woman. A young woman. Somebody knocked her on the head and killed her, then tried to burn her body. Probably the night you fell down the stairs."

Put to her thus tactfully, Lucy went into a fit of convulsive weeping. The chief waited impatiently, but when he left he still knew nothing more. But he was satisfied at least that there had been no fire while she was lying at the foot of the stairs.

"I'd have smelled anything burning," she said, sniffling. "I didn't break my nose when I fell."

"Maybe you passed out."

"I guess I did for a while. But I'd have smelled it when I came to, wouldn't I?"

She was certain, too, that all the doors were locked that night. She accounted for the front door by the fact that who-ever knocked her down must have left it open. But she was still semihysterical when he left her. After that she lay still for a long time, her eyes closed and her hands still clenched. When a nurse came in she roused herself. The story of the murder had reached the hospital, and Floyd's order as he left that Lucy was to see no one and communicate with no one had left it in a state of quivering excitement.

"I want to see Miss Spencer, Miss Carol Spencer," Lucy said feebly. "She hasn't any telephone. Maybe you'd send her a telegram."

"The doctor thought you ought to be quiet today, Mrs. Norton. I'm sure she'll be in as soon as she can."

So that was it, Lucy thought hopelessly. They wouldn't let her see Carol, she wouldn't know anything, and the police—

She lay still in her bed, her face desperate. She couldn't even warn Carol, and they probably would keep Joe out too. Not that Joe knew anything either, but she might have sent a message by him. Only—murder! She shivered and closed her eyes.

It was after that visit of Floyd's to the hospital that he sent for Carol to view the body and attempt to identify it. It was in the local mortuary, and lacking a morgue, it had been packed in ice and covered with rubber sheets. She took only one look, gasped and rushed into the air.

"That was cruel and unnecessary," she said when she got her breath. "You knew I couldn't recognize her. Nobody could."

"Well," he said, "at least you can say that at the inquest. Sorry, Miss Carol. It had to be done."

He did not take her home at once. He drove around to his office and let her out there.

"One or two things we got might help," he said. "Won't hurt to look at them. They won't bother you any," when he saw her face. "Just some stuff she was wearing."

He sat down behind the desk and opening a drawer took out a small box which he emptied onto the blotter. There was a pair of artificial pearl earrings of the stud type, somewhat scorched and rather large, and a ring. He picked up the ring and held it out.

"Might be a wedding ring, eh?" he said, watching her with sharp eyes.

"Possibly. I wouldn't know."

He let her go then, still suspicious, still hoping to break the mystery through her. Then he got busy on the telephone.

"I want the phones put back in the Spencer house this afternoon," he said. "Get a jump on, you fellows. This is a hurry job."

"It will have to go to the War Production Board, chief. Make out your application and we'll send it in."

"The hell you will," Floyd shouted. "You get three or four instruments out of that shed behind the hotel where you've got them stored, or I'll arrest the bunch of you for obstructing justice."

The instruments went in that afternoon, and Floyd walked around to where Bessie Content sat before her switchboard. "Listen, Bessie," he said. "I want you to do something for me, and keep your pretty mouth shut. Make a record of all calls from the Spencer place, and—you don't have to be deaf, do you?"

Bessie smiled with her pretty mouth.

"It gets awfully dull here sometimes," she said, "and my hearing's good, if I do say it."

After telling her to notify the night operator, Floyd went back to his office and again pored over the charred fragments on his desk. When he went home he took with him the fragment of red silk found under the body.

"Ever see a nightgown this color?" he asked his wife.

"No, and I never hope to."

She examined it carefully, going to a window to do so.

"It's good silk. That's hard to get these days. It used to come from China, you know. And it's sewed by hand," she said. "It's been expensive."

"From China, eh?" said Floyd, and lapsed into silence.

Carol in the meantime had not been able to go to the hospital. By the time her car was ready the news had spread, and to a summer colony shrunken by the war, it came as a welcome excitement in what had promised to be a dull summer. Telephones buzzed, where there were any. At the club, usually deserted in the afternoons, small groups of people gathered, and at teatime a few who had known the Spencers well drove or walked up the hill to commiserate with Carol and—if possible—to get a glimpse of the closet.

Carol received them as best she could, the elderly Wards,

old-fashioned and solicitous, Louise Stimson, the attractive young widow who had built a smart white house near the club, Marcia Dalton, the Crowells, and so on. She managed tea and Scotch for them, looking young and tired as she did so, but she could tell them nothing.

Actually the first real information she got came from Peter Crowell, a burly red-faced man with a mouselike wife.

"Well," he said. "I guess they've traced that corpse of yours, Carol. Part of the way anyhow."

The Wards looked pained, and Carol startled.

"Got it from Floyd himself," Crowell went on, enjoying the sensation he was making. "She got off the Boston train at six-thirty Friday morning and took the bus for here. Quite a looker, I understand. Quite a dresser too. White hat, silver fox coat, an overnight bag, and a big pocketbook. The bus driver says she acted queer when she got off. Looked sort of lost, he said. She asked for the drugstore. Said she wanted to telephone. He told her it was still closed, but the last he saw of her she was going that way."

"Tell them about the bag, Pete," said Ida, his wife.

He took a sip of his Scotch and soda.

"That's funny," he said. "The bus driver saw initials on it, only he can't remember them. There were three, and I understand they didn't find it in the closet. You didn't see it, did you?"

Carol's voice was slightly unsteady.

"I didn't look, Peter. All I saw—"

The Wards got up abruptly, and old Mrs. Ward took Carol's hand and held it.

"I'm sure," she said, looking around the room, "that Carol would prefer not discussing what has happened." She turned back to her. "I'm sorry, my dear. If you care to stay with us for the next few days we'd be delighted to have you. That is really why we came."

Carol felt grateful to the point of tears. She managed to smile.

"You're both more than kind. I'd love to, but the servants wouldn't stay here alone. Not after what's happened."

She went out to the door with them. A graveled path connected the two properties, broken only by the lane leading up the hill. She walked to it with them, asking about Terry, their grandson who was flying in the Pacific, and telling them about Greg. They looked much older, she thought, and rather feeble. The war was hard on people like that. She felt saddened, and this was not helped when on her return she learned that the telephones were in again.

She would have to call Newport now. There was no longer any excuse.

The others drifted away slowly, until only Louise Stimson and Marcia Dalton were left. Peter Crowell's departing speech was characteristic.

"Any objection to my looking at that closet?" he said.

"The police have sealed it, Peter."

He looked annoyed.

"Well," he said, "soon as you can, get it opened and have it painted. Then just forget about it. What's it got to do with you anyhow? A strange girl gets herself killed in it. You don't know her. So what?"

She went back to Louise and Marcia. They were smoking, and she lit a cigarette and sat down. She had a definite impression that each was determined to outstay the other, Louise with an amused smile, Marcia's horselike face and tall thin body rather grim.

"So you've met Jerry Dane," Louise said. "Interesting type."

"I wouldn't know. Is he?"

"Definitely yes." She glanced at Marcia. "A wounded hero, isn't he? And good-looking too. Why on earth come here to recuperate?"

"There's no mystery about that," Marcia said tartly. "The Burtons offered him their house. At least," she added, glancing at Louise, "Carol has managed to meet him. That's more than you can say."

Louise got up.

"I didn't have a body around," she said cheerfully. "There's still hope, of course. Most things come in threes, don't they?"

She left on that, but Marcia stayed, planted solidly in her chair, with her thin legs stuck out in front of her. Carol knew her well, and she relaxed somewhat.

"What do you think of Jerry Dane?" Marcia asked abruptly.

"I haven't really thought of him at all. I haven't had time."

Marcia shrugged.

"Well, he's definitely a mystery. We've all asked him to dinner. We've asked him for bridge. We've even, God help us, asked him for backgammon and gin rummy. But nothing doing. He's still an invalid, and goes to bed early. An invalid! He climbs hills like a goat. I've seen him myself."

"Maybe he doesn't like games," Carol said indifferently. "I hope you don't mind, Marcia, but I've had a long day."

Marcia got up, but she did not leave. She stood looking into the patio.

"I suppose this house is an architectural bastard," she said, "but I've always liked it. It's queer Elinor never comes here, isn't it?" She fixed Carol with shrewd eyes.

"She likes Newport better. That's all. It's easier for Howard to get there for weekends."

But she realized that Marcia had dragged in Elinor's name for a purpose, and she felt herself stiffening.

"It's queer," Marcia said, still watching her. "I thought I saw her car about two o'clock last Saturday morning. I'd know that car anywhere."

"That's ridiculous, Marcia."

"I suppose it is. I just thought I'd better tell you. Someone else may have seen it too, or thought so. It was going toward the railroad, and making sixty miles at least. I didn't think there was another car like it in the world."

"There must be. She hasn't been here. I know that. She was in New York."

"Well, if you're sure of that— I'm a Nurse's Aide, and I worked late at the hospital Friday night. When I got home I let that damned dog of mine out. He didn't come back, so I went after him. That's how it happened."

"It's absurd, Marcia. You saw a car. You didn't see Elinor in it, and she wasn't in it. She couldn't have been."

But she was not so sure. She knew the deadly sharpness of Marcia's eyes. She knew, too, how the story would grow if Marcia told it. It was Marcia herself who reassured her.

"I suppose I was mistaken," she said. "Anyhow no use starting talk. You know this place. Any summer colony, for that matter. I'm not telling it, Carol. You can count on me."

It was some time after she left before Carol could control her hands sufficiently to light a cigarette.

SEVEN

SHE CALLED ELINOR that evening, shutting herself in the library to do it. There was something reassuring in Elinor's matter-of-fact voice.

"Hello, Carol," she said. "I hear you've had some trouble there."

"You know about it?"

"The gentlemen of the press," Elinor said lightly. "I've been trying to get you for some time, but you know what long-distance is nowadays. I hope it hasn't been too bad."

"It's been bad enough. Does Mother know?"

"Not yet. Of course when the papers get it— Have they any idea who it is?"

"Not yet."

"Her clothes ought to tell them something."

"They haven't found her clothes. Look here, Elinor. I called you up to tell you something. Marcia Dalton says she saw your car here last Friday night, or Saturday morning. She's just told me."

There was a brief pause. Then Elinor laughed.

"Marcia's seeing things," she said. "Tell her I have a perfect alibi, and that I don't go around murdering people in the middle of the night."

"You did go to New York?"

"I hope the telephone operators along the line are enjoying this," Elinor said coldly. "For their benefit I'll tell you that I left my car in Providence on Friday, took a train to New York, stayed in our apartment that night, shopped all day Saturday, had dinner with my husband that evening and went to the theater afterward."

"You stayed in your apartment?"

"Why not? The club was jammed. So was every hotel. What's

the matter with you anyhow? Do I have to have an alibi?"

Carol felt foolish as Elinor rang off with her customary abruptness. Of course Marcia had been mistaken. What possible connection could Elinor in New York have with a murder on the Maine coast? Or, granting there was one, would she possibly have risked everything she prized so highly on such an excursion? Yet there remained the puzzling question of why the dead girl had come to Crestview, and why Lucy—if she knew about it—had let her stay.

Elinor *could* have made it. She could have come by car, arriving that night, gone back to Providence the same way, left her car there, and taken an early morning train to New York. Only why? Had the girl been Howard's mistress? His money laid him open to that sort of thing. But even then she could see Elinor's sheer disdain of a dirty business. She might leave him, demanding an enormous settlement, or she might choose to stay on and ignore the situation. But to connect her with a crime of passion was impossible.

Carol was still in the library when Jerry Dane tapped at the terrace door. She admitted him, and he looked down at her gravely.

"I'm afraid I was rude to you today," he said. "My leg was hurting damnably, and—well, I'm sorry. I won't do it again."

"It's all right," she told him. "I don't blame you for calling me one of the cumberers of the earth. I just can't help it, that's all. I have to look after my mother."

"Don't make me more abject than I am. I came to tell you I couldn't see Mrs. Norton. Did you?"

"No." She recited her day while he listened, about being compelled to look at the body and the things on Floyd's desk, and the fact that by the time her car was ready she could not go to the hospital. He had taken out a pipe and filled it, and as she talked she watched him. He was hard, she thought, the sort of man who in a war killed without scruple. But he was honest too. Honest and dependable, and she had to talk to someone or go mad.

"There's something else I ought to tell you," she said. "It happened here this afternoon, and it has bothered me a lot. There's no truth in it, of course, but it could cause trouble.

Marcia Dalton claims to have seen my sister's car here the night
Lucy was hurt and this girl was murdered."

"Have you called your sister?"

"Of course. She has an alibi. She was in New York that night.
It's ridiculous, isn't it?"

"Naturally." His face remained impassive. "Is there anything else? Might as well clear the slate, you know."

"Well," she said, her voice doubtful. "I suppose I should
have told the police before this, but I couldn't see Lucy, and
the place has been full of people this afternoon." She looked at
him apologetically. "I don't even like telling you, but I suppose
I must."

"I see," he said patiently. "Just what is all this about?"

"It's about the yellow room, the room over this. Somebody
had been staying there, and taken a bath."

His voice sharpened.

"Didn't the police look over the house?"

"I suppose they glanced in. They were looking for her
clothes, weren't they? They wouldn't notice anything else. They
probably thought Lucy Norton slept there. But the bed's been
used, there's powder on the toilet table, and there are cigarette
ashes on the floor. Lucy doesn't smoke, of course, and she slept
in the service wing."

"And her clothes?"

"There were no clothes there when I saw it."

There was a longish pause. His pipe was dead, and he did
not relight it.

"They didn't find her clothes," he said at last. "I was here,
you know. Mason came back empty-handed. But if she slept
here she undressed here. The simplest answer is that whoever
killed her took her clothes away so she wouldn't be identified.
That and the fire— See here, Miss Spencer, do you still main-
tain that you have no idea who she was? Or why she was here?"

She shook her head.

"No to both," she said. "So far as I know I've never seen
her before, or heard of her."

"Well, let's put it another way. Who knew you were coming
back, and when?"

"Quite a lot of people. It was no secret."

"Isn't it possible she was waiting here to see you?"

"Why on earth would she? There's a hotel in town. Lots of people rent rooms, too. To come here, with the house cold and empty—"

"She did come, you see," he said, still patiently. "She came, or she was brought here after her death. What you say about the yellow room seems to indicate that she came. When she came is another matter. If she slipped in at night after Mrs. Norton had gone to bed it might explain some things."

"Explain what?"

"Explain why Mrs. Norton apparently knew nothing about her being here." He got up. "Mind if I look at the yellow room? Unless you've had it cleaned."

"It's the way I found it. The door's locked."

He nodded his approval, and they went up the stairs together.

The yellow room was as she had left it. She noticed that he touched nothing when he went in. He inspected the bed, where a spot of lipstick showed on one of the sheets. He bent over and looked at the cigarette ash on the floor. And he stood for some time at the bathroom door.

"Was this left as it is?" he asked rather sharply. "Soap and towels, and so on, when you left last year?"

"Soap? I hadn't noticed. I supposed Lucy puts such things away when she closes the house."

"Then this girl seems to have known her way around pretty well," he said grimly. "Either that, or Mrs. Norton knew she was here. What about these towels? Are they from the servants' rooms?"

"They're guest towels. That's queer. Lucy must have given them to her."

He turned to a window and stood there, looking out. There was still some light, and a breeze was covering the bay with small white-capped waves. Except for a few fishing boats the harbor was empty, and overhead an army plane was making its way to some inland field. He was not thinking of the harbor, however, or even of the war at that moment.

"Floyd is going to trace her further, if he can," he said, without turning. "Whether anyone in the town saw her. Whether she made any inquiries to find this place. He's a small-town policeman, but he's nobody's fool."

He was still at the window when they heard a car chugging up the hill. He put out the light quickly.

"Sounds like his car," he said. "Better get downstairs. And let me do the talking if you can."

They were in the library and Dane was filling his pipe when Nora announced the callers. They came in rather portentously, Floyd, Dr. Harrison, the state trooper, and still another man in plain clothes. Floyd was carrying a bundle under his arm.

The chief introduced the strangers, Lieutenant Wylie and Mr. Campbell.

"Mr. Campbell is the district attorney," he said impressively. "Seems like we're getting famous all at once."

"That's hardly the word," said Mr. Campbell dryly, as Floyd placed his package on the center table. "We don't like to disturb you, Miss Spencer, but we're trying to identify the—this woman. It seems likely that she had a reason for coming here. After all"—he cleared his throat—"there are a good many houses here not being opened for the summer. It seems strange her body was found in this one."

It was Dane who answered that. He was standing by the fire, looking interested but nothing more.

"Probably most of them are boarded up," he said. "This one happened to be open."

"With a caretaker in it," said Mr. Campbell. "Why take a chance on a thing like that?"

Carol asked them to sit down, and offered them cigarettes. Lieutenant Wylie produced a pipe and asked if she objected. Then Mr. Campbell cleared his throat.

"I need not stress the need of identification of this woman, Miss Spencer," he said. "I believe you have said you don't know her."

"I didn't say that," she protested. "How can I tell? I hardly saw her, and when I did— I can't think of anyone who would come here, or why they would be killed here. All I know is that she *was* here."

Her voice sounded strained, and the doctor smiled at her.

"No need to worry, Carol," he said. "It's only a matter of

identification. She may have been killed outside and her body brought here."

"But it wasn't," she said, half hysterically. "She had slept here. Go up and see for yourselves. She had slept in the yellow room."

If she had tossed a bomb into the room, the reaction could hardly have been greater. They poured out into the hall and up the stairs, and Carol found Dane's hand on her arm.

"Better not say I've been up there," he said cautiously. "Let them look for themselves."

She nodded. Dr. Harrison knew the yellow room, and the others were already inside when they got there. The place spoke for itself, the bed, the toilet table, the tub in the bathroom, and the district attorney looked at Floyd.

"Missed this this morning, didn't you?" he said unpleasantly.

"How the hell could I know Jim Mason hasn't the sense of a louse?" Floyd said. "I had my hands full as it was." He turned to Carol. "When did you find out she'd slept here?"

"One of the maids saw it."

"When was that?" he barked.

"Around noon, I think."

"And you didn't report it?"

"I thought someone would be back. I had no telephone, and the house was full of people all afternoon. I locked the door so it wouldn't be disturbed."

He eyed her suspiciously.

"It wasn't locked just now, Miss Spencer."

The lieutenant had opened the closet door.

"Nothing here," he said laconically. "Unless—"

He was a tall man. He ran an exploratory hand over the closet shelf, and when he brought it out it was holding a small white hat. It was a gay little hat, crisp and new, and all the eyes in the room were turned on Carol.

"Belong to you?" the lieutenant inquired.

"No," she said faintly. "I never saw it before."

She sat down on a chair inside the door. More than anything else the little hat had brought the real tragedy of the murder home to her. She felt dizzy and her heart was pounding furiously. She did not realize that Floyd was standing over her until he spoke.

"You missed it, didn't you, Miss Spencer?"

"Missed it? I never saw it."

He looked triumphantly around the room.

"I'm wondering," he said, "just what became of the rest of her clothes. She came here in a black dress and a pair of pumps, and she had a purse and an overnight bag. She undressed in this room. Look at that hat. Now what I want to know is who disposed of them, and how?"

Carol stared at him.

"Why would I do it? When she was killed I was at my sister's in Newport. I didn't come into this room until Freda reported it to me. And I didn't even need to tell you about it. I did. Isn't that enough?"

"Somebody got those clothes," he said doggedly.

Sheer indignation brought her to her feet.

"Why don't you go down and look in the furnace?" she said indignantly. "That's where I would burn them, isn't it? Go on down, all of you, sift the ashes—that's what you do, isn't it? And I hope you get good and dirty!"

"Don't you worry about me getting dirty," Floyd said grimly, and after locking the door led the way downstairs again.

In the library once more the state trooper placed the hat beside the package on the table, and Floyd went over what he had so far discovered. The girl had got off the bus at half past six or thereabouts on Friday morning, June the sixteenth. She had asked the driver for the drugstore, but he had told her it would not be open yet. After that nobody saw her in the town that early morning until at seven-thirty or so Mr. Allison who owned the local Five-&-Ten, saw a girl in a white hat, a fur jacket and a black dress sitting in the public park near the bandstand. When he looked again, she was gone.

After that the trail picked up somewhat. She had had a cup of coffee at Sam's hamburger stand when it opened at eight, and asked for a telephone book. Apparently she did not find what she wanted, and Sam had told her half the telephones in town had been taken out. She had not seemed worried, however. She had merely said a walk would do her good, and asked the direction of Shore Drive, which led to Crestview.

Sam had said she was pretty, about twenty-five or so, and very well dressed. What he actually said, Carol learned later, was that she "looked like some of the summer crowd," and that he didn't think she would walk far "in them spike-heeled shoes she wore."

None of the taxi men in town had seen her. Apparently she had walked to her destination, whatever that was.

Dane did not interrupt. He listened intently, but when the district attorney made a gesture toward the package he made a protest.

"Is that necessary?" he asked. "Miss Spencer has had a bad day. She looks exhausted."

"We have to do what we can, major. There may be something here she will recognize."

It was Floyd who opened the bundle, carefully saving the string his big fingers working at the knots. Opened and spread out on the table was what was left of the short fur jacket, badly burned, the scorched pair of bedroom slippers, and a few scraps of cloth, one of them red silk or rayon. Over all was the odor of burned fur, and Dane quickly lit a cigarette and gave it to Carol.

It helped somewhat. She was able to face the table, even to go to it. Floyd was holding up the scrap of red material and once more all the faces were turned to her.

"What's this, Miss Spencer?" Floyd asked.

"I wouldn't know. It looks—it might be part of a kimono or a dressing gown. It wouldn't be a slip."

"That's what my wife says." He looked around the room. "So what? So she was undressed. She wasn't expecting any trouble. She undressed and went to bed in that room upstairs, and what happened to her happened to her in this house."

Dane spoke for the first time.

"That doesn't follow," he said. "She might have gone outside, for some purpose."

"What difference does it make?" said Floyd belligerently. "She's dead, isn't she?"

"It might change things somewhat." Dane picked up one of the slippers and shook it. A pine needle slipped out and lay on the desk, and Floyd flushed angrily. "Whether she was killed in this house or not," Dane said casually, "she was outside that night. What does Mrs. Norton say?"

"That's my business," Floyd said gruffly, and proceeded to tie up the package again, crushing the white hat in with the rest and fastening it carefully with the string he had saved. They left after that, all except Dane, but following a colloquy at the front door the state trooper came back to the library.

"I'm afraid I'm going to bother you some more, Miss Spencer," he said apologetically. "I'd like to look over the house, if you don't mind, and . . ." He hesitated, then smiled. "The district attorney thinks it would be a good idea to clean out the furnace. It's lighted, I suppose."

Carol had rallied. She even managed to smile at him.

"Of course," she said, "I had to burn up the evidence somehow. It's been going all day."

He grinned back at her.

"Some things don't burn, you know," he said cheerfully. "You'd be surprised how many. Nails out of high-heeled pumps, snaps off clothes, buttons, initials off bags, all sorts of things. You sift them out of the ashes and there you are."

The last they saw of him he was going lightly up the stairs, and for some time they heard him moving about in the yellow room overhead.

Dane was thoughtful.

"Just remember this," he said. "Even if they find those things have been burned in the furnace, it doesn't connect you with the case."

"You think they will?"

"It's possible, if not particularly intelligent. Of course Mrs. Norton's accident may have prevented it. Whoever did it couldn't know she'd broken her leg. They might have expected her to run screaming out of the house."

He left soon after that, telling her to lock her door but that otherwise she was safe enough. "There will be troopers in the basement all night," he said. "Better get all the sleep you can. I may need you tomorrow."

With which cryptic statement he departed, going out through the door to the terrace and motioning her to lock it behind him.

EIGHT

CAROL DID NOT SLEEP MUCH, although she felt relaxed. Through the old-fashioned register in the floor came the muffled sound of men's voices from the furnace cellar, and she learned in the morning that the lieutenant and one of his men had spent most of the night there. They had made a thorough job of it, emptying the furnace itself and coming up to wash looking as if a bomb had buried them. But all they found was the melted remains of what looked like a teaspoon, which Maggie had reported as missing since the year before.

The word had gone out by that time. Floyd may have lacked a camera, but he knew police procedure. He had sent out a description of the girl to the Missing Persons Bureau and by teletype all over the country. The newspapers had been busy too, and evidently Elinor had been unable to keep them from her mother. Carol, still keeping up largely on coffee, was called to the telephone to hear Mrs. Spencer's voice, shaken and hysterical:

"What sort of a mess have you got yourself into? The papers are dreadful."

Carol controlled herself with difficulty.

"It was done before I got here, mother. Please don't worry."

"It's easy for you to say that. When I think of the notoriety, the disgrace of the whole thing— I'll never live in that house again. Never. And I want you to leave, Carol. Do you hear me? Come back here at once."

"I'll have to wait for the inquest, mother."

"Good heavens, are they having an inquest? Why?"

Carol finally lost her patience.

"Because it's a murder," she said. "Because they think we had something to do with it. And I'm not so sure but what we had."

She rang off, feeling ashamed of her outburst but somewhat relieved by it.

There was a new development that day, one which seemed to justify her last statement to her mother, although it was some time before she learned about it. On that same morning, Tuesday, June twentieth, a caller appeared at the East Sixty-seventh Precinct station in New York City. He looked uneasy, and he carried a morning paper in his hand. The desk sergeant was reading a paper, too. He looked up over it.

"Anything I can do for you?"

"I'm not sure. It's about this murder up in Maine. I think maybe I saw the girl, right here in town."

"Plenty of people think that. Had five or six already."

But later the visitor's story proved interesting, to say the least.

He was the doorman at the apartment house on Park Avenue where the Spencers lived, and on the morning the family had left for the country, a girl had called. She had asked for Miss Carol Spencer, and seemed greatly disappointed when told she had gone. What had taken him to the station house was that the description fitted this girl, white hat, fur jacket and all.

"She acted like she didn't know just what to do," the police reported his statement. "I thought maybe she'd just got off a train. She had a little bag with her, as well as a pocketbook. I don't know what she *did* do, either. The elevator man was off, and just then the bell rang. When I came down again she was gone."

That, he said, had been about ten o'clock the previous Thursday.

Carol did not learn this until later. She was worried and upset that morning. She had called the hospital, to learn that Lucy Norton was allowed no visitors, and to suspect that the police were keeping her incommunicado until the inquest. Also both the younger girls were threatening to leave, Freda declaring that she had seen a man in the grounds from her window after she had put out the light the night before. Only dire threats by Maggie that the police would follow and bring them back kept them at all.

She was unpacking her trunk when Nora came up to tell her

Colonel Richardson was downstairs, and she went down reluctantly. He was standing by the library fire, and looking shocked.

"My dear girl!" he said. "I just heard, or I'd have come before. How dreadful for you."

"It's all rather horrible. We don't even know who she was."

"So I understand. I learned only just now, when I went to the village. But surely Lucy Norton would know. I saw her husband bringing her that morning."

"The police aren't letting her see anyone."

He considered that. She thought he looked very tired, and his lips had a bluish tinge. His heart was not too good, and he had probably walked up the hill.

"Well, thank God it doesn't concern you," he said. "I'll not keep you, my dear. And don't worry too much. Floyd is an excellent man."

He left soon after. She went with him to the door and watched him start down the drive, leaning rather heavily on his stick. When she turned to go in she saw Dane. He was still in slacks and sweater, and he was carefully surveying the shape of the hill behind the house. When the colonel had disappeared he walked over to the drive and, stopping, examined the grass border beside it.

He straightened and grinned at her.

"Hello," he said. "Colonel know anything?"

"No. He'd just heard."

He lit a cigarette and limped over to her.

"How about helping me with a little job this morning?" he inquired. "I'm no bird dog, with this leg. I could use an assistant."

"What sort of job?"

"Oh, just hither and yon," he said vaguely. "Know if anybody tramped around this drive lately?"

"Outside of a half dozen men I don't think of anybody."

"Up the hill, I mean."

"Oh, that?" She looked up the hill. It was heavily overgrown with shrubbery, and on the crest was an abandoned house, gray and forlorn in the morning light. "I wouldn't know. I don't think so."

"How about the tool house? That's it up there, isn't it?"

"There's a path to it. Anyhow George Smith is in the hospital. He hasn't been around lately."

"Well, someone's been up that hill lately. The ground's dry. There hasn't been any rain for weeks. But the faucet for the garden hose has dripped in one place, and somebody stepped in it."

"That doesn't mean a thing," she said. "The deer sometimes come down at night."

"The deer don't wear flat rubber-heeled shoes," he said shortly.

"I'm afraid I don't know what you mean."

"Well, look," he said rather impatiently. "According to Alex, those troopers didn't find anything in the furnace last night. So there are several alternatives. Her clothes were burned elsewhere, they were shipped out of town—which they weren't—or they're hidden someplace."

"And you think they are hidden?"

"Hidden. Possibly buried. Look back, Miss Spencer. Things didn't go according to schedule. Lucy Norton awakened. That was a bad break. Then she fell down the stairs. That gave whoever did it a bit of time, but not much. And there was a lot of stuff to dispose of, the woman's clothes, her pocketbook, and her overnight bag. How far could the killer travel with all that? With air wardens patrolling for lights, and fire watchers looking for fires ever since the drought? Not to mention lovers on back lanes like the one over there."

"I see. You think the things are on the hill."

"I think it's possible. That's all."

"But if they meant to burn the house, why bother with them at all?"

"Remember what I said about Lucy. There wasn't a chance to set a fire that night. It was done later. It had to be."

They started slowly up the hill, beginning at the leaking pipe and being careful not to step on the mark he had discovered. It was small, either from a woman's flat shoe or from that of a rather undersized man. There were no prints beyond it. The hill stretched up, dry and dusty, and before long Carol's slacks were covered with sandburs and her stockings ruined. Dane did not move directly. He circled right and left, but when they reached the deserted house above neither of them had found anything. Dane sat down abruptly and rubbed his leg.

"Damn the thing," he said irritably. "I'll get hell from Alex for this."

He gave her a cigarette and lit one himself.

"You might call this a preliminary search," he said. "They're not on top of the ground. They may be under it."

"Buried?"

"Maybe. It's been done, you know. The idea is to lift a shrub, say, and dig a hole. After that you replant the shrub and pray for rain. Otherwise the thing may wilt and die. There hasn't been any rain." He gave his slightly bitter smile. "Someone around here may be watching the sky this very minute, hoping for rain," he said. "Pleasant thought, isn't it?"

He got up and dusted off his slacks.

"I don't like your being in that house alone," he said abruptly. "Oh, I know. It's all over, and you're a damned attractive girl and nobody would want to hurt you. So was that other girl, remember. But I was a fool to bring you up on this hill. If anybody gets the idea that you're looking for something here— There's one thing to remember about murder. It's the first one that's hard."

"I ought to be safe enough. We haven't found anything."

"That's not what I said."

They went down the hill, this time by way of the tool house, and outside it he stopped.

"Mind if I go in?" he asked.

"It's probably locked."

It was not locked, however. George's appendicitis attack had probably been sudden. Dane opened the door and went inside. It was orderly in the extreme, a table with an old oilcloth covering, a chair, a shelf with a hit-or-miss collection of dishes, and around the walls garden implements in tidy rows, an electric lawn mower, rakes, spades, wicker brooms, and coils of hose.

"Neat fellow, George," he said, and looked around him. "About the way he left it last fall. Except—" He stopped over something, but did not touch it. "Come in," he said. "It looks as though we may be right, after all."

What he had found was a spade. It was deeply encrusted with clay, and a few dried leaves were still stuck to it. Carol stared down at it.

"You think they were buried with this?"

"There's a good chance, isn't there? In that case whoever buried them knew about this tool house. Knew where it was and what was in it. Interesting, isn't it? Don't touch it. There may be prints on it."

Carol did not hear him. She was standing in the doorway, looking at the shelf, her eyes incredulous.

"There's mother's Lowestoft tea set," she said slowly. "And father's picture, and the sampler Granny did when she was a little girl."

"Maybe George liked them!"

"You don't understand." She was fairly drugged with amazement. "They were all in the house last fall. I don't understand. George wouldn't touch them, or Lucy. It looks as though someone meant to save them."

She reached up for the china, and Dane slapped her hands smartly.

"Don't touch," he said. "You've got to learn this game, my girl, and it isn't a pretty one."

She was still bewildered.

"I wonder," she said. "Freda says she saw a man in the grounds last night. Do you think he was after these? It sounds silly, doesn't it?"

He did not think it sounded silly. He thought it sounded rather sinister, in fact. But he said nothing. He found a battered tin tray and using his handkerchief to move them he placed the china, the photograph, and the framed sampler on it. Then, tucking the spade under his arm and remarking that he felt like a moving van, he left her, taking a short cut through the trees to the Burton house and grinning when he saw Alex's face. He put the tray down on the living-room table and eyed it lovingly.

"What's Tim Murphy doing these days?" he inquired.

Alex rallied.

"Not so much, sir. You know the private detective business.

It's kind of up and down."

"Good," Dane said cheerfully. "Let's hope it's down. I think we need him here, Alex. Better see if you can locate him. And don't call from the village. I have an idea Floyd has the telephones pretty well tied up."

Alex looked rebellious, but Dane ignored it.

"Tell him to take the night train from Boston if he can make it," he said. "You can meet him tomorrow morning with the car. And have him bring a camera. I want the prints on this stuff."

"Isn't that Floyd's business?"

Dane's strong thin face hardened.

"Listen," he said harshly. "I'm making it my business, and I'm working fast. There's a girl over there who may not be safe, and I can't bother with small-town police just now. Get that, and keep your mouth shut. Tell Tim to bring some old clothes too, the worse the better. He may have to do some gardening."

This idea cheered Alex so enormously that he made an excellent imitation of an omelet for lunch, singing over his frying pan as he did so.

Carol did not tell Maggie about her discovery in the tool house. She felt tired and discouraged. The mystery was deepening, and a second attempt to see Lucy brought no results. The hospital reported over the telephone that she was still not allowed visitors.

Because she was weary she did something she had not done since she came. She used the elevator to go upstairs, and it was in the elevator that she found something. She had not turned on the light, but she felt something under her foot as it slowly climbed, and reaching down felt for it. It was only a bobby pin, so she held it indifferently until she reached her room.

There she glanced at it. It was a pale color, and there was a long hair caught in it. She felt rather sick as she looked at it, for the hair was blond, and she was certain it had belonged to the murdered girl.

She put it on her toilet table, and lay down on the chaise longue. She did not realize that it had any significance, except that the girl had at one time or another been in the elevator.

And she had not much time to think about it. Nora reported a message that the inquest would be held on Thursday, and that she was to attend. But there was a second message, which filled her with dread. Colonel Richardson hoped she would dine with him that night.

She had known it must happen. Ever since Don's plane had crashed into the sea she had had these solitary meals with his father, here in Maine last summer, once or twice in New York when he was on his way to Florida or coming back from there. Always she dreaded them, his obstinate refusal to accept his son's death, his determined cheerfulness and plans for her future—and Don's.

Nevertheless, she sent word that she would go, and getting up drearily hunted out a dinner dress and sent it down to be pressed. She did not lie down again. She pulled a chair to the window and sat there looking out.

Could Elinor have been in Bayside when Marcia claimed to have seen her? And if so, why? She went over Elinor's conduct at Newport. She had certainly been unlike herself. She did not often have headaches, yet she had spent one whole afternoon and evening shut away with one. And there was the time when Carol had found her at the safe in her bedroom. She had been surprised, not too pleasantly.

She knew Elinor through and through. Behind her lovely face was determination and a certain hardness. If she cared for anyone it was for Greg. But if Howard was threatening her position and security she might go to any length to preserve them. Still, Elinor and murder!

She tried to think clearly. If the girl had come deliberately to the house it had been to see someone. Not Lucy. Surely not Lucy. Then it was either her mother or herself, or both. But what story had she told, that Lucy Norton had put her in the yellow room? It must have been good, for Lucy to accept a stranger. For a moment she wondered about Greg, then she dismissed him. He had been away for a year, and he was deeply in love with Virginia. Turn things about as she would she came back to Elinor, Elinor who would have known how her mother valued the tea set and the other things now in the tool house.

Having reached that point she picked up the telephone and called long-distance; and Bessie at her switchboard in the village pricked up her ears.

She got Elinor without trouble.

"I want you to come up here," she said without preamble. "I'm not taking this thing alone, and the inquest is on Thursday."

"Don't be ridiculous," Elinor's voice was sharp. "Why on earth should I come? Anyhow, we're giving a dinner that night. I couldn't possibly get away."

"A dinner? Who for? Greg?"

"Greg's in New York, and Mother's having a fit. But he has no idea of going to Maine. I know that. Why don't you close the house and go back home? Mother won't go to Crestview now, and she loathes it here."

"Aren't you forgetting something?" Carol said tartly. "We've had a murder here. I can't leave. You'd better come, Elinor. Your name may be dragged into this yet."

"If you mean that story of Marcia's, don't be a fool. You know Marcia."

"I do. And I know you could have been here. You'd better bring your alibi with you."

Elinor laughed, without mirth.

"I suppose you know that that girl was asking for you in New York. The doorman reported it to the police this morning. That leaves us all involved, doesn't it?"

"The more reason for you to come."

There was a brief silence. Carol could almost see Elinor, her active mind weighing the pros and cons of the situation. When she spoke again she had evidently decided.

"I dare say the telephone operator will testify if Marcia doesn't," she said. "You've certainly given her plenty to think about. I suppose I'll have to come. It's absurd, of course. I can take the train Wednesday night. You'd better meet me."

"I'll send a taxi," Carol said shortly. "And listen, Elinor. Don't bring your maid. I can't take care of her, and it's quiet here anyhow. She'd be bored to death."

"Quiet!" said Elinor. "You don't sound quiet." She rang off, and Carol went back to her chair. Her room usually quieted her, with its picture window looking out over the water, its dusty rose walls, its French blue furniture and white rug. It had been an oasis of peace, too, after the shock of Don's death. Now she glanced at his picture. Incredible that he was gone, she thought, and that she was here alone. He had been so alive; he and Terry Ward tramping in and out of the house, raiding the kitchen together, golfing and swimming together, with her tagging along. They had all been too young for Greg and Elinor, of course. And Don had never liked Greg. She didn't know why, unless he was jealous of him, his plane, his good looks, the big house and the money.

Greg had only laughed about her engagement.

Nevertheless, she felt better now that Elinor was coming. They were not particularly congenial, but Elinor had brains. She was far more intelligent than Greg, who was in some ways still the little boy who never grew up. And Elinor's hard common sense was what she needed now. She had put her head back and closed her eyes when Dane found her there, late in the afternoon.

He had had a busy time. He had called Floyd at the police station, but he was out, and Jim Mason innocently gave him a piece of news; that the doorman at the Spencer apartment house had notified his precinct station house that somebody answering the dead girl's description had called there last Thursday morning.

"They'd gone," Jim said. "She must have followed them."

"Not here," Dane said shortly. "They weren't here. Who did she ask for?"

"Carol Spencer, he says. Wait a minute. It's here somewhere."

Dane could hear him shuffling among some papers. When he spoke again he was evidently reading.

"Stated that she asked for Miss Spencer, and that he told her the Spencer family had left for the summer," he read. "Did not say where they had gone."

"Thanks, Mason."

He rang off. It was another thread, he thought, pointing in the same direction. The dead girl had known where to find Carol Spencer. But that had been on Thursday, and she had reached the village Friday morning. She had evidently not known about the Newport visit.

Out on the porch he wondered why the case was interesting him so much. He had had worse ones, many of them. And he knew he was not helping his leg any. Alex's disapproval followed him wherever he went. He sat there for some time, feeling tired and uncertain. The breeze was ruffling the surface of the bay, and a great sea eagle was drifting with the wind. A navy dirigible was moving oceanward, and he watched it, scowling. For the climb up the hill had told him something. He was not ready to go back to his work. If he did, they would put him on a desk job. He had missed so much, he thought savagely, and now here he sat like an old dog, licking his wounds.

His inertia did not last long. When he heard Alex snoring after the lunch dishes had been washed he tackled the hillside once more.

This time he did not go by way of Crestview. He went up through the woods from the Burton place and, concealed by the trees and heavy undergrowth, began to work down the slope. The air was cooler by that time, although the light was not so good, and it was by pure chance that he stumbled on something which proved his theory correct.

He had thrown away his cigarette and ground it out with his heel. Within five inches of his foot something partly hidden by dead leaves was shining. He stooped and picked it up.

After dropping it in his pocket he turned and retraced his steps, taking a line from the tool house to where he had found it and going on from there. The growth was particularly heavy. There were times when he had to crawl, and other times when an outcropping of rock forced him to detour. But he found nothing more, and at last, dirty and discouraged, he went down to the Spencer house and to follow an astounded Nora up the stairs.

"That Major Dane is here, miss," she said. "I told him you were resting, but he said it was important. He said not to get up. He'll take only a minute."

"I'll go down. Ask him to wait."

Dane was behind Nora, however, and he came without ceremony into the room. Distracted as she was, Carol smiled when she saw him. His slacks were stained, his sweater was snagged, and there was a long scratch along one cheek. He grinned sheepishly.

"You'd never guess they're after me for the movies, would you?" he said. He pulled up a chair and sat down. "Sorry to barge in like this. You look as though you needed a rest. Delayed shock, probably."

She turned wide candid eyes on him.

"Not delayed shock. Just one shock after another. I don't believe that girl was killed in the house, Major Dane. I think she was brought in later. That's why the front door was open."

"That doesn't necessarily follow. Who opened it in the first place?"

"Perhaps she did it herself." She got up and going to her toilet table picked up the bobby pin.

"I found it in the elevator," she told him. "It's a bobby pin, if you know what that is."

He took it and went to the window with it.

"In the elevator?" he said, after a minute. "Where's that? I haven't seen an elevator."

"You can't tell it's there unless you know about it. The doors are solid. There were two large closets, one on each floor, and Mother had it put there."

"Where is it?"

"The upper door opens next to the linen closet. I just happened to use it today. I was tired."

"It hasn't been used since you came?"

"I suppose the bags were brought up in it. They usually are. But that pin is for light hair, and the hair in it is blond. None of us here is a blonde, and—she was, wasn't she?"

He nodded absently. Of course the elevator had been used, he thought. If there had been any prints they would be gone now. Like the linen closet. Probably like the spade handle. Probably like everything in the whole damned case. But if the elevator was concealed it meant that someone who knew about it had used it to carry the girl's body to where it had been found.

"I suppose it was well known? The elevator, I mean?"

"Mother always used it. It wasn't any secret."

He said nothing. He folded the bobby pin in a clean handkerchief and put it back into his pocket. Then he opened his hand and placed something on the chaise longue beside her. She raised up to see it better. It was a large metal initial, such as is fastened on a woman's handbag. It was an *M,* and she looked from it to his impassive face.

"Where did you find it?" she asked.

"I went up the hill again this afternoon. It wasn't far from the top."

"Anyone could have lost it, couldn't they?"

"Not where I found it," he said grimly. "No woman ever carried a handbag through that brush. It hadn't been there long either. It's not even tarnished."

She began to feel frightened. It had nothing to do with the metal initial on the couch. It concerned the man beside her. Elinor could laugh at Marcia. She could and probably would wrap Floyd and the district attorney and all the rest of them around her delicate finger tips. But this man was different. He had a bulldog tenacity, an unsmiling determination that began to alarm her. He must have seen it in her face, for he got up impatiently.

"I wonder what you're worrying about," he said. "You know this is part of that dead woman's outfit. You know her clothes are somewhere about, or at least you did this morning. What's happened since? What are you afraid of? Your sister?"

He didn't wait for an answer. He stalked to the window and stood there, looking out.

"Nice view you have," he said, in a different voice. "Better than mine, I think." He turned then, came back, and picked up the gadget from the couch. "I'll let you rest now. I have to bathe and shave. I'm dining out tonight."

She was definitely uneasy now. If he was dining out, he must have a reason. But she tried to make her voice light.

"Don't tell me you've succumbed at last. Who succeeded in getting you?"

"Miss Dalton. She likes to talk, I gather, and I need some information. This working in the dark——" He saw her expression, and his voice changed. "I'm sorry," he said. "I've hurt my leg again, and this thing's getting me down. Don't mind if I'm rough. I've been living a rough life."

He was ready to leave when he saw Don's picture. He went over and looked at it, the helmet, the haggard eyes, the boyish face.

"This is not your brother."

"No. It's Donald Richardson. He was lost more than a year ago, in the Pacific. I—was engaged to him."

"Sorry," he said. "A lot of fine fellows gone."

He went soon after, telling her before he left that Alex had found a man to cut the grass for her. "Not a gardener," he said, "but a useful person to have around. Name's Tim. Tim Murphy, I think. If you like he can sleep in the house. You'll be less nervous with a man around. And so will I."

NINE

THE COLONEL LOOKED BETTER that night. He wore the dinner clothes without which he was never seen after six o'clock, alone or not, and for once he did not talk about Don immediately.

He made her a cocktail, admired her summer evening dress, and served her an excellent small dinner, with some fine old claret. He did not even discuss the murder, except to say that he hoped the police were not troubling her. He rambled on. Old Nathaniel Ward was not looking well. There was a barmaid at the club, doing nicely too. The idea that women couldn't mix drinks—

He came at last and deviously to Elinor.

"She hasn't been here lately, I suppose?"

"She doesn't like it. No. She's at Newport."

"And you were with her last week?"

She felt herself stiffening. There was something coming, she knew. It came, almost immediately.

"I was quite sure of that, of course," he said, in his courtly manner. "It just happens that Mrs. Ward said something about somebody seeing a car like Elinor's here one night last week. I'm glad you can say where she was."

She took a hasty sip of claret.

"There are a number of cars like Elinor's in the country," she managed to say. "Of course it's absurd. What night was it?"

"I think it was Friday. Don't worry about it, Carol. You know how stories spread here."

He did talk of Don after dinner, and she found it for once a relief. Not that he said much. There was a map pinned on the wall, but he did not refer to it. However, she sensed in him a concealed resentment and fear of Dane.

"Who is the fellow anyhow?" he asked. "Just because the Burtons loaned him their house doesn't mean anything. I've looked him up in the *Army and Navy Register*. He's not there."

"I suppose, with all these new officers . . ."

"I'd be just a little careful, my dear. All sorts in the service now, and he's a bit of a mystery. I remember in the last war we got a lot of good men, but we got a lot of bounders too."

She had walked down, and he took her back home up the hill. Neither of them saw Alex, on guard among the trees and burning a hole in his pocket with the cigarette he had hastily stuffed there.

He remained on duty until two o'clock, when Dane relieved him, a Dane in a dark outfit and with a revolver in his pocket. They wasted no words.

"Okay?"

"Okay."

Then Alex went home, and Dane began his cautious circuit of the house. Nothing happened, and at dawn he disappeared. But not to sleep. What he had learned from Marcia Dalton that night looked as though Carol's family was involved in the murder, and he did not like the idea.

He had driven down to the Dalton place. Two or three cars were already parked in the drive, and he cursed himself for letting down the bar he had so carefully erected. But he had at least a chance to see a dozen or so of the summer people, the Wards, the Peter Crowells, Louise Stimson, a few others. He stood, stiff in his uniform, through several rounds of cocktails, watching and listening, but he learned nothing from any of them except the prospects of the approaching election and the cost of living. Then at the table Marcia, beside him, had abruptly turned to him.

"You're interested in our murder, aren't you?" she asked, her sharp eyes on his.

"Merely as an observer," he said lightly.

"Well, I don't think Carol Spencer ought to be alone in the house. She's a nice child. Where's her family?"

"I understand her sister is coming."

Marcia looked surprised.

"Elinor!"

"Why?"

She gave him a long look, then turned abruptly to speak to

Peter Crowell on her left. She talked to him through the lobster and up to the saddle of mutton. Then, as though she had made up her mind, she turned back.

"I'm going to tell you something I've promised not to tell," she said in a low voice. "I've known Elinor Hilliard all my life. I don't like her much. I know her car. It's a foreign job you can't mistake, and I'm pretty sure I saw it the night that girl was killed."

He duly registered surprise.

"That's hard to believe," he said.

"Carol doesn't believe it. I told her, and she said Elinor couldn't have been here. But there's nothing wrong with my eyes, and if you're interested you ought to know. I haven't told anyone else," she added. "And don't let Carol know I spoke to you, will you? I'm fond of her, and I think she's in a jam."

He played a rubber or two of bridge after dinner. His mind was not on the game, but he won ten dollars from Peter Crowell and that gentleman was not pleased. He got out his wallet and eyed the scratch on Dane's face.

"Saw you on the hill above the Spencer place this afternoon," he said. "What are you looking for? More bodies?"

"You never know your luck," Dane replied indifferently, and was to remember that later with what amounted to horror.

He had gone home, relieved Alex, and was in bed at six o'clock the next morning when a highly disreputable-looking individual with a battered suitcase got off the train ten miles away. He looked around, saw a car at a distance, and after the crowd dispersed moved casually toward it. Once inside he grinned.

"What goes on?" he inquired. "Don't tell me he's on the old job again. I don't believe it. Not in this neck of the woods."

Alex shrugged as he started the car.

"He'll tell you himself," he said, his one eye on the road.

"I thought he was resting that leg of his."

"Not him," Alex said disgustedly. "He's been working his head off to get well so he can go back. Bored stiff, too. He was fit to be tied until this happened. Now his leg—"

"Well, what happened, for God's sake? Why the fingerprint stuff? Is it this Spencer murder?"

"I'd rather the major told you himself."

It was Tim's turn to stare. Then he burst into raucous laughter.

"The major!" he said. "When did he get to be a major?"

"They move them up fast these days," Alex said imperturbably.

"Yeah, but they don't move them from a sergeant in the army to a majority in six months. The last time I saw him he was lugging a pack, and don't think I'm fooling. What are you doing? Kidding me? He's in some special branch of Intelligence, isn't he?"

Alex slowed the car for a curve. His one eye was wary.

"Look, Tim," he said. "A lot of fellows got queer jobs in this man's army. Now they're there, now they're here. Maybe they're in Japan or the Philippines. Then before you know it they're somewhere else. He was a major when he got shot in Italy. I was there."

"That where you lost your eye?"

"I got off easy," Alex said comfortably.

Tim was silent. He was a typical Brooklyn Irishman who had fought his way from the police force to a business of his own, and just now his expression was one of amusement.

"Okay," he said. "So he's a major, and what am I? A tramp?"

"I imagine you're to be a gardener."

Tim stared.

"Well, I'll be God-damned," he said, suddenly sour. "A gardener! What the hell does that mean? I never saw a blade of grass until I was thirty."

"You can run a lawn mower," Alex said, enjoying himself hugely. "You know. You just push the thing. It cuts the grass. Then you rake it up."

Indignation kept Tim quiet for a time, but his curiosity was too much for him.

"All right. I cut somebody's grass. Then what?"

"I expect you're to keep an eye on the Spencer girl. The major thinks she may be in danger."

It was Tim's turn to enjoy himself.

"So he's fallen for a girl at last," he said. "Always said he'd fall hard when he did. What's she like?"

"Just a girl. You'll be seeing her when you're digging in the garden."

"I'm doing no digging," Tim said firmly, and relapsed again into silence.

He cheered over his breakfast, however, and he was loading his camera when Dane appeared at noon. Tim grinned.

"Morning, major," he said. "Hear you've been promoted."

"Temporarily, Tim. Don't bother about the rank stuff unless there are people around." He glanced at the camera. "I see you're ready."

"All set."

For the next hour or so they worked, as they had worked together before. They ate lunch while Tim's films were being developed, and inspected them later. There were prints on all the china, and on the photograph frame as well. Tim looked up.

"Looks like a dame's," he said. "Kind of long and tapering. You take a man's, even if he's got a small hand, the prints are broader."

Dane nodded. He had no longer any doubt that they were Elinor Hilliard's, and the whole picture looked clear. She had been in Bayside the night of the murder, and she had somehow managed to save her mother's treasures before she set fire to the house. He halted there. She had not set fire to the house. That had been done later, Saturday or Sunday night. So what?

But it was the spade that added to the confusion. There were smudged prints on the handle, but one or two were clear enough to prove that they did not resemble the others. They were not large, but Tim was confident they were a man's. Without much hope Dane sent them to Washington, using the post office at the railroad for reasons of his own, and going to the hospital that afternoon.

He did not ask for Lucy. He found George Smith sitting up in bed, and took a chair beside him.

"Doing all right, are you?" he inquired.

"Be better when they take me off this pap they're feeding me," George said sullenly. He surveyed Dane's uniform. "You're the fellow at the Burton place, aren't you?"

"Yes. I thought I'd better see you. I can get a man to do your work until you're able to carry on, if that's all right with you."

"Sure is," George said more cheerfully. "All I got done was a bit of mowing. Then this pain hit me."

"You hadn't done any work in the garden, I suppose?"

"Nothing but the grass, and not much of that. You tell the other fellow he'll find everything nice and tidy in the tool house, and to keep it that way. I'm particular about my tools."

Before he left Dane resorted to the old device of offering George his cigarette case, and carried away with him excellent impressions of five large and calloused fingers. He did not even need to compare them with the ones on the spade handle.

Tim spent an hour or two that afternoon sauntering over the hillside. To any observer he was merely hunting a dog, whistling now and then, and occasionally calling an imaginary Roger. But he covered considerable ground and found nothing. He spent the evening with Dane going over the case, but in the end he gave it up.

"Sounds like the sister," he said. "Only she didn't work it alone. Who helped her?"

"That's what I'd like to know," Dane said soberly, and went back over his notes again.

TEN

Elinor arrived early the morning of the inquest, Thursday. She came by taxi, surrounded by luggage and irritable at the hour, the trip, at Carol's insistence that she come at all, that she had had to abandon her dinner party, and been obliged to leave her maid behind.

If there was anything else, her manner did not show it. She went up to Carol's room and surveyed her as she lay in bed.

"You look like the wrath of God," she said. "Don't tell me the story now. I've read it in the papers. That's a hellish train. I need a bath and some food."

But she did not bathe at once. When Carol had dressed and gone downstairs she found her in the library, her breakfast tray almost untouched and she herself with a cigarette, staring down through the French door at the harbor.

"I can't see why you wanted me," she said fretfully. "As to that car business, there are hundreds of cars like mine. Marcia only wants to make trouble. She's always hated me. I don't have to testify today, do I?"

"Not unless you know something. If you do, I advise you to tell it."

Carol's voice was dry, and Elinor looked at her sharply. Then she laughed.

"It was you she asked for in New York, not me," she said.

She went upstairs after that, and Carol heard her bell ringing in the pantry. She knew what that meant. Without her own maid Freda would be pressed into service, to draw her bath, to press her clothes, to help her dress and fix her hair. But Elinor had had to come, if only to confront Marcia if necessary.

When she herself went up later it was to find Elinor in bed, with the odor of bath salts heavy in the air and Freda opening a half dozen bags. An elaborate traveling toilet set was already on the dressing table, and Freda was looking sulky. Elinor's voice was sharp when she saw her.

"I don't see why you leave the linen closet like that, Carol. Surely you can have it cleaned and painted. Those red seals on it make me sick. They look like blood."

"The police want it that way."

"And these sheets!" Elinor said crossly. "Why in the name of heaven sheets like these?"

Carol kept her temper, although she flushed.

"You might remember our own are scorched. I wouldn't use them anyhow, Elinor. And I can't buy sheets. There are none in town."

She sent Freda out, for the house was still only partially livable, and did the rest of the unpacking herself under Elinor's watchful eyes. But her heart sank when, on the toilet table, she saw a number of pale bobby pins, the color of Elinor's hair. She finished however before she began to talk. Then she sat down on the edge of the bed and smiled at her sister.

"I wish you'd trust me, Elinor," she said. "I don't think you killed anybody. That would be idiotic. But if you were here that night—"

"What on earth would bring me here?"

"I haven't an idea," Carol said candidly. "But you see I found a bobby pin in the elevator, and it looks like yours."

Elinor's astonishment was real. She sat up in bed, staring. Then she laughed.

"A bobby pin! My God, Carol! And in the elevator! I haven't been in it for years. I'd forgotten there was one."

There was the ring of truth in her voice, and Carol drew a long breath. She felt a vast sense of relief. She was even able to laugh a little herself.

"Well, that's that," she said, and slid off the bed. "It had me scared, you know. Marcia was so certain."

"Tell Marcia where she can go," Elinor said vindictively. "And now get out and let me sleep. What time is this inquest? And why do I have to go?"

"It's this afternoon. You don't have to go. I just think you'd better."

They were more amicable by that time. Elinor asked about

Lucy Norton and if she could see her. But when she was told about the yellow room her expression changed.

"Will that have to come out at the inquest?" she asked.

"Why not? She was staying here."

"And you don't know why? What did she tell Lucy, Carol? She must have had some sort of story for Lucy to put her up here. What does Lucy say?"

"I don't know. The police won't let her see anybody."

She was certain now that Elinor had learned something which had terrified her. Lying there in her bed, with no make-up on and her face heavily creamed, she looked white and drawn. Beyond asking to have the shades lowered and saying she would try to sleep she did not speak, however. Carol went downstairs, somewhat dazed and highly apprehensive.

Below, the house was gradually becoming livable again. The long drawing-room rug was down, the covers off the furniture, and as Carol went forward she saw a man carrying chairs and tables onto the terrace. He looked up and grinned at her.

"I'm the new man," he said. "Tim Murphy. Just call me Tim. Major Dane said to go right ahead, and do anything I could."

She smiled in return.

"We're glad to have you, Tim. We needed help badly."

"I'm no gardener, miss. I can cut the grass. That's about as far as I go."

"That's about as far as you need to go."

He nodded and went back to work, but Carol was aware that behind his grin he had inspected her sharply. She dismissed the thought, and getting her car drove into the village for supplies. Elinor had not brought her ration book, of course, and Carol, struggling over butter and bacon and buying the chickens she was beginning to loathe, wondered if her sister even knew about rationing. But she was more cheerful, now that she was out of the house. She had only imagined the fright in Elinor's face, she thought, and this was borne out when she found Elinor downstairs on her return. She was as carefully dressed as usual, but she was looking perplexed.

"What's wrong on the hill?" she inquired. "There's a man wandering around up there. I saw him while I was dressing."

"I didn't see him. What did he look like?"

"I don't know. He kept stooping over, as though he was looking for something."

Carol put down her bag and confronted her.

"There are some things you ought to know, Elinor," she said. "You know how they found the—how they found the body. She was in a nightdress and a dressing gown, with a fur jacket over them, and she had been sleeping in the yellow room. At least she'd gone to bed there. But we've never found her clothes. They have to be somewhere."

"So they think they're on the hill?"

"Maybe not on it. Buried in it."

She repeated what Dane had told her, about the possibility of such a method, the digging of a hole and the replanting over it. But Elinor thought the idea farfetched.

"Why not burn them?" she said lightly. "Why go to all that trouble, if they had to be got rid of? And why are they so essential? After all, she's dead."

"They want to know who she was," Carol said patiently. "It's almost a week, and they still don't know."

Dane was gone—if it had been Dane—when she saw the hillside again. She viewed it from the servants' dining room, with an upset Maggie at her elbow.

"I don't mind Miss Elinor," she said. "I know her ways. But if Freda's to spend all her time with her I'll have to have more help, Miss Carol."

She conciliated Maggie as best she could, and she and Elinor ate lunch almost in silence. With Elinor there the days of trays were over, and lunch was served in the dining room, at a small table near the window. A Coast Guard boat was taking a practice run up the bay, and beyond one of the islands they could see the white sails of a yawl. Carol had always loved the view, but this day the approaching inquest hung heavy over her. Elinor, too, was absorbed and silent. She smoked steadily and only looked up once to ask a question.

"Do you think Lucy Norton will be able to testify?"

"I don't know. I shouldn't think so."

But she was wrong. Lucy did testify that day.

The inquest was held at the town hall. Long before two o'clock the street was lined with cars, and half a dozen reporters and cameramen were on the pavement. Elinor faced them with stony calm, but Carol was less lucky. She sneezed just as one shutter clicked, and later she was to see that picture, her face contorted in agony.

"Miss Spencer showed great distress" was what it said beneath.

The hall was jammed. The coroner, Dr. Harrison, sat at a small table below and in front of the stage, with certain articles covered by a sheet; and the six jurymen sat at one side. They had been shown the body, and looked rather unhappy. Over all was the noise of chairs scraping and people moving and talking. Elinor looked around her distastefully.

"It sounds like the zoo at feeding time," she said. "And smells worse."

Nevertheless, she put on a good act, smiling and nodding to the people she knew, and ignoring the others. She had dressed carefully in a white sports suit and a small white hat, painfully reminiscent of the one which probably lay under the sheet on the table, and she looked calm and detached. Carol, watching her smile at Marcia Dalton, felt a reluctant admiration for her.

With the first thump of the gavel the noise subsided, and the silence was almost startling. The coroner's voice was quiet when he began. There had been no identification of the body. Under the circumstances that had been impossible. Later they hoped to learn just who the young woman was who had been done to death in such a tragic manner. In the meantime an inquest was simply an inquiry, to get such information as they could. The witnesses would be under oath to tell the truth. Any failure to do so would be considered as perjury, and the person guilty under the law.

After that introduction came the report on the autopsy. The medical examiner from the county seat had conducted it, and he read his report. The body was one of a young woman, between twenty and thirty probably. There had been no assault. The internal organs were normal, and there were indications that she had borne a child.

The crowd stirred at this. Heretofore she had been merely a girl, dropping, so to speak, out of the blue to be killed mysteriously in the vicinity. Now she became a young mother, and suddenly pitiful.

The medical examiner went on. Deceased had eaten her last meal probably six hours before death, as the process of digestion was well established. Said deceased had been a blonde, and very little work had been done on the teeth. In spite of the situation in which she had been found she had been killed by a blow that had fractured her skull.

The fire which had burned her hair and clothing had been started after death. There was no smoke or soot in the lungs, or any indication that she was alive when it took place. It was even indicated from the effect of the burns that she had been dead for some time before the attempt had been made to incinerate the body.

He paused here, for the coroner's questions.

"Would it be possible to state how long this interval might have been?"

"No. Except that death was already well established."

Chief Floyd was the next witness. He told of Carol's arrival at his office, and of going back with her to Crestview. He had found the body in the closet and had it removed after Dr. Harrison had examined it. No, he had taken no pictures. No one had a camera; or if they had, there were no films.

Asked about the position of the body, he said it was on the floor of the linen closet, with the head toward the rear, and what he called the limbs neatly arranged. Most of the clothing, he said, had been burned, but it was there in that bundle if the jury cared to see it.

The jury did care. It came forward solemnly and stared at what lay on the table. None of them touched anything, and they filed back, more sober than ever and somewhat shocked. Elinor Hilliard, too, had lost some of her poise. She was pale and evidently shaken.

"It's horrible," she said suddenly. "I want to get out, Carol. I'm going to be sick."

But Carol caught her arm.

"Be careful," she said. "You have to stick it, Elinor. It will be over in a minute."

Dane, standing at the rear of the hall, saw the bit of byplay;

Elinor's attempt to rise, and Carol restraining her. He had, as a matter of fact, been watching Elinor from the beginning. She knew something, he was convinced, but what or how much he was not sure. Now as the exhibits were re-covered he saw her relax, and puzzled over that too.

There followed an interval while a blueprint of the house was circulated among the jury, and this was still going on when there was some movement at the rear entrance doors. People were craning their heads, and to Carol's surprise she saw that Lucy Norton was being brought in. She was in a wheel chair, and her leg in its cast was carefully propped in front of her. A nurse in uniform was pushing the chair, and Lucy was staring straight ahead, looking pale and nervous.

Her arrival, Dane saw, was a shock to Elinor. He could not see her face, but she sagged in her chair and Carol looked at her anxiously. The audience, however, did not notice this. It was absorbed in Lucy, in her wheel chair now beside the table, with the nurse bending over her.

They did not call her at once. Freda was the next witness, and a nervous one. She had gone upstairs to fix Miss Spencer's room for her, and had gone to the linen closet for sheets. There were black smears all around the door, and she rubbed at one with her finger. "It came off like soot." After that she opened the door and saw somebody lying on the floor inside. That was all she knew. She had run down the back stairs and fainted in the kitchen. "I was sick to my stomach," she said.

They did not keep her long, nor Nora, nor Maggie, who followed them. Even Carol was asked only perfunctory questions, about verifying the fact and notifying the police. Asked if she knew the identity of the deceased she said she did not, nor had she any idea why she was in the house.

So far there had been no mention of the yellow room. Evidently that was waiting for Lucy. The bus driver testified as to the arrival at six-thirty on Friday morning of the week before of a young woman dressed as the deceased was supposed to have been dressed. Sam of the hamburger stand stated that such a young woman had had coffee in his place early that morning and looked at the telephone book, but did not call anybody. And some of the interval between her arrival and that time was bridged by Mr. Allison of the Five-&-Ten. He told of seeing such a young woman sitting in the public park opposite his store.

"It was early, a little after seven o'clock," he said, "And I'd just opened the place. She was on a bench by the bandstand, looking as though she was waiting. She wasn't in any trouble that I could see. There was a squirrel there, and she was trying to coax it to her. Then I went away. When I looked again, about ten minutes later, she was gone."

Lucy was better now. Dane saw that she was listening carefully. She was slightly deaf, and her chair had been wheeled well forward. But Carol, closer to her, saw her holding her hand behind one ear, and was certain that the hand was trembling.

When at last she was called, Dr. Harrison treated her with considerable gentleness.

"We appreciate the willingness of this witness to appear," he said to the audience. "As you all know, she has had a serious injury. But her testimony is important. Now, Mrs. Norton—"

She took the oath without looking at the crowd. There was no noise now. Some of the people at the rear of the hall were standing up, to see or hear better. But the early part of her testimony was disappointing. The girl had arrived at Crestview about half past eight on Friday morning. She had asked for Miss Carol Spencer, and had seemed disappointed that she had not arrived.

"She kind of hung around for some time," Lucy said. "She claimed to be a friend of Miss Spencer's, and she said Miss Spencer was expecting her. I didn't know what to do. I had plenty of work on my hands, but she didn't go away. She just sat in the hall and waited. It was cold there, so I asked her back to the kitchen. I'd lit the stove.

"I told her nobody was coming until the first of the week, and I said she'd better go down to the village and telephone to Mrs. Hilliard's at Newport, where Miss Carol was staying. But she said her feet hurt her, and couldn't she at least clean up after the train trip. That's how she came to be in the yellow room. I didn't see any objection to that. She was well dressed and looked like a lady. But I thought she was kind of nervous."

She went on. She had got soap and towels, and the girl took a bath and came down in a red kimono. She talked pleasantly, and she offered to pay Lucy five dollars to let her stay the night. Her railroad ticket back was for the next day. She had showed it. And with travel the way it was now she would have to stay somewhere.

Apparently she had won Lucy, although she refused the money "except for enough to get some food for her. All I had was what I'd brought for myself."

She had gone to the village for more groceries, and she cooked a nice lunch and carried it up on a tray. The girl stayed in her room all afternoon. She thought she had slept. But when she carried up her supper the door to the yellow room was locked, and she wouldn't open it until she told her who she was.

"She tried to laugh. She said it was just habit. She'd been staying in hotels. But I wasn't comfortable after that, although she seemed to know the family all right. She asked about Mrs. Hilliard and Captain Spencer, and how Mrs. Spencer was. She'd asked for cigarettes and I brought her some, but she didn't leave the room again, so far as I know."

She had given Lucy the name of Barbour, Marguerite Barbour, and the initials on her bag were M.D.B. That seemed all right, and there wasn't much in the house to steal anyway, Lucy said. Nevertheless, she was uneasy. She slept badly that night, and when it turned cold she had got up for an extra blanket. As the electric current had not been turned on she took a candle and went to the main linen closet, since the servants' blankets had not yet been unpacked.

Her voice grew higher at this point, as she relived the terror of that night.

"I'd just got to the closet—the door was open an inch or so—when something reached out and knocked the candle out of my hand. I was too scared to move, and the next minute the closet door flew open and knocked me down. I—"

"Take a minute," said the coroner kindly. "I know this is painful. Take your time, Mrs. Norton.

She drew a long breath.

"That's about all anyhow," she said, more quietly. "When I got up I guess I was screaming. Anyhow I wanted to get out of the house. But it was black-dark, and that's how I came to fall down the stairs."

"Did anyone pass you after that happened?"

"I don't know. I must have fainted. I don't know how long I was out. I don't remember anything until I heard the birds. That was at daylight."

"When you came to, did you notice anything burning?"

"No, sir. There was nothing burning, or I'd have known it."

They asked her very few questions. She had not really seen the hand that knocked over her candle. As to what ran over her after the door knocked her down, she didn't remember any skirts. But who would, with dresses only to the knees anyhow, and women wearing slacks half the time?

They wheeled her out after that, and Carol was recalled. She knew no one named Barbour, certainly no Marguerite Barbour. And she had no idea who could have been using that name.

"You wouldn't recognize the description of her clothing?"

"They are practically uniform for spring or early summer. No, I don't."

"It is possible of course that she gave a name not her own. Would that help any?"

Carol shook her head.

"No one I know is missing," she said. "I have no idea who she was, or why she wanted to see me." She looked around the room. It was a sea of faces, curious, some of them skeptical, and not all of them friendly. She stiffened slightly. "If she was frightened enough to lock her door she was certainly not afraid of Lucy Norton. But she might have been afraid of someone else."

"You are not accusing anybody?"

"Certainly not," she said, her color rising. "I know nothing about this girl. I don't even believe she came to see me. That was an excuse for some purpose of her own. But there may be someone who does know why she came. That's all."

They excused her then, and the coroner made a brief summary. It was hoped that the identity of the deceased would soon be established. She was evidently in good circumstances. The face powder she used had been analyzed and was of a fine quality. Her feet and hands had apparently been well cared for. And young women of that walk of life did not disappear easily. It was, of course, one of their difficulties that her purse as well as her clothing had not been found. They hoped to do that eventually, unless it had been destroyed, and all over the country authorities were trying to discover if a young woman of this description was missing.

In the meantime this inquest was an inquiry into the cause of death, whether it had been accidental, suicide or murder. He felt he should say here that it was considered impossible that she could have so injured herself, or—as had been suggested—that a cigarette could have caused the fire. However the jury had heard all the evidence, and must make its own decision.

And they did, without leaving the room. It was murder, by a person or persons unknown.

ELEVEN

DANE HAD LEFT HIS CAR in an alley some blocks away from the hall. He slipped away to it quietly as soon as the verdict was in, and sat thoughtfully smoking until Tim Murphy joined him, when he took a back road home.

"Well," he said, "what did you think of it, Tim?"

"Phony," said Tim, biting off a piece of cigar and lodging it in his cheek.

"The Norton woman's story?"

"Sure. Look at her! She's nobody's easy mark. None of these New Englanders are, especially the women. So what? She gives the girl a room, she buys groceries for her, and she carries trays up to her. It doesn't make sense."

"No," Dane said, still thoughtful. "She didn't perjure herself, but she didn't tell the whole story. Find anything on the hill this morning?"

"That's the hell of a place to search. I picked up a bushel of burs. That's all."

Dane glanced at the sky.

"There's one thing," he said. "If this dry spell keeps on we may get a hint. It's no weather to replant anything, and if you see some shrubbery wilting— Did you notice Miss Spencer's sister, Mrs. Hilliard?"

"Who could help it?" said Tim, with appreciation. "Not so young, but a looker all right."

"She's supposed to have been seen here—or, rather, her car was—the night of the murder."

Tim whistled.

"Think it's true?" he inquired.

"I think it's possible. She married Howard Hilliard. You know who he is. Money to burn. She's not going to let anything interfere with that. Place at Newport, house at Palm

Beach, apartment in New York, a yacht when there were such things. The whole bag of tricks."

"I see. Think this dead girl was Hilliard's mistress?"

"It's possible. Only why come here?"

Tim spat over the side of the car.

"Well, you sure bought yourself a job," he said philosophically. "You can have it. How long have I got to search that hill or push that lawn mower? I got blisters already."

Dane did not reply at once. He was in uniform, and he ran his finger around the band of his collar as though it bothered him.

"We got one thing there," he said. "The girl's name, or the name she gave. Marguerite D. Barbour. The police will go all out on that. Me . . ." He hesitated. "The initials are probably right. They were on her bag. How about calling up your people in New York, Tim? If she spent a night there at a hotel she'd use those initials, but maybe another name."

Tim demurred.

"Know how many hotels there are in New York?"

"You can get help. I'm paying for it."

"It's a damn good thing you don't have to live on your service pay, whatever that is, or whatever your service is for that matter," Tim said resignedly. "All right. My best men are gone, but I can cover this, I suppose."

"Not from here. Drop me at the house and drive over to the railroad. There's a booth in the station there."

"What about dinner? I have to eat sometime."

"Get it over there," said Dane heartlessly. "I've never known you to starve yet. And listen, Tim. If you don't pick up anything by midnight take the train yourself. I want to beat the police to it."

"Why, for God's sake?"

"Call it a hunch. Say I don't trust this bunch up here. It's a big case, and they're likely to go off on a tangent that may damage innocent people."

"Such as the Spencer girl?"

"She's out of it," Dane said dryly. "Go and get your toothbrush. Alex will take you over, and you can get a taxi back."

He rested until dinner. He had found that he could still do

only a certain amount before the old trouble asserted itself and Alex began to baby him again. It annoyed him that night to find his dinner coming up on a tray.

"Damn it," he said irritably. "I can walk, can't I? And where's the coffee?"

"Drink the milk," Alex said firmly. "Coffee keeps you awake, and you know it."

"No word from Tim?"

"He's probably eating a beefsteak somewhere."

Dane smiled. The matter of ration points was a sore one with Alex. But he dutifully drank his milk, and as a result he was sound asleep when the fire started on the hill above Crestview.

Tim had telephoned. The only one of his assistants he had been able to locate had found nothing so far, and he was taking the night train to New York.

"On his hunch!" he told Alex with some bitterness. "And in an upper. I'll do it, but I don't have to like it, do I?"

The fire started late. Carol and Elinor had dined at the Wards' that night. It was Elinor who accepted over the phone.

"If we bury ourselves it will make talk," she told Carol. "There's too much of it now, after that story of Lucy's today."

"Lucy isn't a liar."

"Oh, for heaven's sake!" said Elinor impatiently. "That's the point. She *was* telling the truth. But now everybody knows that awful girl had some reason for coming here. She wasn't using this house as a hotel."

In the end Carol agreed. They walked over to the Wards', using the gravel path that connected the two properties, and lifting their long skirts as they crossed the dusty lane. In the summer twilight they both looked young and lovely in their light dresses, Elinor's hair piled high—with Freda's assistance, of course—and Carol's brushed back smoothly from her forehead. When they went in they found the colonel there, rather guiltily trying to hide a map.

Mrs. Ward put down her knitting and got up.

"How nice to see you," she said, "and how beautiful you both look. How are you managing, Carol?"

Carol said she was getting along, but inwardly she was

shocked. Mrs. Ward looked ill. She had changed since the preceding Monday when she had been at Crestview. So had Nathaniel, for all his smiling hospitality. Only the colonel seemed himself, defiantly hopeful, as though he were daring fate to deal him its ultimate blow.

No one mentioned the inquest, or that strange story of Lucy's. Mrs. Ward had picked up her knitting again but her eyes were on Carol with an odd intentness.

"When do you expect Gregory?" she asked.

"We don't know. I suppose he's still in Washington or maybe New York. He may not come at all, of course. He's going to be married. And the way things are now . . ."

Mrs. Ward inspected her work. Their grandson, Terry, had been flying in the South Pacific, and she was knitting socks for him.

"Even there their feet get cold, poor dears," she said. "They fly so high, you know. How frightful this war is!"

The other three were talking together over their cocktails, and Mrs. Ward lowered her voice.

"I don't think Gregory ought to come up, Carol," she said. "After all, why should he? It will only spoil his leave. He has seen enough of death where he has been. I might as well tell you. Floyd was here today after the inquest."

"Floyd? What did he want?"

"Just to know if we had seen or heard anything that Friday night. But he asked about Gregory."

There was no mistake about it. Mrs. Ward's veined old hands were shaking. She gave up all pretense of knitting.

"But that's absurd," Carol said stormily. "Greg was in Washington. Floyd's crazy. He has only to use the telephone to learn that."

Dinner was announced then, and they went out to the vast baronial hall that was the dining room. Carol's color was still high, but Elinor was her usual self. She talked about Greg's decoration, and his approaching marriage, and she inquired about Terry Ward, who it seemed was either on his way back on furlough or about to be.

Nevertheless there was constraint at the table. They ate the usual soup, fish and chicken, and there was the inevitable discussion of ration points and thin cream. But neither of the Wards ate much, and Carol was glad when the meal was over and old Nathaniel took Elinor out to see his garden.

They left early, Elinor pleading fatigue after her journey, and Nathaniel seeing them home and then returning for what he called his nightly game of chess with the colonel.

"He can't do much else," he said. "His heart's not too good. Fine fellow, the colonel. We're very fond of him."

He left them at the door, saying a rather abrupt good night, and turned back, his small figure almost immediately lost in the shadows. Carol had the feeling that he was relieved to get rid of them, and wondered why. It was not until they were inside the house that its possible meaning began to dawn on her. Elinor had started up the stairs when she stopped her.

"Wait a minute," she said. "Elinor, when Marcia saw your car that night was Greg in it?"

The hall was dark. She could not see Elinor's face, but her sister turned and stared down at her.

"How often," she said, "do I have to tell you Marcia did not see my car?"

"Have you seen Greg at all?"

"How could I? He's been in Washington and New York. What's the matter with you, Carol? If you start suspecting your own family—"

"It's only because old Mr. Ward has insomnia," Carol said, rather wildly. "He gets up and takes walks at night. And tonight Mrs. Ward said Greg oughtn't to come here. She looked queer, too. Elinor, I can't take much more. If you know anything, tell me. I won't run to the police, but at least I'll know where I am. Major Dane—"

"What about Major Dane?" Elinor said sharply.

"I don't know. I think he's Intelligence or something. I saw him at the inquest today. I don't think he believed Lucy."

"He'd better mind his own business," Elinor said inelegantly, and went up the stairs.

It was one o'clock that morning when Carol heard the fire siren. She roused from a deep dream, in which Greg was hiding from her and she was following him, to hear the noise and sit bolt upright in bed. She got up, feeling for her slippers in the dark, and went to the window. The village seemed to be all right, but there was a reddish glare reflected on the clouds above the house, and the siren kept on. It was calling the volunteers now, and the engine was already on its way, its own shrill clamor adding to the din. She was still in her night clothes when she ran to Elinor's room, to find her standing at the window in a pale negligee, gazing out.

"It's the hill," she said. "I think that empty house up there is going. It's lucky the wind is in the other direction, or we'd go too."

Carol looked out. The fire had already roared up the hillside. It had escaped the tool house, but as she looked the dried shingles on the roof of the abandoned house above began to catch, and the hill itself was a roaring inferno. The engine had gone to the fire hydrant up the lane, but she could hear the cars of the volunteer firemen as they began to roar up the Crestview drive.

She realized that it was hopeless, although men were shouting and running, and she even saw Maggie rushing out with a broom. The lane would probably keep it from Rockhill, and a cement road beyond the burning house would stop it there. But the hillside was gone. Even its trees were burning. Her first thought was the trees.

"I can't bear it," she said. "They've been growing there for years. Greg built me a swing there once. Remember?"

Elinor nodded. She looked somber in the red glare, but she said nothing. It was some time before Carol remembered that the firemen would want coffee. She dressed rapidly and went to the kitchen, to find the two maids huddled there and a bedraggled Maggie standing over the stove, with the coffee under way.

"They turned the hose on me," Maggie said calmly. "Who started that fire, Miss Carol? Don't tell me somebody dropped a cigarette. I saw it before it had gone very far. It looked like it began all over the place." She turned to the other women. "One of you girls run out and tell those men to come in for coffee when they're ready."

But it was three in the morning before they wanted coffee. They straggled in then, tired and dirty and some of them with small burns. Maggie used some precious butter on them, lacking anything else. Most of the men of the summer colony had turned out, and they were as dirty as the rest. The house above was gone, and the hillside was burned, wiped out completely. They had saved a few of the trees, however.

They stood around, eating sandwiches and drinking coffee. A bewildered lot. The air warden who had turned in the alarm was Sam Thompson, who ran the hamburger stand in the village, and he told his story to an interested audience.

"I went up the lane just before one o'clock. It was all right then, but five minutes later I saw a glare and ran back. Looked like there were five or six fires, all going like mad. I raced over to the Wards'. There was a light on there, and it was the nearest house from where I was. Mr. Ward was still up, and he telephoned the fire department. When I got back the whole hill was one solid blaze."

"Think somebody set it?"

"Maybe. Maybe not. With the wind the way it is, and everything dried up, it could spread itself."

That was when Carol saw Jerry Dane. He was in his pajamas with a dressing gown over them, and he was as dirty as the rest. She took him a cup of coffee, and he regarded her coolly.

"Nice work!" he said. "How many people besides you knew I was looking for something up on that hill?"

"You're not invisible," she said, her voice as cold as his. "And don't look at me like that. I didn't do it."

"Well, somebody did." He put down his cup and his face softened. "Listen, Carol," he said. "Someday you may decide to tell me what's behind all this. You may save a life or two if you do. Perhaps your own. So don't wait too long."

She did not reply, and she did not see him again. By four o'clock in the morning the house was empty. The girls were washing up, and she found Elinor in the library making herself a drink from the small portable bar table there. At some interval she had gone upstairs to do her face; but she looked tired and irritable.

"What was that Dane man saying to you?" she asked. "He looked nasty."

"Only asking me why I started the fire," Carol said ironically. "And what I was keeping from him. He thinks I know something."

"And do you?"

"What do you think?"

There was a rather pregnant silence. Elinor said nothing. She sipped at her drink, and Carol lit a cigarette and watched her. Which was the precise moment which Captain Gregory Spencer chose to return to his summer home.

He came in from the terrace, a tall blond man in uniform with Elinor's good looks in masculine mold, but with Carol's candid eyes and Carol's smile. He was smiling then as he dropped a bag and straightened to look at them.

"Well," he said. "Here's the sailor home from the sea, and the hunter—"

Elinor looked stunned.

"Greg!" she said. "What are you doing here?"

He did not reply. He held out his arms and Carol went into them. He held her close.

"Poor little girl!" he said. "Been going through hell, haven't you? I couldn't get away any sooner."

Out of sheer relief she began to cry. She stood in the shelter of Greg's arms and felt safe and protected again. And Greg held her off and gave her a little shake.

"Stop that," he ordered. "Didn't you know I'd come? Where's your hanky? Here, use mine." He wiped her eyes, and over her head looked at Elinor. "What's the matter with you? Why shouldn't I come? I thought that was the big idea in opening the house."

He released Carol and poured himself a drink.

"Quite a fire, wasn't it?" he said. "I've been hiding out for the last couple of hours. It looked as though they had plenty of help, and this is my best uniform. I thought it was this house at first. What on earth happened?"

"Probably someone dropped a cigarette," Elinor said calmly. "There hasn't been any rain for ages."

He seemed satisfied. He finished his drink and yawned.

"What about bed?" he suggested. "Plenty of time to talk tomorrow. I drove up, and I'm tired. You look as though you could stand some sleep, Carol." He inspected her closely.

"Taken quite a beating, haven't you?"

Suddenly Elinor got up.

"Everybody has taken a beating," she said furiously. "It's not over, either. Why should you come here to be dragged into it? I thought you were going to be married right away."

"So I am," he said, "God willing." He looked at Elinor. "But I'm not letting Carol take this mess alone. It's got her down already. Look at her."

"Then I think you're crazy," said Elinor, her voice sullen.

Carol went up to see to his room, which was still closed, but the first excitement and relief of seeing Greg were gone. There was something behind Elinor's semihysteria, and the look Greg had given her. It had almost been as if he was warning her, and alone upstairs, fumbling in the dark back hall for sheets from the service linen closet, she felt once more the old closeness of the two downstairs. They might quarrel—they had always quarreled—but they would stand together, against her, against the world.

By the time she had made the bed and seen to towels and soap Greg had come up. He stopped in front of the sealed closet door and inspected it.

"Why all this stuff?" he inquired. "I thought the thing was more or less over. It's horrible, right here in the house."

"Maybe you can get them to take it off."

"I'll do my damnedest," he said. "It makes me sick to look at it. I suppose they have no idea who did it?"

She looked up at him, and at once she felt that she had to talk to him, to tell him what was driving her into a nervous collapse. He looked big and reliable, and he was Greg, whom she had always adored. She lowered her voice.

"I hate to tell you, Greg," she said, "but I'm frightfully worried. Marcia Dalton says she saw Elinor's car here the night it happened."

She had been prepared for surprise, perhaps for indignation. She was not prepared for the stricken look he gave her.

"Oh, my God!" he said. "What was she doing here?"

He tried to pass it off, of course, said the whole thing was preposterous and to forget it. But he had had a shock, and she knew it.

It was faintly daylight before she went to bed. She left a note on the kitchen table saying that Greg had arrived and not to disturb him, and before she went up to her room she glanced out the kitchen window. There were still men around, watching, for fires like that had a way of eating for hours under the leaves and then flaring again. But in the gray of the dawn the blackened hillside stretched up to the skeleton of what had been a house above, its green beauty destroyed and small patches here and there still smoking.

Her car was still in the drive where she had left it. It looked shabby in the morning light, but at least the fire had not touched it. And already the birds were singing, although some were fluttering about with small frightened chirps. Their nests were gone, she thought tiredly. Their nests and their babies. Even the old orchard where in the autumn the deer came at night to stand on their slim legs and eat the apples.

In her room she undressed slowly. The patio was gray with the dawn, and across it she could see faintly the outline of Elinor's door. As she looked she saw it open and close, and realized that Elinor had gone to waken Greg and talk to him.

She was too exhausted to wonder why.

TWELVE

DANE SLEPT LATE the next morning. He did not waken until noon, when Alex called him to the telephone. It was Tim in New York.

"Think I've struck oil," he said. "Registered as Mary D. Breed." He gave the name of a hotel. "Answers description. Gave residence as St. Louis. May be phony, of course. Only arrived Wednesday evening. Checked out the next morning."

Dane was making notes on a pad.

"Seen the room?" he asked.

"Look, Dane, you know what hotels are like. There have been half a dozen in that room since. Yeah. I looked at it. Seven dollars a day. Worth about three. Paid in cash."

"Anybody remember her?"

"The porter thinks he does. Says he carried down her suitcase. Gave him fifty cents. Remembers the fur coat and white hat."

"A suitcase? She didn't bring it here with her. Probably checked it at the railroad station."

"With the stub in her bag. Sure," Tim agreed. "New Haven Railroad to Boston. From Boston to Maine. Could have left it anywhere."

"It may have her initials on it."

"Yeah, and it may not. Have a heart, chief. Have you seen the checkroom at any of the railroad stations lately? Anyhow, I can't get hold of it if I do locate it. Unless you want the police in on this. Maybe they could get it. I can't."

"Keep the police out. That's why you're there, Tim."

"I'm damned if I know why," Tim grumbled. But Dane was not listening.

"Better take a plane and go to St. Louis," he said. "We'll have to try. How about money? Got enough?"

"I get airsick," Tim protested. "Besides, I hate flying."

"I'm sorry, Tim. I haven't much time, you know. I'll soon be back in service. Make it on a plane, and go to the police there. Give both her names. Chances are they don't know any details about the murder. It's just a hope, but it's all we've got."

Tim was still protesting when Dane put down the receiver. He went to the window and looked out toward the hillside which had burned the night before. Somebody had been smart, he thought. Alex had been down by the stable when it started, and he had seen nobody. The first warning he had had was the glare, and by the time he reached it it was too late.

"Started in half a dozen places," he had reported, his voice sulky. "Gasoline, probably."

Dane was worried, too, about Tim's call over the telephone. If Floyd was as smart as he thought he was it had been unfortunate, to say the least. And from his point of view it had indeed. At that moment Bessie at her switchboard had plugged into the chief's office.

"I've got something for you," she said excitedly.

"Good girl. What is it?"

"A man named Tim called Dane from New York. Said she spent the night at a hotel there, and registered from St. Louis. Name Mary D. Breed. He's gone on to St. Louis. Tim, I mean."

"Fine work, Bessie. Get the chief of police in St. Louis and call me back, will you? We're getting hot. Who's this Tim? Did he say?"

"No, he didn't. But he called Major Dane 'chief,' if that means anything."

If Dane did not hear this conversation he was fairly sure it had taken place. He was still annoyed when Alex brought his lunch to the porch. Alex's eye was bloodshot and his eyebrows singed, and Dane found himself grinning in spite of his irritation.

"Good place we chose for a rest, isn't it?" he observed.

"It might be, if we'd mind our own business," said Alex, and added a "sir" with some reluctance.

"At least we know we were on the right track. The stuff is buried there, or was."

"Much good that does," Alex grumbled. "I went over it this

morning. It's burned, and burned good. You couldn't find your
grandmother in it."

Dane disclaimed any intention of looking for that aristo-
cratic old lady in such surroundings, and ate a good lunch.
After that he inspected the hillside. As Alex had said, it was
hopeless. It was covered inches deep with charred wood and
ashes, and the skeletons of blackened trees towered over it.

It was the border that interested him, however. It was
irregular as though the fire had started in several places at
once, and he was inspecting it when someone spoke behind
him. He turned sharply, to find a youngish man eying him.

"Quite a fire, wasn't it?" he said amiably. "Spoils the place,
rather. I always liked that hill. Used to play on it when I was
a kid."

Dane inspected him. He saw a big good-looking man in
slacks and sweater, rather like his own outfit, who was smiling
as he offered a cigarette.

"I'm Greg Spencer," he explained. "Only got here last night
after the show was about over. Drove up. My sisters were pretty
much upset."

"They've had a good bit to be upset about. Especially Miss
Carol."

Dane was not certain, but he thought Gregory Spencer's
pleasant face became rather wary.

"Yeah. Terrible thing," he said. "She's a courageous child,
or she'd have got out before this. How she kept the servants—
I came as soon as I could. I've been in the South Pacific, and
I'm trying to get married before I go back."

Dane introduced himself. They had been in different theaters
of war, but the service was a common bond between them.
Also Dane found himself unwillingly liking the other man.
They went in together for a drink, to find Elinor there alone.

"Carol's gone to see Lucy Norton," she said. "We've had
Floyd and his outfit here all morning. To hear the way they
talked to the servants you'd think we had set that fire last
night."

"Why think that?" Dane asked.

"I don't know," she said pettishly. "It's silly, of course. It
spoils the place dreadfully."

She did not look well. She was as carefully dressed as usual, but she looked her age and more. Dane took his highball and went to the fireplace, where he could face her.

"I was looking at it. I think it was deliberately set."

If she knew anything about it she was good, he thought. She lifted her carefully penciled eyebrows in surprise.

"But why?" she asked.

"The dead girl's clothes were never found. They might have been hidden there."

"That's rather farfetched, isn't it?"

Gregory put down his glass.

"Oh, come now, major," he said. "Why go looking for trouble? The place was dry, and probably somebody dropped a cigarette."

"Dropped six cigarettes, in that case. It started in half a dozen places."

There was an uneasy silence. Greg picked up his drink again.

"What you're saying is that it was set to burn the—to burn the girl's clothes. Is that it?"

"It looks like it. That's why the police have been here. They're used to forest fires, you know. I expect they had a ranger with them, didn't they?"

Elinor didn't know. She had slept late, and they had not come into the house. The servants had told her. And for goodness' sake let her forget it. She was giving a dinner that night at the club. She went back to her list, using the telephone now and then while the two men talked, about the war, about their respective services, even about the political situation. Carol found all three of them there when she came. She came in tumultuously, flinging off her hat and ignoring Dane completely. Greg looked at her.

"Well, did you see Lucy?" he asked.

"If you can call it that. They kept a nurse in the room every minute. I tried to get rid of her, but she said she had orders. I think Lucy knows something, but she doesn't intend to tell it."

Dane, conscious of tension when Carol came in, now sensed relief in both Elinor Hilliard and Greg. Especially in Elinor.

"What makes you think she knows anything?" she inquired.

"The way she looked at me. The way she tried to send the

nurse on an errand. She wouldn't go, of course."

"Rather highhanded of Floyd, eh?" said Greg. "Have a drink and forget it, Carol. So long as the old girl minds her own business, why worry?"

Carol refused the drink. She picked up her hat and prepared to leave and Dane, seeing her almost for the first time—except for a glimpse at the inquest—without the slacks and sweater which had made her look young and boyish, realized now that she was neither; that she was indeed a highly attractive if indignant young woman, and that she was still angry with him. In fact, at the door she turned on him sharply.

"I suppose all this pleases you," she said. "You think I started the fire last night, don't you? You told Floyd to keep Lucy from talking, too. He'd never think of it himself."

"Perhaps you underestimate Floyd," he said gravely. "I didn't advise him about anything. I rather think we have different ideas about the whole business."

She did not leave, after all. She was still in the doorway, looking uncertain, when Floyd accompanied by Mason, came along the hall. Mason was carrying a largish package wrapped in newspaper, which he held onto even after he sat down. Floyd did not sit at all. His big face showed excitement and something else.

"Sorry to bother you all again," he said. "Hello, Greg. Didn't know you were back."

"Got back this morning. Drove up."

"After the fire?"

"After the fire. Yes."

The chief looked around the room.

"Well, folks," he said, "that's what I came to talk about. Seemed queer to me, that fire. It spread too fast. It looked like it had started all over the place. So I got one of the forest rangers here this morning. He thinks the same as I do. Somebody set it."

No one spoke. He braced himself on his sturdy legs.

"Now it isn't as though things were just as usual around here. Maybe we've got a firebug. Maybe we haven't. What we know we've got is a murderer, and that ain't common. Not here it isn't. So I begin to think. That girl's clothes were never found, but she was staying in this house, and she didn't come in a red wrapper. So—well, there's the hill. Lots of places to hide clothes there." He glanced at Dane. "I reckon Major Dane had the same idea. He's been snooping around some. So the hill gets burned and the clothes with it. That's the general idea."

He fished in his pocket and brought out something which he held in his hand.

"It's still burning in places up there," he said. "Likely to go on some time. So I put a man to watch it. This is what he found." He opened his hand and held it out. On his broad palm lay another metal initial letter, this time a B. It was blackened by fire, but it had not melted. "Off the bag she carried," he said, and looked around the room. "Anybody recognize it?" he inquired.

No one spoke until Elinor rose abruptly.

"This is all very interesting," she said, "but I can't see how it concerns us. None of us were here at the time this girl was killed, and I object strongly to your attempt to involve us. It's ridiculous."

"Whoever set that fire knew the girl's stuff was on the hill," he said stubbornly.

"How do you know who set the fire?"

"Sit down, Miss Elinor," he said. "I'm not through yet. Give me that package, Jim."

Mason placed it on the table. This time it was not fastened, and he simply unrolled it and exposed its contents. What lay there was an old-fashioned pitcher, of the sort that belonged with a washbowl in the days before modern plumbing. It was chipped here and there, but the pattern was clear and distinct. Floyd stood off and let them see it.

"No prints on it," he said. "The gardener over at the Ward place, Rockhill, found it in the shrubbery near the lane there this morning. It might have been hidden there a year or so ago, but old Nat Ward took a notion to clean out that corner today. So here it is."

Dane glanced at Carol. She was staring incredulously at the pitcher and her color had faded.

"Maybe some of you remember it," Floyd said. "Probably

not you, Miss Carol. You're too young. But you might, Greg. Miss Elinor too."

Elinor shook her head, and Greg looked puzzled. Dane pursued his policy of watchful waiting.

"It looks familiar," Greg said slowly. "It's years since I saw a thing like that, but the pattern—"

His voice trailed off, and Floyd smiled.

"It just happens," he said, "that I know where it came from. I took it to old Annie Holden at the China Shop, and she remembered it all right. It was a special order. She got out her books and showed it to me. Your grandmother bought it thirty-odd years ago before your father built in the extra bathrooms."

"But what has it got to do with the fire?" Carol asked, looking bewildered. "I don't see—"

"Only that it's had gasoline in it," Floyd said. "That fire was set with gasoline, Miss Carol, and it was poured out of this."

There was a stricken silence. Dane, watching all the faces, realized that the difference between surprise and fear was very small. They all looked shocked. In a way, they all looked guilty.

"Of course," he said quietly, "you have to show that it came from this house. Things like that can be given or thrown away. Unless the rest of the set is here—"

"You needn't bother," Carol said, her voice flat and expressionless. "It's been in the attic for years. I saw it there the other day. You can go up and look if you like. One of the maids can show you the way."

Floyd nodded to Mason, and he went out. No one said anything. Floyd replaced the monogram letter in his pocket and looked at Carol.

"Your car was in the drive last night. I saw it there when we were working on the fire."

She nodded.

"It's too far down to the garage. I've been leaving it there at night. The weather was all right."

"All right for a fire too," he said. "Got any rubber hose around?"

"Rubber hose? There is plenty in the tool house."

"Narrow hose, I mean. Tubing."

She tried to think.

"I suppose there is," she said. "For shampooing hair. We usually leave such things here. Why?"

"Siphon out the gas. You can't turn a tap and let gas out of a car, you know, Miss Carol. You have to siphon it." His voice was milder when he spoke to her, almost apologetic. "Miss any gas today? That thing there"—he indicated the pitcher—"holds quite a bit."

"I didn't notice," she told him, and fell silent again.

There was a rattle of crockery from the stairs and Jim Mason came in. He was carrying an assortment of heavy porcelain, a washbowl, soap dish, tooth mug and so on, and his manner was triumphant as he placed it on the table.

"There's another piece up there, but I didn't bring it," he said, wiping his face with a dusty hand. "Ladies present. Guess this is enough anyhow."

There was no argument about it. Except that it had been wiped, the pitcher was obviously a part of the set, and Floyd's face was uneasy as he looked at Carol.

"Now," he said, his voice still mild, "why did you hide that girl's clothes, and set fire to the hill, Miss Carol? Who are you trying to protect?"

THIRTEEN

AN HOUR OR TWO LATER Dane left the house, as did Floyd and Mason, the latter still carrying the crockery and putting it carefully in the chief's car. Floyd looked disgruntled. His questions had got him nowhere. Carol had simply looked confused.

"I don't know," she said over and over. "Yes, I did go with Major Dane to the hill, but I never thought of burning it. Why should I?"

People were already coming to call by that time. The news that Greg was in town had got around, and the summer colony came in numbers to see its returned hero. Also of course to look at the burned hillside, and to conjecture once more about the murder.

The chief in disgust had wrapped his pitcher and escaped, with his satellite trailing him. And Dane had had to admire the three Spencers. Blood always told, he thought; Elinor delicately pouring tea, Carol seeing that the men—and most of the women—had drinks, and Greg hearty and cheerful, apologizing for his impromptu costume and shrugging off his new honors.

He did not stay long after Floyd's departure. The pitcher was a solid if chipped piece of evidence, and Carol had known about the metal initial he had found on the hill. On the other hand, she had looked, he thought grimly, as confused and guilty as the innocent often did look.

He stopped by the fountain, a monstrosity of yellow marble with a tall bronze figure on top, and around the basin a row of grinning satyrs, some holding goblets aloft, some playing on pipes or cymbals. He lit a cigarette and sat down on the rim of the basin. Only two or three days earlier he and Carol had sat here, after a futile search of the hill. His leg had hurt damnably, and she had asked him how he got it.

"In Italy," he had told her. "Old Alex got me back, or I wouldn't be sitting here. That's how he lost his eye."

And later that day Freda had walked across with a beef-steak and kidney pie, not for him but for Alex, with a card which said: "For Alex, with thanks." Alex had blushed with embarrassment.

"What the hell you been telling?" he demanded. "I'm no bloody hero. If that gets around—"

Dane had laughed.

"I don't think it will," he said pacifically. "Calm yourself, old boy. If ever a man deserved a steak and kidney pie you do."

And now Floyd suspected her of burning the hill. He was not fooling himself. She could have done it, have learned something that made it imperative to destroy the dead girl's identity. But she was not under arrest. There had been time before the first callers were announced and had traveled the long hall around the patio for Floyd to tell her so.

"I'll just ask you not to leave this town," he had said. "I think you'd better stay too, Greg. We're not at the bottom of this yet, but we're still digging. As for you, Miss Elinor—well, I wouldn't be in a hurry if I was you."

"Why should I stay here?" Elinor had demanded. "I'm needed at home. I have a husband there, and a mother."

"From what I hear they won't suffer any," Floyd said dryly. "You got plenty of help, haven't you?"

Greg's protest had been violent. He was about to be married, and part of his leave was gone already. But his real resentment had been at the accusation against Carol.

"Preposterous," he said. "Why would she do it? Ruin a place she's loved all her life? And you can't connect her with the murder. Don't try to push us too far, Floyd."

"All right," Floyd said. "Explain that pitcher. That ought to be easy."

Dane went over that in his mind. The chief was shrewd. Only perhaps he was beginning at the wrong end. What was the motive for the murder? Who was the girl? Why had she come to the Spencer place, claiming to know Carol? And why had she got up late at night, left her room and gone outside. For sometime that night she had been outside. There was the pine needle in her slipper to prove it. Why had she gone out, clad only as she was with her fur jacket to keep her warm? Whom had she met that June night? A woman?

He thought it possible. Could it have been Elinor Hilliard? There was that story of the Dalton girl's about seeing Elinor's car. But Elinor had an alibi, or so she claimed. Gregory? He considered Greg Spencer carefully. He might have used his sister's car, and he was the kind to be tied up with women. Dane knew the type well. Yet there were one or two things against the theory. The dead girl had been small and light, but her body had almost certainly been taken up in the elevator. Gregory, in a hurry as he must have been, would not have needed to use it, not with Lucy in the house.

The bobby pin had belonged to her. He knew that, if Carol did not. The hair caught in it had been bleached and showed dark at the root, whereas Elinor Hilliard was a natural blonde.

All right. Go on from there. Greg would not have used the elevator, even allowing for Lucy's slight deafness. He had investigated it after Carol had given him the bobby pin, and it made an unmistakable rumbling sound. But Elinor Hilliard could have, taking the desperate chance it must have been.

He considered that carefully. She had presumably been seen that night, or her car had. Also no sooner had she arrived yesterday than the hillside had been burned that night. There was a resemblance here too, he thought. In both cases fires had been set. But once again he found himself up against Lucy's definite and, he believed, truthful statement that there had been no fire while she was still in the house.

He lit another cigarette and straightened his leg.

Was it possible, he wondered, that the girl had not been killed on Friday night, after all? That she had stayed on for another day, living in the yellow room and eating what she could find? He thought it unlikely. Not only had the postmortem fixed the approximate time as Friday. There was also Lucy's story of the hand reaching out from the closet door. That had been real enough for her to break a leg, trying to escape from it.

He got up rather drearily and limped home. There was no

news from Tim, but he had not expected any. Tim had only had time to reach St. Louis. But Alex found him irritable and without appetite that night.

"For a man who's trying to get back in this war," Alex said somberly, "you act like you never heard of a kraut. You eat that custard. It's good for you—sir.".

He did not eat the custard. He pushed it away and lit a cigarette.

"The police think Carol Spencer set the fire last night, Alex."

"That girl? I don't believe it, sir."

"Nor do I. Just the same she's in real trouble. A little more and they'll arrest her for arson, and possibly for concealing evidence of a crime."

Alex fixed his one eye on the view.

"I've been thinking, sir," he said. "Maybe somebody chased that girl outside."

"In a fur coat?"

"We don't know she had it on, do we? It was easy enough to put it on later. As I get it, the idea was to make it look as though she was killed in the house."

"Why?"

"Well, to let the murderer get away. The Norton woman mightn't have found her right off. She had a lot to do before she made the beds. Take her two or three days, likely, before she needed to get into the linen closet."

"And how would you get in the house?"

Alex was thoughtful. His big body tensed with the effort of thinking.

"Well, if you didn't have a game leg you could shinny up the pillars of that little porch off the kitchen. You can break the lock of a window easy enough, and maybe nobody would notice it up there."

"Any other way you can think of? As I recall, one window in the yellow room was open when I saw it. That's where the girl was staying. How about a ladder?"

"There's a pruning ladder down by the stable. I seen it myself. It's close up. You don't notice it unless you're going by. I use that way for a short cut."

"You might look at it sometime and see if it's been moved."

He sat still for a long time, smoking one cigarette after another. It was useless to try to see Lucy Norton, who was, he was confident, holding in her stubborn head the key to the mystery. He knew, too, that it was possible Carol Spencer had set the fire after all. She would do it if she was trying to protect someone. But whom was she trying to protect? Elinor Hilliard? Her brother? Then again he gave her credit for too much intelligence to have left the pitcher where it was found. It would have been easy to bring it back to the house, wash it and return it to the attic.

Or would it? The fire must have caught fast, and the drive been brilliantly lighted almost at once. Had she found herself more or less cut off, unable to get back with the incriminating pitcher in her hand? He considered that. An air warden on his rounds had seen the blaze and run to the Wards' to telephone. He would have used the path that led to the Spencer place. In that case she could have been cut off, have heard the warden running, taken refuge in the Ward property, and in panic had dropped the thing where it had been found.

The same applied to Elinor, of course. Either one of them could have hidden until the warden had entered the Ward house and then by way of the lower garden and the trees have worked her way back. Gregory he eliminated. It was unlikely that he had known what was in the attic. Unlikely, too, that his surprise when he saw what Mason had carried down could have been assumed.

He looked at his watch. It was almost nine. If Marcia Dalton was at home she would have finished her dinner, and it was time he had a further talk with her.

He said nothing to Alex, except that he was to keep an eye on the Spencer place until he got back, and he did not take his car. He walked down the drive and toward the beach to the Dalton house. A big dog came running at him, but let him alone when spoken to. And he found Marcia alone, playing solitaire in the living room. Her long face lighted when she saw him.

"Well!" she said. "Don't tell me this is a dinner call. I don't believe it."

She was obviously flustered. She insisted on getting him the highball he did not want, informed him that the servants had gone to the movies, and ordered him into a comfortable chair without giving him a chance to speak. Then she sat down, eying him shrewdly.

"So you're not asked to the party either!"

He looked surprised.

"What party?"

"Elinor Hilliard's giving one at the club. She left me out too. I suppose Carol told her I'd seen her car, so here I am, *sur le branche*. I can't say I mind. I'm a Nurse's Aide and I've been at the hospital all day." She gave him a sharp glance. "Still on the trail, major?"

His lean face did not change.

"On what trail, Miss Dalton?"

She made an impatient gesture.

"I'm not an idiot. Maybe you're in love with Carol, I wouldn't know. But you're interested in this case. You won't get far with it, of course."

"That's rather an interesting statement."

"Sure it is. I mean it, too. We're pretty much of a clan here. We stick together. We have our differences, but when it comes to trouble— You'll find Carol and Greg Spencer are part of us. Not Elinor."

"So, granting that I am puzzled by this, I can expect no help. Is that it?"

She did not answer directly.

"You're up against something more than that," she told him. "Greg and Elinor will stick together through wind and high water. They're like twins, only she's bossed him for years. If Greg set that fire last night, Elinor knows about it. I think he did."

"I see. And the murder?"

"I never claimed to see anybody in Elinor's car that night. All I know is that the car was here. I'll swear that on a stack of Bibles. But go down to the club some morning and watch them there. I haven't told them anything, but someone else has. If Elinor was here that night, Greg was with her. At least some man was. He comes back this time, and the hill is burned.

Think about that, Major Dane. If this Barbour girl's clothes were hidden there—"

"Who saw Greg in the car?"

"I didn't say it was Greg. That's not only what I think, but what a lot of other people think too."

"All right," he said patiently. "Who saw this man in the car?"

"Old Mrs. Ward. Mr. Ward's a bad sleeper. He walks around sometimes at night, and this night it seems he was gone so long she got worried. She went after him, but she didn't find him. She saw a car that looked like Elinor's going down the drive at Crestview, only there was a man in it. He wasn't driving it. Somebody else was, and that puzzled her. There hadn't been a murder then, so far as anybody knew, and she happened to speak about it to someone the next day. She thought if it was Greg it was odd he hadn't stopped to see them. He was a friend of Terry, their grandson."

Dane sat upright in his chair, staring at her.

"Good God!" he said. "Are you telling me that this summer colony knows a thing like that and won't tell it?"

"I warned you," she said comfortably. "We stick together. I'm furious at Elinor tonight, or I'd probably still not be sticking my neck out. Then of course old Mrs. Ward doesn't see very well. There's one school that believes she was mistaken. The other school thinks Greg was here; but he's the local hero, so what the hell?"

He was still astounded. He got up and took a turn or two around the room before he spoke.

"I wonder why you're telling me this, Miss Dalton. It's not just because you're left out of a party."

For a minute her mask dropped.

"No," she said. "It's because Greg needs a friend. I'm fond of him, you see. I never had a chance, of course. But this crowd has got him tried and convicted, and someday Floyd and his bunch will hear it. Maybe Greg did it, I don't know. But he never planned to do it. He's not that sort. Only remember this. Lucy Norton had a better reason to let that girl stay in the house than she told at the inquest. And Greg likes women. I guess he's had his share of them."

Dane looked undecided. He looked at his watch.

"Maybe I'd better see Mr. Ward," he said. "If he's a bad sleeper he may still be up."

But, although he found Mr. Ward awake and reading in his library, he left at the end of a half hour completely baffled. Mr. Ward was courteous, even affable. He offered a chair and a drink, only the first of which Dane accepted, and he brought up at once the matter of the fire.

"Bad thing," he said. "I always liked that hill. Of course we're all a little overgrown. Too much enthusiastic planting in the early days. But a fire . . ."

When Dane broached the murder however he became reticent.

"Horrible thing," he said. "Terrible for Carol Spencer, too. I'm glad some of the family are with her. It was no place for her to stay alone."

That gave Dane his opening. He was quick to take it.

"I understand your wife saw a car leaving the Spencer place the night of the murder. Can you tell me anything about it?"

Mr. Ward frowned.

"I see you've heard that story," he said. "There's nothing to it. Absolutely. She saw a car, certainly, but it may have backed into the drive to turn around. That's all I know, sir, or my wife either. The amount of gossip here in the summer is outrageous."

"She didn't see who was in it?" Dane persisted.

"She thought it was a man, but she can't even be sure of that. Her eyes are not what they were, and it was a dark night."

He rose, and Dane saw he was expected to go. He waited a moment, however.

"You yourself didn't see this car, Mr. Ward?"

"Certainly not," the old gentleman said testily.

But Dane persisted.

"The police might like to know all this, Mr. Ward."

"Neither my wife nor I run to the police with all the tittle-tattle of a place like this. As for the car, it was a car. It might have been anybody's."

He himself showed Dane out, but he did not offer to shake hands. He stood in the doorway, small and wiry and watchful, until he could no longer hear Dane's footsteps on the drive. After that he locked the door, put out the lights and went upstairs to his wife.

"I wish to God," he said, "that you'd learn to curb your tongue. They've learned about Elinor Hilliard's car. Major Dane has just been here."

Mrs. Ward sat up in bed. She had lost color, and she wrung her thin old hands.

"Oh, Nat," she said. "What are we to do? What *can* we do?"

He was still upset, but he went over and patted her on the shoulder.

"I'll have to go out," he said. "Try and sleep, my dear. I'll not be long."

She protested almost wildly, but he did not listen. His small neat body was erect and purposeful as he left her, and he stopped long enough in his dressing room to slip a revolver into his pocket.

FOURTEEN

LUCY NORTON DIED that same night.

It happened either during or some time after Elinor Hilliard's dinner at the club. Characteristically, Elinor's reaction to Floyd's visit had been to insist on going on with the party. Greg had protested.

"Don't be a jackass," he said. "Whom are you trying to fool? The police? What do they care? If it's the summer people, I imagine there's plenty of talk already without your trying to show you don't give a damn. Call it off. Have a headache. You've done that before when it suited you."

"And let everybody know something new has happened? Let me alone, Greg. We've got to carry on."

Carol felt helpless between the two of them. When Greg appealed to her, however, she sided with Elinor.

"I don't see what else she can do," she said. "You can't ask twenty people to dinner, let their cooks have the evening off and then tell them to eat scrambled eggs at home. What about that pitcher? It got out of the house somehow. It didn't have legs."

"Why worry?" Elinor said lightly, and looked at her watch. "Good gracious, I have to get my hair done. I'm taking your car, Carol. Greg's going to the barber. He needs his."

"Why can't you walk? If I'm to fix your bridge tables and take the champagne—"

"I'll be back in plenty of time."

She was not, of course. Carol dressed early, putting on a white dress which made her look gayer than she felt, and getting to the club just in time to place the cards on the table before the first guest arrived. It was Colonel Richardson, imposing as ever in dinner clothes, and bringing his own contribution of a bottle of old brandy.

"Nothing in the club like it," he told her, handing it over carefully. "I laid up some for Don years ago, but there's plenty left. You're looking very lovely, my dear."

He wanted to talk about the fire.

"Most puzzling," he said. "Of course the weather is dry, but to spread as fast as it did! Who raised the alarm?"

"One of the air wardens saw it first."

"I was wondering," he said. "I saw that man of Dane's around your place late that night. You remember I stayed at the Wards', playing chess. I certainly saw him—Alex, I think they call him. Rather odd, don't you think? Being out at that hour?"

Her nerves were none too good. She put down the last place card and looked at him.

"If you mean he set the fire, I think you're wrong, colonel. Both he and Major Dane worked hard to put it out."

But Henry Richardson had something to say, and proceeded to say it.

"I've been coming here for a good many years," he said with dignity. "We've never had anything worse than a burglary, and that was by a waiter at the hotel. Then this Dane arrives, with a servant who looks like a thug, and we have both a murder with an attempted fire—in your house, my dear—and another fire last night."

Carol flushed.

"Isn't that rather ridiculous? After all, he's an officer in the army. Even if you can't find his record."

"There have been bad hats in the services as well as everywhere else."

Good gracious, she thought wildly, *I'm quarreling with Don's father, and Don is dead.* She forced a smile.

"I'm sorry," she told him. "I haven't had much sleep lately, and I'm certainly not interested in Major Dane. Now do go and help receive these people. Elinor's late, as usual."

He was not entirely reassured, however. He put his hand on her arm before he left.

"Just don't see too much of the fellow," he said. "He's hard, my dear. Not the sort I like to see with you."

The party was a success, at least at first. Elinor's parties always were. She had skimmed the cream of the bridge-playing crowd, the food was good, the drinks plentiful. The noise rose over the cocktails until Carol felt her head buzzing. She drank two herself, and Greg had more than were good for him. But looking around the table Carol wondered why Marcia Dalton was not there. Pete Crowell was being the life of the party, so far as noise was concerned. Louise Stimson was wearing all her pearls over a black dress that was a trifle low for wartime, and watching that Greg's wineglass was kept full. But Marcia was not there.

It was a deliberate affront, she realized, because Marcia had claimed to have seen Elinor's car the night of the murder. It was stupid of Elinor, she thought. Marcia had a bitter tongue.

She was roused by seeing Greg, his voice slightly thick, lifting his glass. She tried desperately to catch his eye, but he did not look at her. He was on his feet, his eyes slightly glazed, but with his usual beaming cheerfulness.

"To Floyd, our remarkable chief of police!" he said. "Who suspects the Spencer family of both arson and murder!"

There was an appalled silence, but there was nothing to do about it. Elinor had heard him, and was forcing a smile.

"Don't try to be funny, Greg," she said, across the round table. "People might misunderstand you."

He shut up then. But the damage had been done, and those who had not heard him were being informed by the ones who had. Perhaps Carol imagined it, but the gaiety seemed to have gone out of the party. There was low-voiced conversation, a hint of caution, and now and then a face turned curiously toward herself. She was relieved when Elinor got up, and the men drifted into the smoking room for cigars and brandy. Carol herself managed to get away from the women, and outside to the pool.

There was a fog coming in. It crept along like thick white fingers among the islands, bringing a chill with it, and already the village lights had practically disappeared. She heard a car starting up somewhere close by, but paid no attention. It was twenty minutes later when Elinor called sharply from the porch of the club.

"Greg! Where are you, Greg?"

"He's not here," Carol answered. "Perhaps he's gone home."

She went back into the club. Elinor was almost in tears with rage.

"It wasn't enough for him to get tight and say what he did," she said furiously. "He's walked out on a bridge game. You'll have to take his place, Carol."

Afterwards she remembered that night with horror: Greg gone in the fog, herself at the bridge table, bidding, doubling, winning or being set; and sometime, perhaps as she sat there, Lucy mysteriously dying on the floor of her hospital room.

That was where they found her, on the floor and without a mark on her. She had gone to sleep around ten o'clock, a hysterical nurse reported the next morning, and she had been all right then. She had been nervous since the inquest, and she had taken a sleeping tablet at nine.

"I didn't look in after that," the nurse said, sniffling. "I was busy, and she wasn't sick. Then when I carried in the basin to wash her for breakfast— She would never have tried to get out of bed. Never."

Floyd and Dr. Harrison reached the room almost simultaneously. There was nothing to be done, of course. The doctor said she had been dead for hours. Rigor had already set in. And Floyd looked infuriated.

"Mark or no mark," he said, "she's been murdered. She knew something she wasn't telling, so this is what she got."

The doctor got up from his knees.

"Looks like heart, Floyd."

"Heart! With her on the floor like that?"

Both men surveyed the body. It lay beside the bed, in its cotton nightgown, the small face relaxed and peaceful. On the bed itself the covers had been thrown back, as if Lucy herself had done it. The only indication that anything was wrong was that the cord of the pushbutton, which had been fastened to the lower sheet with a safety pin, had been torn away and lay on the floor. Floyd pointed to it.

"Who did that?" he demanded, his face red with anger.

"It happens," the doctor said, still calm. "It slipped and when she felt the heart attack coming on she got out of bed to get it. You've got murder on the brain."

Floyd was still suspicious. He went out into the hall, where an uneasy intern was waiting.

"Any way anybody could have got in here last night?"

"The doors are locked at ten o'clock, chief, when the watchman takes over. She—wasn't killed, was she?"

"That remains to be seen," Floyd said loftily. "Any empty rooms around here?"

"Eleven. Patient went out late yesterday afternoon."

The chief grunted and looked around. Eleven was across the hall. He strode in there and looked around him. The bed had been stripped and not yet made up, and a window was open. The intern had followed.

"Who was in here?"

"The Crowells' little girl. She had her tonsils out a couple of days ago."

Floyd examined the window. The fire escape was just outside, and he grunted again. There were scratches on the rusty edge of the ladderlike steps, and some of the paint had been scraped off.

"Come in here," he said, almost cheerfully. "Bring the doc over, will you?"

But the doctor was not convinced. Someone might have come in. He didn't dispute that. Lucy however had not been killed. "She might have been frightened," he said. "Nobody laid a hand on her, Floyd. Take it or leave it."

"What about these Crowells? Know anything?"

"They're all right, so far as I know. I operated on the girl. I don't know much about them. Get her down to the mortuary, Floyd. I'd better do a post-mortem."

It was the doctor who notified Joe Morton, Lucy's husband, and after a brief hesitation called Carol Spencer. She did not understand at first.

"Dead?" she said. "Lucy! But she was all right yesterday. She was getting better."

"She died suddenly."

"You mean her heart?"

"I think so. She tried to get out of bed alone."

"But she'd never do that," Carol protested. "I can't believe it."

She put down the receiver and wondered what to do. It was still early. The servants had had their breakfast, but Elinor and Greg were not yet awake. She decided to drive to the hospital, and found Joe Norton already there when she arrived. He was sitting on a bench in the lower hall, his face in his hands and his whole attitude one of hopeless grief. She sat down beside him and put a hand on his knee.

"I'm sorry, Joe. Terribly sorry."

He raised his head and looked at her with red-rimmed eyes.

"They say it was her heart," he said bitterly. "Wasn't anything wrong with her heart. That's their way of getting out of it."

"Getting out of what?"

"They killed her. That's what. Somebody gave her the wrong medicine. Or maybe she knew something she wasn't meant to tell."

She had not seen Lucy, and she supposed they were making a post-mortem examination. She herself still felt stunned, and to add to the tension Joe suddenly decided to locate Lucy and was restrained only with difficulty. She quieted him finally. She even succeeded at last in taking him back to Crestview, where he sat in the kitchen, not talking, while a horrified Maggie fried him some eggs and forced him to eat. When Carol went back, however, he had gone.

So great had been her own surprise that it was not until she was in her own room after his departure that she began to wonder why Lucy had been found on the floor, or if heart trouble was really the answer. There had been something in the doctor's voice which puzzled her.

The doctor, to tell the truth, also was puzzled. There was no question that Lucy had died because her heart had stopped, abruptly and finally. But it should not have stopped at all. It was a fairly sound and healthy organ, as was all the rest of what had been Lucy Norton. Shock, he thought, as he put down his scalpel. Shock and fright? He wondered. He reported to Floyd, who was content to take his post-mortems *in absentia*.

"Nothing," he said. "Slight bruise on elbow as she fell. Nothing else, inside or out."

"Maybe *she* climbed that fire escape?" Floyd jeered. "Look

again, doc. Maybe poison."

"The laboratory's doing that now. I think it unlikely."

It was more than unlikely. It was impossible. The lab reported that Lucy had eaten a light hospital supper of creamed chicken and gelatine at five-thirty, and that she had died sometime after midnight, the process of digestion being far along.

Carol knew nothing of all this. She was grieved for Lucy, and slightly annoyed when at eleven o'clock she looked across the patio to see Elinor getting into a taxi on her way to the club. Freda had certainly told her about Lucy, but she was going anyhow, to sit poised and smiling and slightly defiant under one of the big umbrellas by the pool, to gather around her such men as were available, and to drink her before-lunch cocktail as though she had never heard of the death.

It was not normal behavior, even for Elinor. Carol found herself recalling Marcia's story about the car, and the fire which had happened so opportunely. For the first time she began to suspect that her sister was involved, not in Lucy's death but in what had preceded it.

She had to know. It was no use drifting along, with murder and sudden death all around them; with Elinor at the club and Greg still asleep. She had to find out.

Elinor's room was already cleaned when she got there. Freda had gone, and the bottles and jars of cosmetics were in neat rows on the toilet table. The elaborate comb and brushes and mirror without which Elinor never traveled were in place, as well as her jewel case on a small stand beside her bed. Carol only glanced at them, however. She closed the door to the hall and went to the closet.

Considering that she had come merely for the inquest, Elinor had brought a surprising amount of clothes. There were floor-length dinner dresses, high-necked in deference to the war. There were elaborate negligees and sports dresses. On the shelf above, carefully placed on trees, was a row of hats, one of them small and white, and her shoes and slippers were neatly treed on the slanting shelf near the floor.

She examined them all, feeling guilty as she did so. Once Freda alarmed her. She came into the room, saw the closet door ajar and closed it without seeing her. Not until she had been gone for some time did Carol resume her search, moving the dresses along the rod that supported the hangers and inspecting them one by one. She paid particular attention to the dinner gown Elinor had worn to the Wards' the night of the fire, but it told her nothing. She had almost finished when she saw the warm woolen dressing gown hung on a hook behind the rest.

She had not seen it before. It was a practical tailored affair, dark blue, with neat pockets and a cord to fasten around Elinor's slim waist, and she took it down and examined it, her heart pounding in her ears.

It was not only dusty around the hem. There were two or three sandburs caught in it. She stood still, holding it, and trying not to see the picture it painted: Elinor in the attic, getting Granny's old pitcher, Elinor on the drive, siphoning gasoline from the car, and Elinor setting fire to the hillside and then coming back to the house and hanging up the garment, as casually as she did everything else.

When she heard Greg's voice speaking to Freda, she hurriedly replaced the dressing gown where she had found it. But Greg did not come in. She was relieved, although she knew it was only a respite. She had to go on. She found nothing more, however. Among the shoes were bedroom slippers to match the negligees and one practical pair of soft tan leather. Except that these last showed a scratch or two, there was no indication that they had been outside the house.

Greg was on the terrace when she went downstairs. He was staring out at the bay, smoking and depressed.

"I'm sorry about last night, Carol," he said. "Made a fool of myself, of course. What's this about Lucy Norton?"

She lit a cigarette before she could trust herself to speak.

"She's dead, Greg. That's all I know."

"Queer," he said moodily. "Always thought she was a sturdy little thing. Heart, Maggie says. It will be hard on Joe." He put out his cigarette. "I just talked to Virginia on the phone. She's pretty badly upset. Everything's ready, church engaged, bridesmaids ready, presents coming in, and here I sit. *I* didn't set that fire."

She summoned all her courage.

"Are you sure you don't know why it was set, Greg?"

He stared at her incredulously.

"Why it was set? Good God, Carol, I don't understand you. Why would I know a thing like that?"

"I'm not sure," she said wearily. "I only know it was started from this house. There's no other explanation. And at some time or other Elinor has been outside in the grounds at night. I found some sandburs in the hem of her dressing gown. She knew about that pitcher too, and my car was there. She could have got the gasoline from it."

To her surprise he laughed, although rather grimly.

"I can suspect Elinor of a number of things," he said dryly. "I know her. But the last thing in the world she would do would be to soil her pretty hands with gasoline, or go out in the night alone in a dressing gown and carrying Granny's old pitcher to start a fire. That's out, Carol. Don't be a little fool."

Perhaps he was right, she thought. It wasn't like Elinor, none of it, and when Elinor herself arrived soon after, bringing a half dozen people for a drink before lunch she felt still more doubtful. This was Elinor at her best, the perfect hostess, the fastidious, immaculate person she had always been.

They sat around, well dressed and prosperous appearing. Some of them had been on the links. The talk was idle, of golf, of the party the night before, of the war, of politics. It was some time before Lucy was mentioned. Then someone said that Floyd was still clinging to the idea she had been murdered, that he had found where the fire escape had been used.

Louise Stimson looked up at Greg with her faintly malicious smile.

"And Greg with no alibi for last night!" she said. "Where did you vanish to, Greg?"

"Me?" He grinned at her. "I wasn't climbing any fire escapes. I'd had a lot to drink. I drove it off."

She persisted, still apparently only mischievous. "There's a story you were here the night of the murder, you know. You'd better get busy on a couple of alibis."

Greg looked astonished. He put down his glass and glanced around the group.

"I don't get it. What story? I haven't heard it."

"Just that you were seen here, coming out of the drive in

Elinor's car," Louise said pertly.

"In Elinor's car? For God's sake, what would I be doing here in Elinor's car?"

She laughed. "That's the question, of course," she said, and finished her cocktail.

It was Peter Crowell who broke the startled silence that followed.

"Why don't you mind your own business, Louise?" he demanded. "Of course there are stories, Greg. There always are. That's only one of them. Don't let it worry you. Nobody believes it." He got out of his chair. "It's time to go," he said. "More than time, if you ask me."

FIFTEEN

THE NEWS OF LUCY'S DEATH did not reach Dane until Alex returned from his marketing that morning. There was still no word from Tim in St. Louis, and Dane was restless. He had walked again over to the hillside. Most of the watchers had left and the last vestige of fire had gone, but he knew the uselessness of further search. When he went back he had determined to see Lucy Norton, police or no police. There was still the question as to why she had allowed the dead girl to stay in the house, had fixed her bed, even carried soap and towels to her. What sort of story had she put up that Lucy would agree to let her stay there? He felt the whole answer lay there.

He considered that, ruffling through such notes as he had made. He had always believed in following the essential clue, and so far he had considered the dead girl's identity as probably providing that. Now he wondered if her story to Lucy was not more important. These New England women, he knew, were not soft. They were as hard and firm as the soil that bred them. They had character and a certain skepticism, especially about strangers. Yet Lucy had accepted her. Why? What proof had she had? What, for instance, had she shown? A card? A letter?

Some identification she had certainly produced. Something she had carried with her in her bag, something now either buried or in the murderer's possession.

The news of Lucy's death was therefore a shock to him.

"Found her on the floor, sir," Alex reported. "Floyd's running around in circles. According to all I can find out, he thinks somebody climbed up the fire escape and knocked her down."

Dane ate a hasty lunch and drove into the village. He found the police chief grim and not inclined to be communicative.

"She's dead. That's all I'm going to say, Dane. The district attorney's coming over. I wish to God he'd keep out of this.

I've got enough trouble of my own."

"What brings him?" Dane inquired. "If it was her heart—"

"Well," Floyd said grudgingly, "there are one or two things I don't like. Somebody jerked the pushbutton off the bed, for one thing. Then about one A.M. one or two of the patients report somebody opening their doors and looking in. Searching for her, probably. Didn't know what room she was in."

"That ought to let out some of your prize suspects."

"Yeah? Just who? None of the Spencers except Carol knew where she was. And Greg Spencer says he was driving all over the map when it happened."

He did not mention the fire escape, nor did Dane. He blustered about these tight-mouthed women who wouldn't tell all they knew; that he was sorry as hell about Lucy, but if she'd only talked— However he was on the trail of something. That dead girl, now.

"She probably came from somewhere in the Middle West," he said. "Say somewhere about St. Louis, eh?"

He grinned at Dane, and Dane gave him an amused smile in return.

"I imagine we'll both know before long," he said, and went out.

The hospital was quiet when he got there. It was inured to death. It did the best it could. After that things were either up to God or to the patient, depending on your view of things. It was busy, though. No one paid any attention to Dane as he wandered around, first outside and then through the halls. Floyd was right about the fire escape. It showed fresh scratches on the rusty iron. And upstairs he had no trouble locating Lucy's empty room. But he was disappointed in finding it had been stripped and Lucy's small possessions gone.

He was tired and exasperated as he drove home. If something had frightened Lucy into the heart attack that had killed her, what was it? Or who was it?

All along Lucy's attitude had bothered him. So far as he knew she had not mentioned the presence of the girl in the house when she was found and taken to the hospital. All she had told was of a hand reaching out of the closet. Yet at the inquest she had come out flat-footed with the fact.

Had that caused her death? Sent her midnight visitor up the fire escape, to hunt her out and so terrify her that she died of shock? But why such a visitor, unless she either knew or possessed something that might be incriminating?

It was this possibility which had sent him to the hospital; to find if possible what clue to the girl's identity Lucy had in her possession. He was still working on this idea when Tim called him late in the afternoon from St. Louis.

"No soap," he said, "and hotter than the hinges of hell here. What do I do now?"

"Better catch a plane back. I may need you."

Tim protested the plane violently.

"I was airsick all the way out, and how!" he said. "Have a heart! Lemme come on my back, in a good old sleeper. I'm apt to be shoved off the plane anyhow. Any fellow with a brief case under his arm can claim priority."

Dane grinned and agreed. Nevertheless, he was uneasy. There was only one explanation of Lucy's getting out of her bed, and that was fear. If this sort of thing was to go on—

He walked worriedly about the room. His limp was almost gone, and he realized that he had not much time left. Yet if Carol was in danger—and he began to think she might be—the mystery ought to be solved soon. Not that it was a personal matter, he told himself. No man with his type of job had any business falling for a girl. Any girl. But the thing had to be stopped.

That night he drove out to the Norton place, a small frame house on a back road some miles away. A number of cars parked around it showed that Joe was not alone in his trouble. As Dane got out of the car he realized that the drought had broken at last. A fine drizzling rain was falling, making the place look bleak and forlorn. He felt like an intruder as he rapped at the door.

A woman opened it, looking at him suspiciously. She agreed to call Joe, however, and he appeared, haggard and resentful.

"If you're from the police I wish you'd let me alone," he said roughly. "She's dead. That's enough, ain't it?"

"It's not enough if somebody terrified her last night," Dane said. "Better think that over, Mr. Norton. She had a broken leg, but she got out of bed. Why did she do that?"

Joe doubled his hard fists.

"Just let me know who scared her," he said. "He'll never know what struck him."

It was some time before Dane could persuade Joe to let him see what of Lucy's effects he had brought from the hospital. They were disappointing, at that. Joe had cleared the kitchen of people, and under his suspicious eyes Dane examined what he laid out on the table; a few cotton nightgowns, some handkerchiefs, the clothing she had worn to the inquest, and last of all her shabby pocketbook.

There were only two or three dollars in it, proving that the murdered girl had not bribed her way into the house. These, a used handkerchief, and a slip containing a list of groceries bought from Miller's market the day of the girl's arrival merely bore out her story as she had told it at the inquest. And Joe knew nothing more than Lucy had told him, which was substantially what she had testified.

However, when Dane pressed him, he admitted that Lucy had been unlike herself when he saw her at the hospital.

"Seemed like she had something on her mind," he said. "I asked her, but she wouldn't tell me. Said she'd tell Miss Carol when she came. Only thing I got out of her, she said she thought the girl was scared of something the night she was killed. She didn't know what."

So it was back to the Spencer family again, Dane reflected glumly as he drove home. But how? Which one of them was involved? Gregory could have burned the hillside. His easy statement that he had arrived after the fire meant nothing. And so far they had all taken his alibi for granted. But a man could not be in Washington receiving the Medal of Honor for bravery and committing a murder at the same time. Nor could the sight of Greg, knowing him as she did, have alarmed Lucy Norton to her death.

Nevertheless, he called Washington that night, driving over to the railroad station to do so. He asked that no name be used in the return telegram or telephone message, and felt he had done all he could as he drove back.

It was his turn to keep an eye on the Spencer place. Alex

was to relieve him at four in the morning, and was already snoring stertorously in his bed when Dane went out. It was still raining, a thin drizzle which would do little to help the crops but was enough to wet him pretty thoroughly as he went through the trees. It was very dark. His landmark was the light marble of the fountain, and he found it and stopped there. From where he stood the house was a black mass, looming a hundred yards ahead. Its very darkness and stillness reassured him. He moved, limping slightly, toward it.

There was a clap of thunder then, and somewhere not far off a car backfired. Or was it a backfire? He was not certain. The rain had suddenly increased to a roar and made all sound uncertain.

He finally decided it had been a car, and began as usual quietly to circle the house. He moved first along the side toward the sea, where the terrace was empty, the chairs and tables taken in against the rain, and he went on noiselessly, until he had reached the entrance at the rear.

Each night he or Alex had watched the windows and tried the doors. Now, as he felt for the one on the drive, it was open. What confronted him was only the empty darkness of the hall. It startled him by its very unexpectedness, and it was a moment or two before he stepped warily inside. Except for the splashing of the wall fountain in the patio everything was quiet, and he was uncertain what to do. Either one of the household had left the house for some purpose, or someone had been admitted. The door had surely been locked before the family went to bed. But the total darkness made it unlikely anyone had come in. Then who was missing?

He stood for a second or two before he decided to make a move. He knew the house fairly well by that time, and he found the stairs without trouble. Still groping, he passed the door to the yellow room and went on to Carol's. It was closed and locked. He began to feel rather absurd, but he knocked finally, and felt an enormous relief when he heard her voice inside.

"Yes? What is it?"

"It's Jerry Dane," he said. "Don't be frightened. I found the front door open and the house dark. I was afraid someone might have come in."

"Just a minute."

He heard her light snap on, heard her closet door open and knew she was putting on something hastily over her night clothes. She looked very young and startled when she opened the door, her hair loose about her face and her eyes wide.

"Did you say the front door was open?"

"Yes."

"I don't understand. I locked it myself tonight. What time is it?"

"After one o'clock. Perhaps you'd better check up and see if anyone has gone out. I'll look around myself. Somebody may have come in, but I doubt it."

He turned on the lights in the yellow room while she hurried on. It was empty, and the windows were closed. He was still there, remembering it as he had first seen it, when Carol came back.

"It's Elinor," she told him. "I can't understand it. Why would she go out on a night like this? And Greg's asleep. I heard him snoring. She must have gone alone."

He glanced into Elinor's room before they went downstairs. The bed had been used. The book she had been reading was on the table beside it, and a breeze from the open window was ruffling its pages and sending in a thin spray of rain. A pair of sheer stockings hung over the back of a chair, one or two silk undergarments were strewn about, and her evening slippers were on the floor.

"You see," Carol said, her lips stiff. "She had undressed for the night. She had gone to bed too. Why would she go out? Or where?"

"There's a chance she's in the house. I didn't look in the service wing downstairs."

But Elinor was not in the house. Five minutes after he had discovered the open door Dane turned his flashlight up the hill and saw something lying there among the burned and sodden bushes near the lane.

It was Elinor, and she had been shot.

She was not dead. She had been shot through the thigh, and she was bleeding so profusely that Dane was afraid to move her. She was unconscious, and she remained unconscious through much that followed: the rousing of the household, Dr. Harrison on his knees in the rain and mud beside her, the arrival of the ambulance, and Carol's departure in it while Greg dressed and got his car.

Dane was glad to have a few minutes to himself, but he learned little. There had been footprints both in the lane and on the hillside, but either the rain had obliterated them or the ambulance had destroyed them. He did find a small pool of what looked like bloody water in the lane itself, and within a foot or two of it a small shell comb, like those Elinor wore in her hair. She had been shot there, he decided, shot and then carried a few yards up the hill.

He was still there when Greg called him to the car. Greg was badly shocked. His hands were shaking, and after a look at him Dane told him to move over and took the driver's seat himself.

"That shot," he said as they started. "It was fired pretty close to the house. Didn't you hear it?"

Greg shook his head.

"No. I don't hear much once I'm asleep. It was an accident, of course."

"Why?"

Greg stared at him.

"Don't tell me you think somebody tried to kill her," he protested. "Why would they? She doesn't even belong here. It was someone after a deer. They come down from the hills at night, you know."

"Rather early for deer, I imagine," Dane said dryly.

"I've seen them as early as this."

"It was no deer who carried her from the lane to where we found her. And it's a pretty stormy night for hunters, you know. Why don't you face it, Spencer? Someone tried to kill your sister tonight."

"Oh, for God's sake!" Greg groaned, and lapsed into bewildered silence.

SIXTEEN

ELINOR WAS IN THE OPERATING ROOM when they reached the hospital. Carol, white-faced and quiet, was waiting outside in the hall. Dane thought she looked heartbreakingly anxious, when Greg went to her and took her hand.

"She'll be all right, kid. You know that, don't you?"

She roused and tried to smile at him.

"You'd better call Howard, Greg. It's Saturday. He may be in Newport."

He seemed relieved to have something to do. He went down to the telephone, leaving Dane awkward and tongue-tied. When Greg came back he reported he had failed to locate Hilliard, he was neither at his apartment in New York nor at the Newport house.

"Probably at one of the golf clubs," Greg said, "but I can't chase him all night. I left word at both places to have him call. It's all we can do."

Dane listened glumly. He was restless. In his slacks and rubber-soled shoes he had been pacing the hall, feeling that somewhere he had fumbled. He was convinced that all these people, Elinor and Gregory and even Carol, had known something they had not told anyone. Had Gregory actually been here in Elinor's car the night the girl was murdered? Was that what they were hiding? Yet looking at Carol, clinging to Greg as if she found him a tower of strength, it seemed impossible to believe that she knew or even suspected such a thing.

Greg's distress, too, was evident. Always Dane had realized that the tie between Elinor and Greg was very close. He would never have shot her. But he was conscious of a faint stir of jealousy when Greg put his arm around Carol and she rested her head on his shoulder.

"You've helped me weather a lot of storms, kid. We'll

weather this all right." He beamed down at her, his pleasant
face strained and tired. "She'll be all right. Lost a lot of blood,
that's all. And blood's what I ain't got anything but!"

It was three o'clock in the morning by that time. Somewhat
belatedly Floyd had been notified, and he stamped out of the
elevator in a bad humor, followed by Mason, who looked only
half awake. Dane took advantage of his arrival to slip downstairs and telephone Alex.

"Get the car down to the hospital as fast as you can," Dane
told him. "Don't ask any questions. Just get here."

He did not leave at once, though. Floyd had followed him
down. He had to tell his story, and to realize that the chief of
police was regarding him stonily.

"It's a queer thing, Dane," he said, "but you've been mixed
up with this funny business from the start."

"What do you mean by that?"

"You walked up the drive to the Spencer place every morning, didn't you? Maybe you were there when this girl arrived."

"So I killed her!"

"So maybe you knew who she was," said Floyd, still cold.

"Oh, for God's sake!" said Dane wearily. "I didn't know her.
I never even saw her before. And I'd never seen Mrs. Hilliard
until she came here."

"So you say. What were you doing out at Joe Norton's last
night looking over Lucy's things? Did she have something you
wanted?"

Dane laughed mirthlessly.

"I'll tell you someday," he said dryly. "And I'll tell you this
now. Either Mrs. Hilliard was knocked out on the lane, or she
was shot there. In any event she was dragged or carried to
where she was found. And I didn't do it."

Floyd was still watching him with cold unblinking eyes.

"All right," he said. "Then maybe you'll explain why you
were around the Spencer place tonight in the rain. Carol says
you came in and wakened her. That might be damned smart of
you, Dane, if you knew what you were going to find."

"I'll tell you that right now," Dane said sharply. "I was doing
what you ought to have been doing. I was keeping an eye on
Crestview. Somebody around here is dangerous, Floyd. Maybe

you'll get that into your dumb head someday."

But Floyd was not dumb, and Dane knew it. As he waited for the car he went over what he knew. Elinor had not been taken out of the house. She had gone out for some purpose of her own and, unlike the murdered girl, she had been fully dressed, even to the heavy shoes on her small feet and the light raincoat which had enabled him to find her.

Where had she been going? To the Wards'? There was the story that Mrs. Ward had seen a man in her car the night the girl was killed. It might have worried her. But at such an hour? And in a storm?

He dismissed the Wards for what he was beginning to call X, the unknown. X, he thought grimly, would solve the equation, only he had none of the other factors.

He got away finally, irritated and taciturn. The rain was still heavy, and the night air cold. In the car he told Alex nothing except that Elinor Hilliard had been shot, and left that individual in a state of smoldering resentment. And at the entrance to the Spencer place Dane told him to turn in, without explanation.

"You might hang around," he said. "I may be some little time."

"And what will I be doing while I'm hanging around?" Alex demanded, his voice sulky.

"Try taking a nap," Dane said hardheartedly, and got out as the car stopped.

The house was still brightly lighted. He found the front door locked, rang the bell without result, and going around to the kitchen saw through a window the women inside, gathered in a close group and obviously terrified. He knocked on the glass and heard one of them scream.

"It's only Dane," he called reassuringly. "I've come from the hospital."

The noise subsided and Maggie admitted him, looki... re-lieved.

"I'm sorry," she explained, "but we decided ... 's how any-one in. There's a coldhearted murderer arou... would

"You're probably right," he told her ...
I happened to be here tonight. I w...
happen."

The girls looked panicky again, and he hastened to reassure them. He felt that it was over now, and Mrs. Hilliard would certainly live. In that case she might tell them who had shot her. There was no mystery about her being out. She had gone out, perhaps for a breath of fresh air, and had probably been attacked in the lane and carried—he did not say dragged—to the hillside.

Maggie gave him some coffee, her consistent remedy for all emergencies, and only after he drank it did he tell her he would like to go up to Elinor Hilliard's room.

"There may be something there to indicate why she went out," he said. "Anyhow I'd like to look at it. Did Mrs. Hilliard get a telephone call tonight?"

If she had they did not know it. They let him go up alone, and after a brief survey which showed him nothing he wanted to know he went on to the yellow room. The lights were turned off, although he did not remember that either Carol or he himself had done so, and when he switched them on he stared around him in astonishment. The room had been hastily searched. One window was open, the edges of the rug had been turned back, the mattresses on the twin beds displaced, and a loose baseboard had been pried away from the wall near the mantel.

Dane stood looking at this last for some time. It had been a good hiding place if she had used it, he thought sourly. And either someone who had known it was there or who had better eyes than his had seen it.

He went back over the night's events. Carol had had no chance. She was in the house only long enough to notify Gregory and call the doctor. Gregory himself? He had come on the run, still pulling on his dressing gown as he came. Anyhow why should he? He had several days in which to search the house. After that, with the exception of the servants, the house had been empty. But the lights had all been on, and it seemed unlikely that anyone could have entered the front door while they were on the hillside. He was certain, too, that the windows of the room were all closed when he saw it last.

Later, he thought, his mouth tight. He had slipped up. He should have seen that it was taken away.

Before he went downstairs he examined Gregory's room. It was furnished as it probably had been since his boyhood holidays there: his college photographs on the wall, a snapshot of a grinning youth who might have been himself at sixteen holding a string of trout, a shelf of books, and a glass-topped box of slowly desiccating moths.

The room was kept with military tidiness. Greg's uniforms were hung up, the drawers in the bureau neatly in order. The closet door was open as Greg had left it, and Dane looked at the suitcase on the floor. It was closed but not locked. He opened it, to find a service automatic. It had not been fired recently, however, and he put it back and shut the case.

There was no sign of any intruder downstairs until he reached the side door. This, more or less under the staircase, opened on to a grass terrace, and the door was unlocked. Careful not to disturb any possible prints he went outside and found what he had expected. The ladder was lying on the ground under the windows of the yellow room. The picture was clear now, so far as it went. Whoever had entered the house had used the ladder, but had left by the side door.

Once more he cursed Tim for his refusal to fly back. He left the ladder where it was, and going back to the car found Alex asleep in it, which added to his irritation.

"No hope you saw anybody around, I suppose?" he said, taking the wheel himself.

"You told me to take a nap." Alex was aggrieved. "Who'd be hanging around a night like this anyhow?"

Dane drove home, to call the hospital and learn from Carol that Elinor was out of the operating room, and that lacking a blood bank they had typed Greg and were giving her an infusion.

"They think she has a good chance. She's stronger than she looks, you know."

"Good. What about you?"

She seemed surprised.

"Me? I'm all right. Anxious, of course. I'd better come back and get dressed."

"Listen," he said earnestly. "I want you to stay there until full daylight. If you won't I'll come for you myself. I'm not taking any chances on you."

There was something new in his voice, a sort of protective tenderness she had not heard in it before. It made her feel a little happier. She had not had much affection since Don's death, and even Don himself had been a casual, debonair lover. After a moment's silence, she said, "You think it's a homicidal maniac, don't you?"

"I told you once, the first murder is the hard one."

After some argument she agreed to stay, and at last he relaxed and went to bed. Not to sleep at once, however. He was puzzling over the yellow room and what—if anything—had been hidden in it. And for some reason he was seeing Mr. Ward, small and elderly and wary, saying that he did not run to the police with what he called tittle-tattle, and rather abruptly ending the interview and not shaking hands when he left.

He would have been greatly surprised had he known that at that same moment Mr. Ward was putting his car away with as little noise as possible, and stealthily entering his stately house. Or that when he went up to his dressing room he took a revolver out of his pocket and placed it carefully in a drawer, under a tidy pile of the stiff-bosomed dress shirts he so seldom used these days.

Dane was up and out again at eight that Sunday morning. The rain had stopped, and except for Maggie returning from early Mass there was no one in sight at Crestview. He waited until she was safely in the house, then going through the woods to the crest of the hill he began to work his way down. No one had traveled in that direction, however. He crunched and slid through the debris of the fire, watching the ground intently, and was brought up suddenly by a small shallow hole.

It was freshly dug. A pool of rain water lay at the bottom, and a garden trowel had been dropped a few feet away. Dane examined the hole carefully. It was only a foot or so deep and as much across. The ground around it was trampled, and he thought the digging had been hasty.

He picked up the trowel with a handkerchief. The handle was fairly clean, and he wrapped it in the fresh linen. He was still carrying it when, having followed down to where he had found Elinor, he came out on the lane once more. The road was muddy, and the heavy rain had washed away all traces of the bloody water he had seen the night before, as well as any possible footprints. There was one, however, which remained fairly intact. He measured it beside his own, and decided that it had been made by a fairly tall man. He was still stooping over it when he heard someone behind him. It was Mr. Ward.

He wore an overcoat against the cold morning air, but he was bareheaded. Instinctively Dane glanced at his feet. Even in galoshes they were small, and Mr. Ward saw the look and smiled frostily.

"It might have been mine," he said. "I'm often here. I don't think it is, do you?"

"Doesn't look like it." Dane straightened. "There was some blood here last night. It's been washed away. Did you hear the shot, Mr. Ward? It was fired about here."

"Who hears a shot these days?" Mr. Ward countered. "A shot and a backfire sound much alike. No. I heard nothing. I was asleep, I suppose. I don't even know when it happened. In fact, I've only just heard about it. The milkman is our local paper."

He did not look as though he had been asleep. In fact, he looked old and exhausted, his face a yellow-white and his veined hands unsteady. He looked at the handkerchief-wrapped trowel.

"I see you've found something, major."

Its shape betrayed it. Dane opened it carefully, and Mr. Ward took a step nearer to look at it with nearsighted eyes.

"A trowel!" he said. "What does that mean? We all have them. Where did you find it?"

"It was on the hillside," Dane said carefully. "I wondered about it. That's all."

He did not mention the hole, nor did he have occasion to, for at that moment Nathaniel Ward staggered. He caught Dane by the arm, and the trowel fell to the muddy ground. Days later Dane was to wonder whether that action was intentional or not, but certainly the old man's color was definitely worse. He looked like a man who had received an unexpected blow. He did not even speak for a moment. Then:

"I'm sorry," he muttered. "I'm too old for all this, I suppose. Just a moment. I'll be all right."

Dane held him now with both arms. His body felt small under his heavy coat. Dane managed to reach his pulse, and found it stringy and faint.

"I'd better get you to the house," he said. "Or if you'll sit here on the bank I'll get someone to help you back."

But Ward held up a protesting hand.

"Don't alarm my wife," he said. "I'll be all right. I'll sit down, if you'll assist me."

The trowel was still on the ground. Dane seated Mr. Ward on the bank and then picked it up. Part of the handle was covered with mud, and he swore under his breath. Nevertheless, he rewrapped it. Mr. Ward did not seem to notice. He was sitting with his eyes shut, but his color was slowly coming back.

"I'm most apologetic," he said. "I don't often come out before breakfast, but when I heard about Elinor I decided to walk over to see if I could do anything."

It could have been true. He had come along the graveled path that connected the two properties. But Dane believed that the old man had been shocked to find him there, although the attack, whatever it was, had been real.

"Have you spells often?" he asked.

"I get dizzy now and then. Nothing to do with my heart. Middle-ear trouble probably." He was much better now. He pulled out a clean handkerchief and wiped his forehead. "Don't let me keep you. I'll sit here for a minute. I'm perfectly all right."

Thus dismissed, Dane moved back toward Crestview. He was still suspicious, although he hardly knew why, and halfway along the path he turned and looked back. The immaculate Nathaniel Ward was picking something from the mud near his feet. Even at that distance it gleamed dully, and Dane was certain it had been the shell from the gun with which Elinor had been shot.

He hesitated. He could go back and demand to see it, in which case Nathaniel would certainly deny he had it, or he could go on and pretend he had seen nothing. He decided to go on.

SEVENTEEN

BREAKFAST WAS READY when he got back to the house. When Alex brought in the bacon and eggs he found Dane examining the trowel, and looked astonished.

"What's that, sir?"

"I imagine it was intended to dig up the clothes on the hill. Look here, Alex. What do you know about the Wards? And I wish to God you'd learn how to make coffee."

"I'm no cook, sir. I never pretended to be a cook. If you don't like the way I do things—"

"All right," Dane said impatiently. "What about the Wards?"

Alex scratched his head.

"Well, they're very highly thought of here," he said. "Very rich, but the townspeople like them. They give to the churches and the hospital, all the local stuff. Their son was killed in the last war. They've got a grandson in this one. They've been coming for forty years or so."

"Their grandson been back lately?"

"They expected him, but he didn't turn up."

Dane called the hospital after breakfast. Elinor Hilliard was somewhat better and was conscious. Greg was still there, but Carol was at home, and he went over to Crestview after he had hung up. He had expected to learn she was in bed, but he found her in the library beside the fire. She was looking exhausted, her hands lying limp in her lap, and her eyes lifeless. But she smiled at him.

"I've just had a telephone battle with Mother," she told him. "You would think I had shot Elinor myself. Either I'm to go home, or she will come up."

"And you don't want her?"

"She can't help, and she doesn't understand," she said wearily. "She's used to this house with seven or eight servants in it. And the way things are . . . Howard will be coming, but he can stay at the hotel."

"Then you've located Mr. Hilliard?"

"Not yet. It's Sunday, so his office is closed. He may be weekending anywhere. Mother didn't know."

He gave her a cigarette and took one himself as he sat down.

"Do you mind a little family talk?" he asked.

"I'm used to them. What about?"

"Your sister. Are she and her husband happy together?"

She thought that over, as if she were uncertain.

"It depends on what you call happy, I suppose. They're congenial. They like the same things; you know, parties and bridge and plenty of money. He's frightfully proud of her." She roused then and stared at him. "You aren't thinking Howard shot her, are you? That—well, that would be ridiculous."

"All right," he said. "Cancel Howard. Why did she dress and go out last night, Carol? It was raining, you know."

She gave him the candid glance that always touched him.

"She was after her clothes, wasn't she?" she said. "At least I'm afraid she was. I don't know, of course."

Anyhow that bar was down between them, thank God, he thought. She had been so pitifully alone, with no one to turn to. If she would use him—

"I don't pretend to understand it," she said, closing her eyes. "My brain doesn't seem to work. She's had time enough to look for them, and last night it rained. She's like a cat. She hates rain. Yet she— I don't think she killed that girl, you know. And she liked Lucy. She'd never have bothered her."

"But you think she knows more than she's telling?"

"Yes. That's what frightens me. If she's protecting some-one . . ."

He knew what she meant. Carol thought Elinor was protecting Greg. He changed the subject abruptly.

"Have you been upstairs since you came back?"

"Only to dress. Why?"

"You didn't look in the yellow room?"

"No. What about it?"

She was sitting erect now, and looking frightened.

"It's all right," he told her quickly. "Nothing to worry about. I saw it on my way home. I'd come in to see everything was all right. Somebody had searched it pretty thoroughly."

She relaxed at that, as though the mere searching of a room was nothing compared with the welter of blood and mystery that surrounded her.

"I don't understand," she said slowly. "It's been carefully cleaned. Unless the police . . ."

"I don't think it was the police. It may tie in with your sister's being shot. Suppose she heard someone in the house and followed outside—"

She shook her head.

"She'd never do that," she said and got up. "I'll have to see the room, I suppose. I'm glad Freda hasn't seen it first."

He had prepared her as well as he could, but the first sight of the yellow room certainly shocked her. He had to restrain himself from putting his arms around her.

"Look, my dear," he said, "it's not so bad as all that. Someone was looking for something. That's all."

"So we're just to go on, two people dead, Elinor shot and the hill burned. I can't take much more, Jerry."

She cried a little then, and after a while he held her head against his shoulder and felt for a handkerchief.

"Blow for papa," he said, and was pleased to see her lift her head and smile.

"I'm not really a baby," she told him. "I play golf and tennis and swim and ride a horse. Usually I'm just average. But this has got me down. It's—as Greg would say—it's pretty rugged."

She insisted on straightening the room before the servants saw it, and the next few minutes they spent repairing the damage as best they could. Dane even managed to get the baseboard back in place, somewhat tottery but still, so to speak, on its own. The church bells were ringing when they finished, and she stopped to listen, as though it was strange that people should be going quietly to morning service while her own world was so chaotic. He felt that in her, and he kissed her lightly before he left.

"For being a good girl," he said cheerfully, and limped down the stairs to find Colonel Richardson, breathing hard from his climb, in the hall.

"What damnable thing is going on?" he demanded. "Nobody

tells me anything. I have to hear it from my servants or from someone who happens by. A girl murdered and burned! Lucy Norton dead! Now Elinor Hilliard is shot, and I'm not so much as notified."

"I'm sorry, colonel," Dane said pacifically. "Things have happened pretty fast. Mrs. Hilliard was shot only last night, and it may have been an accident."

He snorted and looked at Dane suspiciously.

"What was she doing outside in the rain?" he demanded. "I know Elinor. I never liked her much, but she wouldn't go out alone at night in the rain for a million dollars. And she likes money at that. What happened? Does she know?"

"She's not allowed to talk. She's barely conscious, I believe. She lost a lot of blood. But she's going to be all right."

Dane got the impression that the colonel had more to say. He stood still for a moment, as though debating something with himself. But evidently he decided against it, for he saluted stiffly, turned on his heel and departed. Dane, watching him as he left, thought that aside from his almost defiant head he was not a well man. His lips after the climb up the hill had been slightly blue. And he was leaning rather heavily on his stick. He was certain too that the colonel had not been entirely frank with him.

There was a car climbing the hill as he was leaving. It came with difficulty, gasping and roaring, and when at last it came into sight he saw an ancient vehicle, driven by a grinning young man who brought it to a stop and then mopped his face with a handkerchief, as though he had been pushing the car himself.

"Got here," he said triumphantly. "She's a good old bus, only a bit on the asthma side."

He got out and looked around him, at the burned hillside, at the house and then at Dane himself.

"Say, what goes on?" he inquired. "Another death and a shooting since I was here last! That's going some. That the hill where the Hilliard woman was attacked?"

"Attacked? Who said she was attacked?"

"Don't tell me she was shot by accident, or that she tried to kill herself by shooting herself in the leg. Who shot her, and why?"

His smile, in spite of Dane's resentment, was engaging.

"Mind telling me who you are?" he inquired. He eyed Dane's slacks. "Are you the brother, Captain Spencer? I'm Starr from the paper over at the county seat. I was here before."

"I live next door," said Dane, somewhat diverted by all this. "I don't know anything. If you want a story go to Floyd, the police chief here."

"Old sourpuss?" Starr laughed. "He'd clap me in the clink as soon as he saw me." He viewed Dane with keen young eyes. "Say, I've seen you before, haven't I?"

"Hardly likely," Dane said dryly. "I've been here only a few weeks."

But the boy grinned and then whistled.

"I've got you! Starr with the eagle eye. Starr the boy reporter who never forgets a face. Remember the time that gang blew into the county seat to order machine guns, and you came up from Washington?"

Dane was annoyed.

"Now listen, son," he said. "I'm in the army, now and until the war is over. I'm getting over a shot in the leg, and if you know what's good for you that's all you know."

"But hell, sir—"

"That's an order," Dane snapped.

Starr subsided. Dane felt repentant as he watched his crestfallen young face, and told him briefly what had happened, the shot followed by the finding of Elinor Hilliard wounded. He intimated, however, that she had heard someone outside and been shot while investigating. And the boy—he was little more—gave him something in return.

"Funny thing," he said. "I saw the body of the girl they found in the closet. She sure as hell was wearing a wedding ring. Floyd never gave that out, did he?"

"It's the first I've heard of it."

He was thoughtful after the reporter left. Did Floyd have the ring and was deliberately keeping quiet about it? Or had this youngster been mistaken? After all, it had not been a pleasant sight.

His leg was better. It had been improving for some time, he realized as he walked home, and the thought cheered him considerably. His voice was almost gay when he was called to the long-distance phone. Nevertheless, the message, couched in careful language, gave him furiously to think. The subject of the inquiry, it said, had received his "what you may call it" in Washington on Wednesday, June fourteenth. He had had a room at a hotel and had stayed there Wednesday night. At some time on Thursday he had packed a bag hastily and said he was taking a plane to New York, giving no address there, and not returning at all.

"Not back yet," said the voice. "Hotel has had no word. Drinking pretty hard before he left. No other details. Corroboration by letter."

Dane thought a minute after he hung up. Then he got in touch with Tim Murphy, who had reported from New York and was waiting for train accommodation north. He knew that Bessie would be listening in, but there was no time to waste.

"About that C.M.O.H., Tim," he said. "Find out if the holder was registered there in New York at a hotel between these dates. It's important. Probably one of the big places, but I'm not sure. And get a move on. We've had more trouble here."

He gave the dates and Tim took them down. He had some trouble with the Congressional Medal of Honor, but finally understood. He had not finished, however.

"I located that suitcase here," he said. "Initials M.D.B. Sounds all right, doesn't it?"

"Sounds fine."

"Railroad company won't let it go. But they can get it opened, or a friend of mine there can. What are they to look for?"

"How the hell do I know?" Dane said irritably. "Papers, documents, photographs—you know as well as I do."

"No panties?"

"No panties," said Dane grimly. "And you'd better come back here as soon as you can. I need you."

Dane rang off, confident that Bessie at least would be puzzled. He was not so sure about Floyd, nor indeed about the whole business. After all, Greg was not only a nation-wide hero, with his picture in all the papers. He was Carol's brother, and Dane was not fooling himself any longer about Carol. Not that it was any use, he knew. This was a long war, in spite of the idiots who were betting it would soon be over. And Carol had waited for Don Richardson. He was not going to ask her to wait for him.

As to Greg he was puzzled. He could have come here by plane, killed the girl and got away. Nevertheless, there was the fact that he had come back, rather cheerfully than otherwise. Murderers did not return to the scene of their crimes, unless they were psychopathic. They got as far away as they could, and stayed there.

He was thoughtful when he called Alex, who came from his kitchen without removing the apron tied around his broad body.

"What about this grandson of the Wards'?" he asked. "You say he hasn't come home lately."

"No, sir. They were expecting him a while ago, but he couldn't get away. They'd planned some sort of party for him, but he had to go back to the Pacific. Old lady went to bed over it. Kinda hard on her."

"That the one they call Terry?"

"Yeah. Not short for Terence. Mother's name was Terry. He's a flier in the Pacific. Good guy, by all accounts. Father and mother both dead. Lived with the old folks."

As usual Dane ate his lunch outside. The weather had cleared, and a plane had ventured out, flying low. He ate at the corner of the porch, so that by turning his head he could see either the bay or the ridge of hills above him. He could see the skeleton of the burned house, a chimney of the gardener's house at Rockhill, and above and beyond them all two or three abandoned summer properties.

He had driven or walked around most of them, with their neglected gardens and their blank closed windows. Now, returning to the X of his earlier equation, it occurred to him that someone could hide almost indefinitely in any of them. He did not admit even to himself that he preferred an unidentified criminal to Greg Spencer. It was merely a part of his system to explore all possibilities. He said nothing to Alex when he took his car that afternoon and drove around over the hill. Owing to the gasoline shortage, the roads back here were completely deserted, and the first two empty houses were closed so entirely that he gave them up after a brief examination. The third was different.

It was also closed, of course. It was almost buried in vegetation, and no tire marks showed on the ragged drive. But a winter shutter was loose, and underneath it in the soft ground he found a footprint or two. He took his automatic from a compartment in the car, and going back to the building managed to raise the window.

It creaked badly. He waited for a while; then, nothing happening, he put a leg over the sill and crawled inside.

The building, shut in as it was, was almost entirely dark. It smelled moldy and dank. But it also smelled faintly of tobacco smoke. It was not fresh. It might have been there for a week or more. Nevertheless, someone had been in the house recently, and might still be there.

The darkness bothered him. He had forgotten to bring a flashlight, and after he left the room by which he had entered only the hall showed a faint illumination from the window he had opened. Using matches he more or less felt his way along, until a blank space indicated a door.

He stepped inside and almost fell over a pile of blankets. They were lying there, abandoned in a heap, as if they had been dropped casually. Otherwise the room was undisturbed. It had been a dining room and some of the old-fashioned furniture still remained. Outside of the two blankets, however, he found nothing. The kitchen, too, was neat and empty. Apparently no one had cooked there for years. But the few dishes in the closet he found remarkably clean, and he was whistling softly to himself as he lit a cigarette and went up the stairs. Here were the usual bedrooms, the beds with ancient mattresses on them and everything else of value gone.

On one bed, however, was a pillow, somewhat indented as though it had been slept on. That the house had been occupied by someone, and that recently, he did not doubt. But he did not doubt either the care with which all evidence of each occupation had been eliminated. The blankets were a curious oversight. He puzzled over them, leaving the house as he had found it and drove slowly home.

EIGHTEEN

CAROL SPENCER was not the same girl who only ten days or so before had kicked Greg's golf clubs out of her way in the train and worried about opening Crestview. That sheltered, carefully set-up young woman had vanished. She was as neatly dressed as ever, her eyes as frank, her smile—when it came—as spontaneous. But there were lines of strain in her face, and she looked very tired. Maggie, coming in after Dane had gone that morning, surveyed her with disfavor.

"Are you planning to stay up all day?" she inquired truculently. "What good will you be to anybody if you get sick?"

"I don't suppose I can sleep. What about the girls, Maggie?"

"Scared of their shadows. That man who was going to help hasn't showed up again, and I'm having to fix the furnace myself."

"That's ridiculous. I'll tell Greg to do it." Carol got up, but Maggie caught her arm.

"There's that newspaper fellow snooping around," she hissed. "Up with you, Miss Carol. I'll tell him you're sick. And sick you look," she added. "I'll bring you some coffee right off."

She whisked Carol up the stairs and stood by until she got into bed. For a second or so she paused indecisively by Don Richardson's picture. Then she faced Carol, her honest Irish face troubled.

"I've got something to tell you, Carol," she said, reverting to years ago when Carol was a child, running in from play to ransack the refrigerator or to find sanctuary from her governess. "I don't like to say it, especially just now, but you'll have to know it sooner or later."

Carol smiled. Maggie's troubles usually referred to her department of the house. This proved to be different, however.

She had been out the night before, Maggie said. At the

Daltons' with the maids there playing hearts. She was surprised when she found how late it was. It was around one o'clock when she put on her galoshes and got her umbrella and started home, and before she reached the main road she heard a shot.

"It could have been a backfire," she said, "but I didn't think it was. I didn't hear any car. I just stood still, kinda scared. I guess I was there five minutes or so. It was raining cats and dogs. And then I heard somebody running. He was splashing down the lane, and—now mind, I don't say he shot Miss Elinor; why would he?—but it was Colonel Richardson."

Carol sat upright in her bed, her face a mask of astonishment.

"It couldn't have been, Maggie. Not the colonel! He never—"

"I seen him plain enough," Maggie said stubbornly. "White hair and all. He looked as though he was wearing a bathrobe or something, and he went into his house and slammed the door as though the devil was after him. Believe me, I got up to the house fast by the short cut from the road. I was plenty scared."

Carol dismissed all this with a gesture.

"He may have been playing chess at the Wards'," she said. "They often play late. And hurrying home out of the rain."

But Maggie shook her head.

"He's been queer lately," she said. "And don't tell me he'd leave the Wards' in that storm and in what he was wearing. I been going over it in my mind ever since. Seems to me he'd had just time to come from the hill where they found Miss Elinor, but I didn't see any gun. Why else was he running like that, with the heart he's got?"

"I'm sure there's some perfectly ordinary explanation, Maggie."

"Well, it's off my mind anyhow, miss." Maggie returned with dignity to her role of cook to a respected family. "I'd rather you didn't mention it to the police, if you please. I don't want that Floyd poking around. The way he went up to the attic where he had no business to be, and carried away your grandmother's washstand set . . ."

This grievance being an old and safe one, Carol let her go on. After Maggie had gone, however, she lay back and thought with some anxiety over the story. Had the shot alarmed the colonel, so that he had run back to his house? Had he already told the police the story? And why had he been in the lane at all, unprotected from the rain? She came back to Maggie's statement that he had been what she called queer. Outside of his obsession about Don, which was largely wishful thinking, he had seemed much as usual to her, courtly and kind.

Greg came in to interrupt her thoughts. He had had breakfast and some sleep at the hospital, and although his handsome face looked weary the news he brought was good.

"She'll be all right," he told her. "Lost a lot of blood, but it missed the big artery. She hasn't any idea who did it. They won't let her talk much, of course, but it's a puzzler, isn't it?"

He wandered about the room, said he needed a bath and shave, and wondered if they could have lunch up there.

"Think the staff will run to a couple of trays?" he asked boyishly.

She thought it would, and they had cocktails and ate the usual Sunday dinner of chicken and ice cream together in her room. It was characteristic of Greg that he threw off Maggie's story about the colonel as easily as he threw off everything which did not immediately concern him. She marveled at that ability of his. He was the old Greg, for all his war record, saying life was fun, even when he had a headache the morning after.

"The Irish are an imaginative lot," he said, amused. "The old boy runs to get out of the rain, so he's mixed up in this mess. Or maybe Maggie shot Elinor herself and makes this up! She isn't fond of Elinor, you know. Never was."

He clung to the theory that the shooting was the result of an accident. Carol found herself accepting it, as the simplest way out. But after he had gone, to bathe and shave and take a nap, she made a decision. She took off Don's engagement ring for the first time since he had put it on her finger, and put it away in her jewel case. She felt freer without it, as though she had finally laid a ghost.

In the meantime Dane took his car and drove down to Floyd's office. He had decided to tell the chief about the empty house. It would at least keep him busy, he thought derisively, and off his own neck. But Floyd was not alone when he got there; he was in angry consultation with Campbell. The district attorney was cold and unsmiling, chewing on an unlighted cigar, his hat on the floor beside him and his expression one of annoyance mixed with contempt.

"What did you expect me to do?" Floyd was demanding savagely. "I'm here alone except for Mason and a traffic man. I can't put guards around the whole town. I haven't got them. If I ask for more help it raises the taxes, and watch the people howl."

"You knew Lucy Norton didn't tell all she knew at the inquest," Campbell said, scowling.

"So what? So I'm to put an intern at the hospital outside her door as a guard? They've got more than they can manage there now. Look at this town, only one doctor left, no men available, no nothing. As for the Hilliard woman, if she wants to wander around at night in the rain and get shot that's her business. I can't keep her in her bed, can I?"

Neither of them paid any attention at first to Dane. He walked to the desk and stood waiting until the argument ceased. Then:

"I was driving around the back roads today," he said to Floyd. "Know a place called Pine Hill?"

"Been empty for years," Floyd said sulkily. "What about it?"

"I have an idea someone's been sleeping there lately. Maybe a tramp, maybe not. Couple of blankets on the floor. Bed upstairs may have been used."

Floyd blew up.

"That's all I need," he roared. "It's an unknown now, is it? That saves your friends at Crestview, I suppose. I may be only a hick policeman, but I haven't lost my senses."

"You might go up and look." Dane's voice was mild.

"You bet I'll go up and look, and if this is a plant, Dane—"

"It's not a plant."

Campbell spoke then.

"What's your idea, major? How did you happen on this house?"

Dane sat down and got out a cigarette.

"I don't exactly know," he admitted. "There are a good many imponderables in the case. You can't leave out X, you know."

"Who's X?" Floyd snorted.

"It's just a symbol I use for myself. Meaning the unknown factor, of course. Has Mrs. Hilliard talked yet?"

"If you can call it talking! Says she doesn't know who shot her. Says she wasn't on the hill at all. Couldn't sleep and went out as far as the dirt lane there. Knows she was shot and remembers falling. That's all."

Dane was thoughtful. Elinor's story did not hold water, of course, except that she had not been on the hill. That was true enough. He looked at Floyd.

"Was the girl who was murdered wearing a wedding ring when you found her?"

"What's that got to do with it?" Floyd was still surly.

"Well, was she?"

Reluctantly Floyd opened the drawer of his desk and took out the box Carol had seen earlier. He shook its contents out onto the desk blotter. "The jury saw these," he said resentfully. "I don't know what right you have to look at them."

Dane surveyed them, the scorched imitation pearl earrings and a narrow gold band. He picked up the latter and weighed it in his hand, then he carried it to the window and examined it. There was a poorly engraved inscription inside it.

"C to M," the chief said grudgingly, "if that's any help to you."

"Mind if I borrow it for five minutes?"

"What for?"

"Just an idea I have. Make it ten. I'll be right back."

He did not wait for consent. As he left he heard the chief's voice raised in protest, and Campbell's milder one.

"If he's got any ideas we need them," he was saying. "So far as I can see—"

Dane was longer than ten minutes. It was a half hour before he had wakened the local jeweler from his Sunday nap, induced him to open his shop and produce his watchmaker's glass. With this screwed in his eye Dane examined the ring carefully. It was, as he had thought, of the light and inexpensive kind, but he focused his attention on the engraving.

His face was sober as he thanked the watchmaker and returned the ring to Floyd. He made no comment as he put it back on the desk. Floyd was less truculent now. He put the ring back into the box, and the box into the drawer again.

"Sorry if I've been kind of rough with you, major," he mumbled. "Fact is this thing's got me. I don't sleep. I don't eat. This is a resort town, and things like these in the papers don't help any."

"Maybe we can clean up some of it."

Floyd eyed him.

"If you've got anything you ought to tell me," he said resentfully.

"I've found Pine Hill."

"Still after X, are you?"

"I think it's worth looking into. You might find some prints, for one thing."

"And then what? I can't fingerprint everybody in this town. Or any tramp who chooses to break into an empty house and sleep there."

Dane drove to the hospital after he left the police station. Elinor Hilliard was still allowed no visitors, but her husband had been located and was expected at any time. He had somehow managed to get a plane and was flying up.

In spite of his new knowledge Dane found himself wondering about Hilliard. So far he had been only a name, but he could not afford to eliminate anybody. And this was corroborated when, on reaching Crestview, he found Carol still in bed and Marcia Dalton and Louise Stimson snugly settled in the library. They had walked up, they said, and finding Carol and Greg both asleep had come in for a rest and a drink.

"How's the sleuthing going?" Louise asked, her smile faintly impertinent.

"Sleuthing? If you mean finding Mrs. Hilliard—"

"The talk is that you were watching this house when you found her."

"Then you'll have to admit I failed pretty completely," he said gravely.

It was obvious that they meant to stay, and he groaned inwardly. They gave him the local gossip, however. According to it, Greg was out. He would never shoot Elinor. And someone, coming home by the back road, had seen a car driving madly along the main road at two o'clock that morning. They had no authority for it. It was being told, that was all.

"What sort of car?" he asked.

"Not Elinor's this time," Marcia said. "A long dark one. I wish I knew how people get the gas they do. I can't."

"It sounds like Elinor Hilliard's husband," Louise drawled. "They seem to have all they want, don't they? And Howard always drove like the devil. Maybe the girl they found here was living with him, and Elinor put her out of the way. She might, you know. She's a pretty cool proposition."

He got rid of them at last, and went back to the kitchen. Greg was still asleep, Maggie said, and the two girls, Freda and Nora, were upstairs packing to leave.

"I can't hold them," she said. "Not any longer. They're scared. So am I, but I'm staying. I can't leave Miss Carol like this. Maybe I can get somebody from the village. Only the town's scared too. It's as much as I can do to get the groceries delivered."

"I might be able to locate the man Alex got you for a day or two. Tim Murphy, wasn't it?"

"A fat lot of good he'd be! He walked off without notice."

"He could wash the dishes."

In spite of what was waiting for him upstairs he smiled to himself. The thought of Tim washing dishes and scouring pans was almost too much for him. But he needed a man in this house, and Tim had done worse things in his time.

"I'll try to find him," he said. "He may have a perfectly valid reason for not showing up."

The two girls were lugging suitcases down the back staircase as he went toward the front of the house. One look at their determined faces showed him the uselessness of protest, and he went forward and up to Gregory Spencer's room.

Greg was awake. His shower was running, and he did not hear the knock at the door. When he came out of the bathroom, clad only in a pair of shorts, he found Dane settled in a chair calmly smoking, and stared at him in amazement.

"Sorry," Dane said. "I rapped, but you didn't hear me. I had a question to ask, and it couldn't wait."

"What sort of question?"

The very fact that Greg's face was suddenly wary convinced

Dane he was right. At least he had to take a chance. He took it.

"I was wondering," he said quietly, "just when and where you married the girl who was killed in this house ten days ago."

NINETEEN

IF HE HAD DEPENDED ON SURPRISE he succeeded. Greg did not even protest. He stood still, his fine big body moist from the shower, a bit of shaving lather on the lobe of one ear, and threw out his hands in a gesture of resignation.

"I suppose it had to come out," he said. "How did you know it?"

"A number of things turned up. For one, she wore a wedding ring. It said 'G to M' inside it."

"A ring? I never gave her a ring."

It was Dane's turn to be surprised.

"She had it. Floyd has it now. His eyes aren't too good. He thinks the G is a C. He may know better by this time."

But Greg was still bewildered.

"I give you my word of honor, Dane, I never gave her a ring." Then the full meaning of the situation began to dawn on him. He sat down abruptly on the edge of the bed. "I didn't kill her, either," he said heavily. "You probably don't believe that, but it's true."

"You must have wanted to get rid of her," Dane said inexorably. "You were engaged to another girl. She was planning to marry you on this leave. And I'm telling you now, you haven't an alibi worth a cent, unless you can prove you were in New York when it was done."

Greg shook his head confusedly.

"I didn't do it. I don't even know who did."

"But you knew she was dead, didn't you? You went ahead with your plans for being married again. How did you know all that, Spencer? Who told you?"

"I'd rather not answer that," Greg said slowly. "I knew it. That will have to do." He drew a long breath. "I'd had a year of hell, Dane. It was a relief."

He dropped his head in his hands. It was some time before he looked up, and his eyes were dull and hopeless.

"Let me tell you the story, Dane," he said. "God knows I'll be glad to get it off my chest. I came back on a special mission last May a year ago. I guess you know how these things are. I did the job—it was in Los Angeles—but I had to wait for a plane to take me back. I fell in with a lot of fellows, and they found some girls somewhere.

"We were drinking pretty hard, and one of the girls seemed to like me. I remember that, and by God that's about all I do remember, except that I woke up a morning or two later below the border in Mexico with this girl in a room with me, and she said I'd married her."

Dane nodded. He knew better than most the strain of the war, and the drinking that was so often an escape from it. He was no moralist, either. He offered Greg a cigarette and took one himself.

"Go on," he said. "It's a dirty trick, of course. It's been done before."

Greg looked grateful.

"Well, figure it out for yourself," he said. "It was true enough. She had a certificate. And until I saw it I didn't even know her name!

"I went back to the Pacific, and I tried my damnedest to get killed. That's why I got that decoration. Believe me, I was sick at my stomach when they pinned it on me. I'm still sick. I'd tried all year to break off with Virginia. Imagine how I felt when I came home and found she had planned our wedding! I couldn't marry her. I couldn't marry anybody. I tried to prime myself to tell her by taking a few drinks, and that turned out as you might expect.

"That's the story, Dane. I didn't kill Marguerite, but I knew she was coming east. She wrote me at Washington. I haven't seen her since I left, more than a year ago, but I sent her a thousand dollars then to keep her quiet. I thought maybe she'd let me divorce her. But she didn't want a divorce. She was coming east to see Carol and my mother. I tried to stop her. I flew to New York, but I was too late. She'd left her hotel. The next thing I knew she was dead."

"You didn't know she was coming here?"

"How could I? Mother and Carol were in Newport. But she must have told poor old Lucy who she was, or she wouldn't have let her in the house. That's what gets me, Dane. I can't pretend I'm sorry about Marguerite, but Lucy—what on earth happened to Lucy?"

He got up. He looked rather better, as though telling the story had given him relief.

"I've wondered," he said. "Lucy was fond of us. She might have killed herself. She was a little thing—Lucy, I mean— but these New Englanders are capable of violence. The way their boys are fighting in this war— But of course that's crazy, isn't it? Who shot Elinor? Who burned the hill? What's it all about anyhow?"

The contrast between the two men was very marked at that moment, Greg's bewildered, not too clever face against Dane's keen determined one. Dane lit a cigarette.

"I can tell you about the fire," he said casually. "At least I'm morally certain. Your sister, Mrs. Hilliard, set it."

Greg's expression changed, hardened. He flushed angrily.

"You'd better have good reason for an accusation of that sort," he said stiffly. "My sister is not mixed up in this. It's my story, not hers."

"You're sure of that, are you?"

"Absolutely."

"She knew you married this girl, didn't she?"

For the first time Greg's frankness deserted him.

"She didn't know it until recently."

"How recently?"

"I don't remember."

He was definitely on guard now, and Dane got up.

"About that ring," he said, "how do you account for it?"

"She must have bought it herself. I never gave her one. I never even saw her, after Mexico."

"Any letters of yours?"

"Only one with the check in it. The check had my name on it. I didn't sign the letter. Only my initials."

"Do you think she brought the letter with her?" Dane persisted. "She brought something, I am sure of that, and something somebody wants. I don't know what it is. I don't even know who wants it. If it wasn't your sister who was shot last night I would think you were that person. Look here, do you remember any of the men in Los Angeles who were in that party?"

Greg shook his head.

"They came and went, the way those things are. I expect some of them are gone by this time. Anyhow I'd had plenty to drink before that. I was pretty well under before the party— if you can call it a party."

"Was young Ward part of the crowd?"

"Ward? You mean Terry? He may have been. I didn't see him."

There was a long silence. Then Greg returned to Elinor.

"What about Elinor and the brush fire on the hill?" he asked. "That's the hell of a thing to accuse her of."

"Her car was seen here the night of the murder, captain. Now wait a minute—" as Greg made a move toward him. "I don't think she killed the girl. It seems unlikely under the circumstances," he added dryly. "The fact remains that she may have known more than she's ever told. For instance, there was a definite attempt to conceal Marguerite's identity. Her clothes haven't been found, not even her overnight bag. Perhaps Carol has told you why we believed her things were buried on the hillside, about the spade we found and so on.

"But she may not have told you that Mrs. Hilliard was pretty badly scared when Lucy testified at the inquest. I watched her. I know. But Lucy Norton was careful. She told only a part of the truth, and Mrs. Hilliard knew it."

"She didn't kill her," Gregory said thickly. "I'll take my oath on that."

"Then why did she set fire to the hill?" Dane demanded. "I think you'll find she did exactly that. She knew the pitcher was in this attic and Carol's car was in the drive. She even had a rubber hose to siphon off the gasoline. I saw it in her bathroom, part of a shampoo arrangement. It still smelled of gasoline, although I imagine she had tried to clean it."

"I don't believe it," Gregory said stubbornly. "I don't believe she was here when Marguerite was killed. Why don't you ask her?"

"Because she had an alibi of sorts." Dane's voice was bland. "She claims to have spent that night in her empty apartment in New York. She certainly was in New York Saturday. She says she had dinner with her husband that night and went to the theater. She probably did, unless he is involved in this too. But she could have been here, you know; have driven the rest of Friday night to Providence and taken an early train to New York. In fact, that's almost certainly what she did."

"So she shot herself!" Greg said roughly. "She went out in the rain, climbed the hill and shot herself in the thigh! For God's sake, Dane, make sense."

"All right," Dane agreed. "Let's try something else. She didn't kill the girl. She came after her, because she knew she was coming here. When she got here the girl was already dead, so she did the only thing she could think of. She took the body upstairs in the elevator and put it in the closet."

"It sounds crazy."

"It does indeed, but something of the sort happened. The body was hidden to gain time, of course."

"So Elinor could get to New York and go to the theater!"

"So she could protect you, captain. And her own position too. Want me to go on?"

"I'll have to hear it sometime," Greg grunted.

"All right. Let's say Lucy's still at the foot of the stairs. She's unconscious, but she might recover any minute. Mrs. Hilliard didn't know Lucy had broken her leg, but she had to get rid of the girl's clothes. She found them in the yellow room, along with her bags. Lucy was stirring by that time, and probably moaning. What could she do? Take them with her? She was going to New York, remember, and Lucy might raise the alarm any minute."

"Can you imagine Elinor burying them in the middle of the night? She could have got rid of them in a hundred places on her way to New York." Greg was openly defiant now. "She has her faults, but she's not an idiot."

Dane nodded, still imperturbable.

"Precisely. That's where I stop. I've been stopped there for ten days; bridges, rivers, empty fields, and those clothes buried up on that hill! Unless she had help, of course."

There was another silence. Greg broke it.

"Who claims to have seen her car?"

"Old Mrs. Ward, for one. She was out looking for her husband. It seems he sleeps badly. She told it quite innocently. But the Dalton girl saw it too. She was out with her dog."

"Looks as though the whole damned town was out that night," Greg commented sourly.

He had commenced to dress. Dane watched him idly, his mind busy with what he had learned. He roused as Greg shrugged into his blouse.

"What about your alibi when your wife was murdered?" he asked. "You left Washington on Thursday of that week. I know that. You'd better be sure you can fill in that interval, Spencer, and don't tell me you don't remember. You'll have to remember."

Greg laughed, unexpectedly and without mirth.

"All right," he said. "I registered at the Gotham on Thursday. You can check that. And I called Elinor at Newport that day. You can check that too. You can check that I got my car out of storage also, to drive to Newport to see Virginia and the rest of the family. But you can't check me for Friday or most of Saturday, because I can't check myself. I'd got that letter from Marguerite, and I told you how I was," he added dryly. "I can drink like any other man most of the time. Then when things get too strong for me I drink myself blind. I came to somewhere in lower New York. I'd been slipped a Micky Finn and robbed. That was at noon on Saturday, and you can ask the hotel how I looked when I got back.

"That's no alibi, and you know it," Dane said sharply. "What was too strong for you? Not that letter, was it? What did Mrs. Hilliard tell you over the long-distance telephone on Thursday? That was it, wasn't it? And who do you think your sister thought she was protecting when she got here that Friday night? You, wasn't it?"

There was another long silence. Greg was obviously trying to think the thing out. When he spoke he did not answer Dane's questions.

"I can't see Elinor in it at all," he said. "I can't see her killing anyone or—you know, digging a hole and burying those clothes. I've done my share of digging since the war began. So have you probably. It isn't easy."

"No," Dane agreed. "And the ground was hard that night. No rain for a long time. How did she know the girl was coming here, Spencer? She did know, didn't she?"

But here again Greg was evasive. He hadn't known it himself, he said. She might have learned it some other way. Dane realized that he was on guard now and got up, looking tired.

"All right, Spencer," he said wearily. "You've got the story now. Where do we go from here?"

"To see Elinor," Greg replied gruffly. "Damn it, Dane, she'll have to talk now, or I'll find myself at the end of a rope."

TWENTY

ELINOR DID NOT TALK THAT DAY, however, or for several days thereafter. She had developed a fever, and no visitors were allowed, not even her family.

Hilliard arrived on Monday, bringing extra nurses and a consulting surgeon on the plane with him. Dane saw him at the hospital, a heavy florid man, on the shortish side, inclined to be pompous, and to regard Elinor's shooting both as an accident and a personal/affront.

"These damned hunters!" he said, red with indignation. "Shooting deer out of season, of course. When a woman like my wife can't even leave her house safely——!"

He succeeded in isolating Elinor completely, although the consulting surgeon seemed undisturbed about her.

"She's all right," he said privately to Dr. Harrison. "A little fever, that's all." He smiled faintly. "Three nurses," he said, "and the country short of them! Well, she's his wife. If he's willing to pay for it, I suppose it's not my business." He glanced at Harrison. "What's she afraid of, anyhow?"

Dr. Harrison looked surprised.

"Afraid? What makes you think she is?"

"Looks it. Acts it. Jumps every time the door's opened. Probably causes her temperature too. Does she know who shot her? Think that's it?"

"I haven't an idea. She doesn't talk about it."

"Maybe she'd better," said the consultant, and took off his mask and white coat. "Well, I guess that's all, doctor. Congratulations and thanks."

Tim had arrived the day of Greg's confession, but he brought little or nothing Dane did not already know, which annoyed him greatly.

"For God's sake," he said, "why send me all over the country risking my neck when you know it all?"

Nor had he discovered much from the suitcase. It had revealed underwear and a dress or two, all of good quality, and a snapshot of a baby a few weeks old.

"You know the sort," Tim said. "No clothes. Legs in air. Kind of a nice kid. Boy."

"She'd had a child."

"Had, eh? Well, that explains it."

Tim's good humor died quickly, however, when he learned that his next assignment was to watch Carol at the Spencer house, and to help Maggie, now alone there. He stalked back to Alex in the kitchen.

"What's wrong with him?" he demanded, indicating Dane in the front of the house. "Is he crazy? Or is he just crazy about that girl next door? It'll cost him the hell of a lot to pay me for washing dishes."

"Money don't worry him," Alex said calmly. "Got plenty, or his old lady has. Father was a senator."

Which ambiguous statement kept Tim silent for a moment. Then: "What's this about the Hilliard woman getting shot? Papers are full of it. Somebody after deer?"

"Sure," Alex said, patting a hamburger neatly into shape. "In June, on a rainy night at one A.M."

Tim whistled.

"Another, eh?" he said. "Well, maybe Dane's right about the girl friend. How about lending me one of those pretty aprons you wear? If I'm to wash dishes all day and stay up all night I won't need anything to sleep in."

Dane himself was at a loose end, with Elinor shut away and no possibility of seeing her. He was confident now that she had not been alone the night Marguerite was killed. Yet his telegram from Washington saying the answer was no, had left him without any specific suspect. And Floyd was still digging. In spite of his skepticism he had investigated Pine Hill. He might already know that the letter inside the wedding ring was a G and be keeping the wires hot about a possible marriage. And in the center of the mystery was Carol, growing thinner and more confused each day.

He went over his notes the day of Tim's return, changing

and elaborating them, and after his custom numbering them.

(1) *The body in the closet. Laid out carefully, and with the
fur jacket not fully on. It had covered only one arm. Had this
been done after death?*

(2) *The wedding ring on body. In spite of the engraving,
Greg claimed he had never seen it. (Can probably be checked
in Los Angeles.)*

(3) *Fire in closet. Set sometime after death. In that case improbable either Greg or Elinor had set it. Lucy Norton's statement at inquest. No smoke or odor of burning that night.*

(4) *The bobby pin found by Carol. Someone not strong
enough to carry the body had taken it up in the elevator. Hair
obviously bleached, indicating it belonged to dead girl.*

(5) *The curious discovery in the tool house. Not only the
spade, but the Lowestoft tea set, and so on.*

(6) *Burning of hillside. Pitcher taken from Crestview attic.
Almost certainly done by Elinor Hilliard to cover evidence.*

(7) *Strange death of Lucy Norton.*

He sat for some time over that. Someone had climbed the
fire escape and found Lucy in her room. She had been sufficiently alarmed to get out of her bed, and to fall dead with a
heart attack. Would she have been murdered otherwise? Had
only the noise of her fall driven the intruder away? But why?
He was convinced now that what she had learned from the
dead girl had been that she was Greg's wife. But she had not
told it at the inquest. After some thought he put an *X* after that
entry and went on.

(8) *Shooting of Elinor Hilliard and moving of her body from
the lane. Why had she dressed and gone out in the rain? To
meet someone, and if so, who was it? Another X here.*

(9) *Why had Mr. Ward stealthily retrieved shell from mud
in lane? Where did the Wards figure in the mystery? The grandson, Terry?*

(10) *Attempt, the night Elinor was shot, to discover and
probably remove girl's clothing if buried on hillside. Elinor?
X?*

(11) Search of yellow room same night, while entire Spencer family at hospital. X again?

(12) Deserted house, Pine Hill. Who had been staying there? Blankets left after all other clues carefully removed. Probably overlooked in darkness and forgotten. X?

After some thought he added another note, thinking grimly that it was the thirteenth.

(13) Terry Ward expected back on leave. Did not apparently arrive.

He put away his notes and began to check the movements of the murdered girl. She had reached New York on Wednesday, June fourteenth, and gone to a hotel. On Thursday, shortly after Carol and Mrs. Spencer had left, she had inquired for them at their apartment house. That left her plenty of time to go to Boston and take the night train for Maine, arriving at the village by bus the next morning.

He sat for some time gazing at this last item. He had missed something here. Boston was only five hours from New York, but suppose she had not gone directly to Boston? Suppose she had stopped off at Newport and seen Elinor Hilliard?

The more he considered it the more certain he was she had done exactly that. If she intended blackmail she would naturally go to Elinor. He leaned back and closed his eyes. He could almost see what happened. The girl, pretty in a common way, in the fur jacket and white hat. Admitted under protests, unless she had said she was Mrs. Spencer. And Elinor sweeping into the room.

"Mrs. Spencer? Which Mrs. Spencer?"

"I'm Greg's wife."

Elinor staring at her, dazed and incredulous.

"I don't believe you. And you're getting out of this house. At once."

"You can put me out right enough. But you can't change things, you know. I've got my certificate."

"I wouldn't believe it if I saw it."

"You're not going to see it. I'm taking care of that. All right,

Mrs. Hilliard. If you feel this way about it, maybe your mother and sister won't. I've looked them up. In Maine, aren't they?"

Leaving, and Elinor rushing to the telephone, telling Greg what had happened, and Greg unable to face it and taking the usual way out. Going to New York on his way to Newport, and starting to drink himself blind on the way.

It had to be something like that, if Greg's story was true and if Elinor had been at Crestview the night of the murder. Why had she come? To buy the girl off, to urge a divorce and promise some considerable sum in return? Or to kill her? Everything else aside, she was capable of going to almost any length to avoid scandal and to save her social position. Even Hilliard would not have taken it well. But if she had killed Marguerite Spencer he was certain she had not done it alone.

He realized that he was going stale on the case, and that afternoon he asked Carol to go for a drive.

"I need exercise," he told her. "Why not leave the car somewhere and do a bit of climbing?"

"I'd love it. How about your leg?"

"I've forgotten I have it!"

They had a happy afternoon. From the top of a low mountain they could see the open ocean, and the bay sprinkled with its low green islands, like emeralds set in blue. Far below, the women on the golf course were bright bits of color, and the town itself picturesque and gay.

Sitting on a rock there he told her a little about himself; about his enlistment in the army, about his having been detached to a special job, and his anxiety to get back to it.

"It takes me around a lot," he said casually. "Trouble is, a man in my position has no business having ties. My mother worries as it is."

"All women have to accept it, don't they? I mean, almost everyone has somebody."

He reached out and took her hand.

"Look, darling," he said, "I'm pretty badly in love with you. I've been fighting it for days, but you might as well know it. I know you still remember Don Richardson, for one thing. The other is—" He threw away his cigarette. "How does any man know he's coming back these days? Or he won't be mutilated, or blind?"

"Would that matter so much?" she asked quietly. "If the woman cared—"

"It would," he said fiercely, and got up. "It would matter my dear. All right. Let's go."

He flew to Washington that night. With Elinor still shut off he felt he had reached a dead end, but there were things he could learn there he could not learn elsewhere. He was not too happy. He had done an idiotic thing, he felt. He had told Carol he was in love with her and in the same breath had said he had no intention of marrying her. Only a damned fool would do a thing like that, he reflected, as the plane roared south.

He did not go to a hotel. He had kept a small apartment there, and he admitted himself, mixing a good strong drink before he turned in. But he slept badly. He bathed and shaved, dressed, got some breakfast at a restaurant, and then reported to an office tucked away among the innumerable War Department buildings. He was not limping at all as he went in, and the man behind the desk surveyed him with a smile as he thrust out his hand.

"Hello, Dane," he said. "How's the Eagle Scout?"

Dane grinned.

"I'm fine. Hard luck, missing the invasion."

"Well, you've had plenty—Dieppe, Africa, Sicily, Anzio beachhead, Cassino. That's a record for any man."

Dane shrugged and sat down.

"I'm reporting for duty," he said, "but I'd like a few days first. Maybe a couple of weeks. There's a case in Maine I'd like to look into."

"That murder at Bayside?"

"Yes." He grinned. "I see you read the papers."

"Greg Spencer's apparently mixed up in it somehow. That puts it up to us in a way. Not our business, of course, but after all a fellow with a record like his— Better tell me what it's about, Dane."

Sitting there, referring to his notes, Dane related what had happened. It was not an uninterrupted narrative. Telephones rang. People came in and went out, quick important decisions were made. But he finished at last, and the man behind the desk made some notes.

"I wired you before," he said. "So far as we can check Terry Ward did not come east on his present furlough. He's still somewhere on the Coast now. Be leaving soon. Of course, all that's not positive. When you can cross the continent in seven or eight hours, and you're a flier with friends in the service, you can get places pretty fast."

"Any way to check on his past? Say the last year or two?"

"What sort of check?"

"Women. Did he play around with anyone like the Barbour girl?"

"My God, Dane, what do you think he is? Just because he flies doesn't mean he has wings like an angel."

It was the best Dane could do. He stayed in Washington for a day or two, learning nothing of any importance, meeting fellow officers, drinking at this bar and that, even going out to dinner once. But he was increasingly restless. On Thursday he flew back to Maine. It was still daylight when he arrived, and Alex met him at the field, an Alex with a long face and his one eye anxious and unhappy.

"I'm glad you're here, sir," he said. "Floyd arrested Captain Spencer for murder this afternoon."

TWENTY-ONE

CAROL HAD HAD A RATHER DIFFICULT TIME during Dane's absence. Greg was taciturn and worried. Tim—the man who was to assist Maggie—had a habit of turning up at unexpected places, particularly at night. And Colonel Richardson had taken it upon himself to see that she was not lonely or downhearted.

It was difficult to see Maggie's picture of him running in the rain in the dignified elderly man who daily brought her flowers from his garden, and who talked garrulously the small gossip of the community. On Tuesday he noticed that she was no longer wearing Don's ring. He picked up her hand and looked at it.

"Have you no faith, no loyalty, my dear?" he asked gently.

"It's so long," she said, afraid of hurting him. "It's over a year. I have tried, but . . ."

"They've been found after longer periods than that," he insisted, and the next time he came he brought a clipping about such a case, and a map.

"Now look, my dear," he said. "You see what I mean. I've drawn in the new routes, ship and plane. This is where he was seen last. That doesn't mean his plane went down there. It might still have gone quite a way, and here's this island."

He pointed at it, his eyes full of hope, his lips slightly blue, and his veined elderly hand tremulous. She quivered with pity for him, but why couldn't he accept it? she thought. Other people did. There were people near-by, among the townspeople and the summer colony, who had had similar losses. They did not talk about them. They went around with quiet faces, or with the forced smiles that made one ache for them.

The situation was complicated by his continued jealousy of Jerry Dane. Not that he spoke about him. It was just there, behind his faded blue eyes as he watched her. In a way it was like a silent battle between them, one of strategy rather than the firing line. But she did not put on Don's ring again.

Greg watched the situation morosely.

"Why don't you get rid of the old buzzard?" he said. "I'm sorry for him. I'm sorry for a lot of other people too. Only they bury their dead decently. He won't."

Tim did not add to her comfort. He was watching her carefully. At night, after she had gone to bed, he prowled around, trying her door to be sure it was locked, watching all doors and windows. At two in the morning Alex took over, but outside the house, and Tim got some sleep. Carol knew nothing of this arrangement, although Greg, coming home late Tuesday night from a dinner and taking a short cut to the house, found himself confronted with a flashlight which blinded him. He was indignant.

"What the devil's all this?" he demanded.

"It's all right, captain. Sorry. Just happened to be passing and saw you."

He had a vision of a big body and a face with a patch over one eye, and went on, still surprised and affronted.

It was almost a relief to Carol when on Wednesday afternoon a sort of inquest on Lucy Norton's death was held. There was no need of an inquiry, Dr. Harrison insisted. He even doubted if it was legal. But Floyd set his heavy jaw and demanded one.

"What's the difference whether she was hit on the head or scared to death?" he shouted. "All right. All right. We won't have a jury. We'll conduct an inquiry, and we'll let the public in if it wants to come. What's wrong with that?"

It was held in Floyd's office, which was jammed to the doors, but it brought out nothing new. Even Joe Norton's statement told nothing fresh.

"She was all right when I seen her last," he said. "Only she had something on her mind. I don't say she was scared. She just wasn't talking. If you ask me, that girl told her something before she got killed and somebody got in her room at the hospital to find out what she knew."

Asked if he had any idea what this knowledge could have been, he had not. "Except that the girl said she was a friend of Carol Spencer's," he said after some thought. "It might have been something about the Spencers."

As having possible bearing on the case, a statement from Elinor Hilliard was read. She had not seen the person who shot her. She had been unable to sleep and had gone out. The rain was not heavy at that time. She had been in the lane when she had heard someone running toward her; in fact, she had thought there were two people, one behind the other. She was not sure, however. It was very dark. But she had not been on the hillside and had had no idea how she got there. She had been conscious when she fell, but she must have fainted almost at once. Someone must have carried her to where she was found.

There was no verdict, of course, and the press went away dissatisfied. There was only one angle the reporters had not already known. This was the fact that several patients in private rooms had had their doors opened the night of Lucy's death, opened and then closed again.

Floyd, realizing that things had fallen rather flat, made a small speech, standing behind his desk to do so.

"I think," he said, "in view of one murder and a shooting; not to mention the death of Lucy Norton, this town should take certain precautions; such as an early curfew for the children and the careful locking of houses at night. Without wanting to cause undue alarm, there seems to be someone around who doesn't hesitate to kill, and I shall inform the state troopers and forest rangers to that effect."

That had been the situation until Thursday afternoon, when Greg was arrested. Alex at the airport, having thrown his bomb, produced a bottle of Scotch from beside him in the car.

"Better take a drink, sir," he said. "There's a fog coming in. It's cold."

Dane drank the liquor straight. It burned his throat, but he felt better after it.

"All right," he said, as Alex put the car in gear. "Let's have the story."

Alex did not know a great deal. What he had had come from Tim, and that gentleman, liking Greg and considering Floyd too big for his pants, had resented the highhandedness of the procedure.

"As I get it, sir," Alex said, "Captain Spencer and Miss Carol were having lunch when Floyd drove up. He had Mason and a state trooper with him, but only Floyd went into the dining room. Tim was in the pantry, and the door has a little glass window in it, so he saw it all.

"The girl got up, but Spencer didn't move. The girl said 'Is there anything wrong chief?' and Floyd didn't answer her. He walked over to Spencer and said he was arresting him for the murder of his wife. Wife! I haven't got that straight yet. But so far as I know Spencer didn't say much. He told his sister not to worry, he hadn't done it, and he asked if he could pack a bag. Floyd sent the trooper up with him, but he didn't make any trouble. Last Tim saw of him he was getting into Floyd's car. He's in jail at the county seat now, and they're going to call a special session of the Grand Jury."

It was a long speech for Alex, so long that he lapsed into complete silence after it. Dane was grateful for it. Floyd must have his case, he considered, to have gone so far. And he knew a good case could be made.

His chief worry was Carol. He looked at his wrist watch when he got home. It showed only nine o'clock, so without stopping he walked over to Crestview. She was standing on the terrace gazing forlornly out at the bay, now misty with fog, and his heart contracted with pity when he saw her. Evidently she recognized his step, for she turned quietly and waited for him.

He was astounded to find her face frozen into a stiff, resentful mask.

"Haven't you a good bit of courage to come here?" she demanded.

"Courage? What do you mean?"

"You've got what you wanted, haven't you? Greg's under arrest. That's what you've been working for, isn't it?"

He lit a cigarette and studied her, not speaking.

"I keep asking myself why," she went on, her voice flat. "Why? He knows Greg didn't do it. He was here when it happened. Maybe he did it himself." And when he still said nothing: "What do I know about you, Jerry Dane? Nothing. Not who you are or what you do. You put a man in this house to watch us, everything we do. Then you get poor Greg's story out of him. He was married to that tart, and that's luck for you, isn't it?"

"You're excited, my dear."

She gave a small hollow laugh.

"That's funny, coming from you," she said, her voice still bleak. "Why wouldn't I be excited? My brother's under arrest for murder. My mother's in bed with a heart attack. My sister's been shot—did you do that too? And Greg's fiancée's driving me crazy over the telephone wires."

"See here," he said authoritatively. "You're not excited. You're hysterical. Sit down and listen to me or I'll carry you up to bed and get a doctor."

He waited until she sat before he spoke. Then his voice was as cold as hers.

"In the first place, I didn't kill the girl. In the second place, your brother didn't do it either. Now stop being a little fool and listen to me. I've been doing my damnedest to keep Greg from being arrested. I couldn't do it in time. But an indictment —if it comes to that—is not a trial, and I'm not through," he added grimly. "Now—did you eat any dinner?"

She was quieter. She was even apologetic.

"I'm sorry," she said in a small voice. "I've been here alone all afternoon, and thinking about Greg . . ."

He smiled at her.

"That's better," he told her. "Now, once again—did you eat any dinner?"

"I wasn't hungry."

"You're going to eat now," he said firmly. "Half of that attack on me was empty tummy. And after I've got some food in you I'm going to see Floyd. I think he's slipped up. At least I hope he has. How is Mrs. Hilliard?"

She looked at him, surprised.

"Elinor? She's doing all right. Howard's going home. Or he was until this happened. He's sent for his lawyer now."

"And your sister is still not talking?"

"What do you mean, talking?"

He eyed her gravely. She could take it, he thought. She had plenty of guts. Nevertheless, he told her as gently as he could.

"I'm afraid she knows some things, my dear. I think she knew of this marriage, which was hardly a marriage at all. Greg was on leave and drinking when it happened, and this girl more or less kidnaped him. But I think she knows something else, or suspects it."

"What? Don't treat me like a baby, Jerry. I'll have to know sooner or later, won't I?"

"I think she knows either who shot her or at least why she was shot, Carol."

She took it well. "Does that mean—do you think she knows anything else?"

"I'm afraid she does, darling."

She was silent when he called Tim and asked for some food for her. And Tim, in a white coat too small for him, took the order stolidly, as if he had never seen Dane before.

"Certainly, sir," he said, in an outrageous imitation of an English butler. "And may I offer the major a cup of coffee, sir? Or perhaps you would favor a ham sandwich."

Dane was not amused. He managed to get her to eat a little, and he saw her go up to bed before he called Alex to bring the car. It was almost ten o'clock by that time, but he counted on Floyd's being still in his office. He had not expected to find Campbell there, however. Both men eyed him with disapproval and resentment.

"I've a damned good idea to arrest you, Dane," Floyd said explosively. "You've known all along this girl was Spencer's wife. You've been covering for him—for the whole family, for that matter—and you know it."

Dane sat down. He was still in uniform, and he put his service cap carefully on a table beside him.

"I suppose it was the wedding ring," he said casually.

"You suppose right. I'm no fool. I got Hodge Hopkins's glass on it myself after you brought it back. That C was a G. How many men's names begin with G?"

"George, Gilbert—" Dane began easily. But Floyd held up a hamlike fist.

"And Gregory," he said. "Not that I was sure. Not then anyhow. In fact he had a bit of luck. The Coast turned up a young woman who had been reported missing by the people who were keeping her baby. Lived outside Los Angeles. She answered the description, clothes and all, and Doc Harrison said the girl here had had a kid. Didn't know that, did you?"

"I did."

"Oh, you knew that too," Floyd said nastily. "Two years old. A boy."

"Not Greg Spencer's child, of course," Dane said, still evenly. "Never saw her until a year ago. Only spent a day or two with her. Very drunk at the time."

Floyd passed that off with a gesture. He was evidently feeling jubilant, although the district attorney was less happy.

"Well, then I got busy," Floyd went on. "The Los Angeles force had no record of a marriage, but they said some parties went to Mexico. It was easy there. No Wassermans, no trouble. Just get married. And there it was, Gregory Spencer and Marguerite Barbour."

"And the date?"

Floyd looked at a telegram in front of him. "May seventeenth of last year. And to save you trouble I'll tell you Spencer was in Los Angeles at that time. *Also* he can't account for his whereabouts the day the girl was killed here." He sat back, looking complacent. "How d'you like it? Even you fellows can slip up now and then, eh?"

"What do you mean by 'you fellows'?" Dane asked dryly.

"FBI man, aren't you? Were before the war, anyhow."

Dane neither denied nor assented. He lit a cigarette and blew out the match.

"We all slip. I suppose he frightened Lucy Norton to death and shot his sister, too?"

"We're not trying him for either of those. We don't have to."

"You can't very well leave them out."

"He may have done them both. I'm not saying. The Norton woman, yes. I expect she saw him that night when she fell down the stairs. His sister, probably no. Somebody took her for a deer."

"And the person who was hiding up at Pine Hill? What about him?"

"I've been up," said Floyd comfortably. "So have the State Police. So has Mr. Campbell here. Know what? Those blankets came from the Ward place. Had the cleaner's tag on them.

Nathaniel Ward says his wife gave them last fall to a fellow who helped their gardener. He's in the Marines now. Nice fellow too. Name's Arthur Scott. Used to go hunting and stay out all night."

Dane got up.

"So Arthur Scott came back from the South Pacific or wherever he is now and slept at Pine Hill within the last week or two. Is that what you're saying?"

The district attorney roused at last. He spoke gravely.

"I undertsand your disappointment, major," he said. "The family is well known, and Greg Spencer has a fine war record. I'm only sorry this has happened. But there is no use dragging red herrings across Floyd's trail. He's done a great piece of work."

"All but finding the guilty man," Dane said curtly, and went out into the fog and dim-out of the night.

TWENTY-TWO

HE DROVE SLOWLY BACK to his house. As he passed the club he could hear the laughter inside and the sound of the jukebox in the bar. He remembered how strange it had felt when he was first brought back from the war, to find people living normal lives. It had been a long time before a plane over the hospital had not caused him to flinch.

Perhaps no man was unchanged after he had been in this war; could take safety for granted, or even the ordinary human happinesses. Had he been wrong, and had this happened to Greg Spencer? At least twice he had admitted to prolonged and heavy bouts of drinking, that usual attempt on the part of exhausted nerves to relieve strain or achieve forgetfulness. And drunken men do strange things, as he knew well.

But again there arose the question of his sister. Guns could be fired and cleaned, of course. Also, people were sometimes shot by mistake. Had Greg meant to kill someone else and shot Elinor Hilliard instead? He tried again to reconstruct the night it had happened, Carol's drowsy response when he knocked at her door, and Greg—

He thought that over, the search of the house and Carol reporting Elinor missing. "And Greg's asleep. I heard him snoring. She must have gone alone."

He remembered Elinor's room, the bed used, the book left as she had put it down, with the wind from the open window ruffling its pages, and her sheer stockings on a chair. If Greg was asleep, who or what had roused Elinor? Had someone seen her light and called through the open window? If so, who had it been?

His mind turned again to the Wards, their blankets in the empty house, the old man's odd behavior the morning after Elinor had been shot, and even further back, to the evening he himself had left Marcia Dalton's and gone to Rockhill. What was it Mr. Ward had said? Something about not running to the police with every bit of tittle-tattle he heard. And his own impression that the old man had wanted to get rid of him that night.

He was not greatly surprised the next morning to learn from Alex that a dozen men or so were working on the hillside.

"Digging all over the place," Alex reported. "Tim called me up to tell you."

Dane dressed and went over. The hill was crowded with men who looked like a hastily assorted group of gardeners from various estates. They had pegged it out, each man with a definite area, and he was still watching them when one of them near the burned house suddenly let out a yell and Floyd hurried across to him.

They had found the cache. Floyd was holding up a small overnight bag, using a bandanna handkerchief to do so, and peering down at something at his feet.

"That's all, men," he shouted. "We've found them. You can quit work. And thanks."

He was still there when Dane made his way over to him. Except for the bag Floyd had touched nothing. He was probably waiting for a photographer, Dane thought, and was not surprised when the reporter, young Starr, came loping across, camera in hand, from his old jalopy. He did not even see Dane. He waved the man back and stood over the hole, focusing carefully.

"Gee, chief," he said. "That's the stuff all right. Bad news for somebody."

Dane could see the pit now, not far from the small shallow one he had seen before. It was wide rather than deep, and the clothing in it had been dropped carelessly. A small black shoe, what looked like a black dress, an edge or two of peach-colored underwear, and the corner of a flat pocketbook were in sight. They made him faintly sick. Good or bad, the girl they had belonged to had lived and liked living. Now—

He went down to break the news to Carol, only to find that she was not alone. He heard a sonorous voice as he walked along the hall.

"But, my dear girl," it was saying pontifically, "I never touch criminal cases. Why Mr. Hilliard sent for me I don't know. As for this fellow Dane you refer to, I've never heard of him."

Thus disposed of with neatness and dispatch, Dane reached the door. The speaker was standing in front of the fire, a short tubby elderly man exuding displeasure from every pore, while Carol was looking crushed. Evidently this was Hilliard's lawyer.

"If—as seems entirely probable—Gregory Spencer has committed—" Hart began. Then he saw Dane and stopped.

"What if he hasn't committed a murder?" Dane said aggressively. "And what about remembering that Miss Spencer has had a shock and ought to be in bed?"

"Who the hell are you?" said Mr. Hart, pomposity lost in indignation.

All the last two weeks of anxiety and frustration came suddenly to the surface in Dane's retort.

"My name's Dane, sir. I gather that means nothing to you. But if you're starting by accepting the fact that Spencer's guilty, I suggest that you take the next plane back. He's better off without you."

Mr. Hart was apparently stunned. He reached for his pince-nez and surveyed Dane through it, uniform and all.

"I see," he said. "Brother officers. The services take care of their own."

Dane took a step toward him, and Hart retreated abruptly.

"All right, all right," he said, the unction gone out of his voice. "I take that back. I'm rather upset. I had no sleep last night. I hate planes, and to be confronted with murder—"

"By a person or persons unknown," Dane said softly. "*Still* unknown, sir."

The learned counsel left after that, presumably headed for the hotel and Hilliard, and Dane, rather ashamed, broke the news about the hill to Carol. She took it stony-faced and unflinching.

"It doesn't prove anything against Greg, does it? After all, since he wasn't here—"

"No, but there are other things not so good."

He could not hold off any longer. He put her in a comfortable chair and then told her the whole story as he knew it. He omitted nothing, but he gave her only facts, not theories. And her wide intelligent eyes never left his face.

When he had finished she nodded.

"I can see why they arrested him, Jerry. I can't see why you think he didn't do it."

"Do you?"

"No. Of course not." She looked startled.

"All right, darling. Now I want you to think, and think hard. What about Terry Ward? He was expected here but he didn't come. Is that right?"

"Yes. But if you're trying to make a case against Terry—"

"He's involved somehow, darling. Pretty seriously, I think. He's on the Coast now, for one thing, although I can't find out if he's been east. He may have been in the crowd last year when Greg met this girl. He may even have been in love with her himself. That's possible, you know. And what's wrong with the Wards? Greg's arrest has upset them pretty badly, or something has. I saw the doctor going in there while ago."

But her mind was still on Terry. He was young and gay. He adored the old people. He had been Don Richardson's friend, and there was some story of the two of them taking up Greg's plane years before, and that Greg in a white fury had threatened them both with jail. Of course that meant nothing, she said. It was just kid stuff, and certainly Terry would never murder anybody.

Dane made no comment. He did not say that this Terry was a different man, one who had been taught to kill. He sat back, watching her and thinking what it would mean to get her away from here, from the neurotic mother, from Elinor's selfishness —if nothing more—and Greg's ability to get himself into trouble.

The mention of Don Richardson had reminded her of Maggie's story about the colonel. She repeated it now.

"So much has happened since," she said, "I simply forgot it. But Maggie's quite positive. It was only a few minutes after she heard the shot. Of course the colonel may merely have been hurrying home from the Wards'. They play chess very late."

He did not ask her for further details. He persuaded her to

try to get some rest, and went around to see Maggie herself. Maggie's story was even more dramatic, the running, the hatless head with its white hair, the dressing gown, the slamming of the colonel's front door. "It was him all right," she said, "and I'm going to that potbellied Floyd tomorrow and tell him so."

He advised against this. He told her he had some ideas of his own, and to keep quiet until it was time for her to speak. But Maggie was still suspicious. She was convinced that the colonel had lost his mind since Don's death. "The way he pesters Miss Carol, poor child." And he lived close enough to Crestview for what she called any sort of monkey business. In the end, however, she promised and he left, puzzled by the incident but also aware of the Irish tendency toward exaggeration. Any man might run if he had heard a shot near him. Only it was rather curious that the colonel apparently had not spoken of it.

He went home, feeling more in the dark than ever. If Floyd had found anything of importance in the girl's pocketbook that morning, he did not know it, would not know it until the trial probably. But there was one angle of the case which he realized he had neglected, and after some hesitation he added it to his notes.

(14) *If Marguerite had been married before she married Greg Spencer, who was the man?*

He could not do anything about it that day. He might indeed have to go to the Coast himself to trace it down. But one thing was obvious. He would have to see Elinor Hilliard, regardless of hospital rules or the small army that supposedly surrounded her.

In the end he found this surprisingly easy. Apparently with Greg's arrest Floyd had taken away the troopers, and the nurse on duty was probably somewhere smoking a cigarette. Because the day was hot the doors were open, and he found Elinor's room without difficulty.

She was more or less lying in state, wearing an elaborate bed jacket, and with her hair freshly done. There was a silk blanket cover on the bed, and a mass of delicately colored small pillows around her. Evidently reinforcements had come from Newport, he thought grimly.

Elinor herself still showed the effects of shock and pain. Even the touch of artificial color on her face and lips did not hide the fact that she was a desperately frightened woman. She almost leaped out of the bed when she saw him.

"I'm sorry," he said, smiling at her reassuringly. "I didn't mean to scare you. Do you mind if I sit down? I want to talk about your brother."

It was the right opening. She looked at him angrily.

"These fools!" she said. "Arresting Greg! He never killed that girl. Never."

He drew a chair beside the bed.

"No," he said. "I don't think he did. But he may go to trial, Mrs. Hilliard. Too many people are not telling what they know."

"What people?"

He watched her carefully.

"The Ward family, possibly including Terry, their grandson," he told her. "And you yourself, Mrs. Hilliard. I think you were here the night your brother's wife was killed. I think you know who killed her."

"You're crazy," she said defiantly, although she visibly paled. "Why would I come here? If you believe that malicious story of Marcia Dalton's—"

"I'll tell you what I believe, Mrs. Hilliard. After you hear it you can decide whether you will let your brother be tried for murder or not. I can easily verify some of it. This girl, Marguerite Barbour—or Spencer—learned of your brother's presence in the country, and followed him east. She may have gone to Washington first. If she did, he did not see her there. I know she spent one night at a New York hotel. I know she tried to see your sister or mother at their apartment, and missed them there. I know she checked her suitcase at Grand Central the next morning, and I think as soon as possible after that she got in touch with you."

"Don't be ridiculous. I won't listen to any more. I don't have to." She reached for the button which would call the nurse, but he took her hand and held it.

"Do you want me to tell you this? Or shall I go to Floyd with it? I don't think Mr. Hilliard would care for that. Do you?"

She said nothing, and he went on.

"I believe she went to Newport and saw you there, probably at your own house. She told her story. She had her marriage certificate, didn't she? You pretended to need time to think things over, or perhaps to raise money for her. But you did not tell her your mother and sister were there at the time. She said she was coming here, and you let her come. Why did you do that, Mrs. Hilliard? To get her out of the way? Or to kill her that night?"

"I didn't kill her," Elinor said hysterically. "She was dead when I got there. She was lying on the upper steps outside the front door, in a wrapper over her nightdress. I—I got away as fast as I could."

"Alone?"

"Certainly I was alone."

"You didn't telephone your brother to meet you here?"

"He was never here at all."

"Now look, Mrs. Hilliard," he said patiently. "Part of the truth is not enough. Who carried her body up in the elevator and left it in the closet, so that it would not be found and you would have time to get away? Who took her clothing and buried it? And who later on set fire to the closet? I need those answers if I'm to save Greg."

"I don't know," she said, despair in her voice. "I never buried her clothes. I never touched—her. And why would I try to burn her? It's terrible. It's sickening to think of."

"You left her where she was?"

"Yes. I thought she was dead. I didn't know. I hoped she was dead. She was dreadful, a common tart and after money, of course. I drove up that night, and I brought most of my valuables with me. I wanted to buy her off, to get a divorce, anything, and I couldn't get my hands on much money without telling Howard."

"And that's all?"

"That's all," she said, and closed her eyes.

Dane felt a momentary pity for her. If she was telling the

truth she was only innocently involved. But he had not finished.

"If that's really all," he said, "I wonder why you set fire to the hill? You must have known what was there."

She shrugged slightly. He felt she was on guard once more.

"What else could I do?" she demanded, her former defiant self again. "Her clothes hadn't been found, and you and Carol were searching the place. You believed they were there, and she had had that dreadful marriage certificate with her in her handbag. I didn't want it found."

"Does Greg know you did it?"

"I never told him. He still doesn't know anything, except that she had written him she was coming east—to blow the lid off, she said."

"You know he has no alibi."

She lay back exhausted on her pillows.

"If you know Greg," she said weakly, "you'd understand. He loathed her. He couldn't even face her. When he got my telephone message that I had seen her he simply went on a binge. He didn't even know she was dead until he saw the papers in New York. Even then he wasn't sure it was the same girl. He didn't really know anything until he got here."

Her voice trailed off, and he got up hastily.

"I'll get your nurse," he said. "Maybe things aren't so bad, Mrs. Hilliard. If you have anything more to tell me let me know."

She did not open her eyes.

"Does all this have to come out?" she asked weakly.

"Perhaps not. I can't promise, of course."

But it was his final question that roused her to genuine surprise.

"Is Terry Ward concerned in all this?" he inquired.

"Terry! Good heavens, what has he got to do with it?"

He stood up, looking down at her. He had not liked her. To him she was the epitome of all grasping self-indulgent women. Now, however, she looked really exhausted.

"Just one thing more," he said. "Your mother's china tea set. How did it get to the tool house?"

She did not even move.

"I can't imagine," she said wearily. "It sounds like one of

Mother's better ideas. She hides things, you know. And who cares anyhow?"

He was only partially convinced as he drove home. He believed that she had told the truth, so far as she knew it. The girl had been dead when she got there on that futile frantic excursion of hers. But he still felt that she was holding something back; that if she did not know she at least suspected the identity of the man who killed the girl and frightened Lucy to death, and later shot her.

On the way out he met Dr. Harrison. He had come from the Wards', and was trying desperately to get a nurse, for the night at least.

"I may have one tomorrow," he said worriedly. "But I need one tonight. Mrs. Ward had a stroke this morning, and old Nat is useless. There's only a maid with her."

"Why not ask Marcia Dalton?" Dane said idly. "She's had some training."

And was only aware after he got into his car that he had had a really brilliant idea.

TWENTY-THREE

MARCIA ARRIVED AT THE WARD HOUSE at nine o'clock that night, looking efficient and calm. Old Mr. Ward himself let her in, and took both her hands.

"My dear girl," he said, "how kind of you. She is—she is quite helpless, you know." To his own embarrassment his eyes filled with tears. He released her hands and got out a meticulously folded handkerchief. "After more than fifty years," he said unsteadily. "It's hard."

"It won't do her any good if you yourself get sick," Marcia said practically. "I'll take over now. You go to bed."

He put the handkerchief away.

"She's been a wonderful wife," he said, still shakily. "I've wired Terry, but you know how it is these days. He may be anywhere. They come and go, these boys of ours— I think she was worried about him, although she was so brave. To say good-bye, and not know if it's the last one or not . . ."

"I didn't know he had been here."

"Not here, my dear. The last time we saw him. That was some months ago. Now, if you care to go up— The housemaid, Alice, is with her, but she has never had any contact with illness. We have sent for nurses, of course, but they are very hard to find."

In spite of her long talk with Dane that afternoon Marcia felt reassured as she followed him up the stairs. Everything looked normal, a quiet house, a little old man grieving for his wife. How could there be any danger in this staid establishment? Yet Dane's last words were ringing in her ears.

"Watch everything," he said. "Talk to the servants if you can. Find out if Terry was here this summer, even for a night. If you can find a way to do it, see if Mr. Ward gave a couple of blankets to an assistant gardener last fall. And look around for a rifle or a revolver. Only for God's sake be careful."

Mr. Ward left her at the top of the stairs. She went into the sickroom, to find Alice, the elderly housemaid, sitting beside the bed. She got up when she saw Marcia, looking greatly relieved.

"I'm glad you're here," she whispered. "I'm no hand at this kind of thing. She can't talk, you know."

Marcia did not whisper. She had been taught never to whisper in a sickroom, and she saw, too, that the woman on the bed was not asleep. She was looking at her with intelligent, despairing eyes.

"What orders did the doctor leave?" she asked in her normal voice.

"Just to keep her quiet. As if she isn't quiet, poor dear thing! He's coming back tonight. She was took this morning. No warning, either. I think she's been worried about Captain Spencer. She was a great friend of Mrs. Spencer's. Then with all those men digging on the hill over there . . ."

When Marcia got rid of her she went over to the bed, where the small thin body of an old woman barely raised the covers.

"I'm going to stay here," she said, looking down. "I won't bother you, Mrs. Ward. I'll just be here. Is that all right?"

The eyelids blinked, whether by accident or design she could not tell.

"I'm to stay until you get some nurses," Marcia went on. "I'll try to get Mr. Ward to go to bed. That's what you want, isn't it?"

There was no doubt now. The blinking was fast and definite.

"I'd better tell you about Greg Spencer, too, so you won't worry. I know you're fond of him. He isn't guilty, Mrs. Ward. Major Dane has been working on the case. He knows a lot the police don't know, so Greg's all right."

There was no blinking this time. The eyes gazed at her steadily and then abruptly closed. There was no expression at all on the wrinkled face, and Marcia found herself as deliberately cut off as though a door had been shut in her face. When Mr. Ward came in she was shading the lights, and his wife was apparently asleep.

She motioned him out into the hall and followed him.

"She's conscious," she said. "I suppose you know that."

"I had thought so. I wasn't certain."

"She seemed pleased when I told her you were going to bed. So please do, Mr. Ward. Show me the linen closet, in case I have to change the bed, and then I'll put on a dressing gown and take over."

"Alice and I did change the bed once," he said awkwardly. "There is a certain incontinence. I'm afraid we were clumsy. I'll wait for the doctor, Marcia. Then I may lie down for a while. It's been a bad day."

He did not go to bed, however. He went into an upper sitting room, and as she moved around she could see him there not reading, just waiting, his hands on the arms of his chair and his eyes gazing at nothing, with all hope dimmed out of them.

After the doctor's visit there was nothing left to do. She managed to get Mr. Ward to bed, and sat down by her patient, apparently still sleeping. The utter silence of the house bothered her. She had a suspicion, too, that her patient was not asleep; that when she moved around the room she was being watched. She was not a nervous woman, however. Even when at midnight the front doorbell rang it was only the wild blinking of the old lady's eyelids that surprised her.

Marcia got up.

"Water?" she inquired, and picked up the cup.

Mrs. Ward refused it. She continued to signal with her lids, however, and when the bell rang a second time it was almost wildly so.

"What is it? The doorbell?"

"Yes," the eyes signaled.

"Mr. Ward's going down. I hear him moving about in his room."

This was clearly wrong. With a look of complete despair the eyes closed, and Marcia went out into the hall. She was in time to see Mr. Ward in a dark dressing gown going down the stairs, and that he was holding a revolver in his hand as he did so.

She was prepared for anything by that time. If she had seen the old man level the gun and fire it she could hardly have been surprised. What she did not expect was to hear the friendly excited voice of Colonel Richardson, and to see Nathaniel quickly hide the gun in his pocket.

"I've just heard, Nat. Why in God's name didn't you send for me? You know I'd do anything I could."

"I know that, Henry. There isn't anything anyone can do. But come in. Marcia Dalton's with her now, until we can locate a nurse. She offered to stay."

"Sounds like her," said Henry approvingly. "Good girl, Marcia. Sound as a bell."

They went into a downstairs room and Marcia found herself still clutching the stair rail. Whom had Nathaniel Ward expected when the doorbell rang? Or before it rang? Why had Dane cautioned her? Did he suspect either of these elderly men of murder? The whole thing was preposterous. Yet she was not sure. Certainly Mrs. Ward had quieted, and not long after, Marcia heard the colonel leaving and old Nathaniel coming upstairs once more.

She dozed a little that night, and when at seven o'clock she heard Bertha, the cook, in her kitchen she let Alice relieve her and went down for some coffee. Bertha was red-eyed but talkative.

"Such a good woman, Miss Dalton," she said as she put the percolator on the stove. "And now to have this happen to her! First Mr. Terry goes to war. That almost finished her. And now this. Alice says she can't talk, or move herself around at all."

"People get over these things," Marcia said consolingly. "She may have some paralysis left, but she may live for quite a while."

She drank her coffee, standing by the kitchen stove, while Bertha talked.

"It happened all at once yesterday morning," she said. "She was watching those men digging up the hill. Then suddenly somebody over there yelled, and I heard Mr. Ward calling. When I got in there she was on the floor, and the poor old man bending over her and looking like death. You know," she said, turning honest eyes on Marcia, "there's been something funny going on lately. You know how honest this place is. Nobody locks anything up, or didn't until that girl was murdered. Well, we lost a couple of old blankets not so long ago. The madam told Alice to air them before she sent them to the Red

Cross in the village and Alice forgot them. The next day they were gone. First time that's happened, and I've been coming here with the family for twenty years."

That would interest Dane, Marcia thought, although she had no idea why. But before she left the kitchen she had learned that Terry had not been there at all that summer, or if he had, the servants did not know it.

She had learned one more thing to report before she left. She had carried her second cup of coffee into the living room, when the telephone rang. She picked it up and answered it. It was a long-distance call from San Francisco, a man's voice speaking.

"Hello," it said. "I'd like to speak to Mr. Ward, please."

"I'm sorry. He's asleep, but I'll get him. Is that you, Terry?"

"I beg your pardon?"

"Is that Terry? Terry Ward?"

"Lieutenant Ward is not here. I am simply giving a message from him. If Mr. Ward's asleep don't bother to wake him. Just tell him everything is all right. Got that? Everything is okay. He's not to worry."

"Everything is all right," she repeated. "Is that message from Terry?"

"Sorry. Time's up," said a voice, and the connection was broken.

Nathaniel Ward was still asleep under the influence of the barbiturate the doctor had given him when the nurse arrived that morning. Marcia wrote the message and carried it into his dressing room, to find him on the couch there, the weight of the weapon in his pocket dragging his robe to the floor. Next door, in the big double bed they had shared for so long, Mrs. Ward seemed to sleep fitfully. The strained look had gone out of her face.

Marcia reported to Dane that morning on her way home, her own long face tired and rather bleak.

"For what it's worth," she said when she finished, "they're both scared. She is, at least. She didn't want him to answer the doorbell."

She was rather surprised to find the emphasis Dane laid on the blankets, however.

"Did she say when this was?" he asked.

"Not long ago. That's all."

But it was his final question that left her in open-mouthed astonishment.

"How good are Mr. Ward's eyes?" he asked. "You know him. Does he have to wear glasses all the time?"

"He's practically blind without them."

He did not explain further. He let her go after that, telling her she was the fine person he had always suspected, and that she had done more than her one good deed that night. What the rest was he did not say, but she drove away that morning in a glow of self-satisfaction slightly modified by bewilderment.

TWENTY-FOUR

THAT WAS ON SATURDAY. For two days Greg had been in a police cell at the county seat. It was not too bad. He had a narrow bed, a chair, and a chest of drawers. He could order food brought in, but he ate very little. He had no knowledge of the excitement his arrest had caused, of the consultations in Washington, or of the reporters milling about the town. One of them even managed to be arrested, to find himself no nearer Greg than before.

He found the lack of action hard to bear. He spent hours smoking and pacing the brief bit of floor space, and in trying to think things out. Thinking, however, was not his long suit. That they were calling a special session of the Grand Jury he knew. Hart had gone, and a famous criminal lawyer was on his way up.

But his real longing was to get out of the mess and join his squadron again. He never doubted that he would, and even his love for Virginia faded beside that. He had wanted to marry her. God, yes. But more even than that he wanted the air again, to be with his own gang, to go out and give the dirty bastards hell, and then to come back, report, eat, and sleep, so as to be ready for the next mission.

He had no idea that Virginia had arrived at Bayside. Nor for that matter had Dane, drinking his before-lunch highball at the desk in what he called his study, and waiting for Alex to return from an errand. The first warning he had was a sort of volcanic eruption, when one of the porch chairs fell over and the front door slammed. The next moment he was confronted by a young and pretty redheaded girl.

"So that's the way you work to help Greg!" she said. "Sitting here and sopping up liquor while these damned fools try to send him to the chair!"

"Not the chair. No chair in this State."

His calmness and his grin stopped her cold. She stared at him.

"I see. It's not your neck, is that it?"

"Why not sit down? How much do you think you help by acting like a ten-year-old, Miss Demarest? I suppose that's who you are."

She subsided into a chair, but she still looked like a frightened willful child. Dane grinned at her.

"That's better," he said, "and just for your enlightenment, more crimes are solved at desks—with or without liquor—than by leg work. It takes both, of course. I might add that Carol Spencer has had enough to bear, without hysteria added to it."

"I'm not hysterical."

"Then behave like it."

He gave her a cigarette, and taking one himself, told her the essential facts; his own belief in Greg's innocence, the fact that he still had a few things up his sleeve, without explaining, and also the fact that if the Grand Jury brought in an indictment it was not fatal or even final.

"The cards are stacked against him at the hearing, of course," he said. "The district attorney calls his witnesses. The defense hasn't a chance. But, as I say, that means nothing."

She herself, completely subdued by that time, could tell him nothing. She knew Greg drank "when he was unhappy." She knew there were girls who married soldiers to get their allotments. But she was in a hell of a mess, to use her own words. She wasn't sending back her wedding presents. She still loved Greg, and she meant to marry him if it had to be in a prison cell. Whereupon she began to cry, produced a handkerchief, said tearfully that she had been an idiot, and departed more quietly than she had arrived.

He went back to his desk and his drink, thinking over the widening circle of every crime, the emotions involved, the people who were hurt, the lives that were blasted. War was different. You killed or were killed, but you left behind you only clean grief, without shame.

After some thought he added to his notes Marcia's report on

the telephone call from San Francisco.

(15) Everything is okay. Mr. Ward is not to worry.

Alex found him still there, the ash tray filled with cigarette stubs, one of them stained with lipstick which he saw immediately and ignored.

"I got Hank Miller alone all right, sir," he said. "Not easy on Saturday morning. I don't think he suspected anything."

"Extra canned goods, eh?"

"Plenty. All sorts. Cheese, sardines when Hank could get them, baked beans, anything that didn't have to be cooked. I said I'd heard it was black market stuff, and Hank showed me his slips."

"Still doing it?"

"Not for a week or so, sir."

"Well, it ought to be easy to find out where it went."

Dane took Carol with him for a drive that afternoon, both to get her away from Virginia and to have a little time with her himself. He had not yet retrieved his error on the mountain. She was too distressed about Greg, and he told himself philosophically that it could wait. But he did not take her to the mountain again. Instead, he circled around until he reached Pine Hill. Here he stopped the car and looked at her, smiling.

"How would you like to look for clues?" he inquired.

"What sort? I'm no good at that kind of thing, Jerry."

"Well, you have good eyes, as well as very lovely ones. Let's see what you can find. Suppose you wanted to hide a lot of tin cans somewhere. How would you go about it?"

"Hide them? You mean bury them?"

"I hardly think so, with all this undergrowth. Still, they might shine, I suppose. Maybe they're covered. Let's look, shall we?"

"Wait a minute," she said, as he started to get out of the car. "Do you mean someone's been living here?"

"There's a chance. That's what we're here to find out."

He did not need to explain further, and it was Carol herself who found them, hidden neatly under an old box near the deserted stable. She stood looking down at them, with Dane beside her.

"Then this means—"

"It may be one thing to help Greg," he told her. "Don't count on it too much, my darling. There's still a lot to be done, but this is the first real step. And it's yours."

When they got back into the car his face was set and so absent that she thought he had already forgotten her.

"I'm going to see Floyd," he told her. "I'll drop you off in the lane. And don't speak of what we've found. Not to anyone. It might be dangerous."

After he left her he drove smartly into the village, to find Colonel Richardson entering Floyd's office, with Floyd at his usual place and Mason with his chair tilted back in a corner. Neither man rose, and the colonel remained standing before the desk. None of them noticed Dane.

"Well, colonel," Floyd said, "anything I can do for you?"

"I have something to tell you," said the colonel, standing with his hat in his hand and his white hair blowing softly in the breeze from an open window. "It will, I hope, save Captain Spencer from an indictment next week. He is innocent, but these things stick, sir."

The chief gave Dane a quick glance but did not greet him.

"You'll be good if you can save Spencer, colonel," he observed casually. "We have enough to convict him two or three times. He was married to the Barbour woman, he was engaged to a redhead—she's here, and a good excuse for murder any time—and he has no alibi for the night the girl was killed. I think he was here and we can prove it. What more do you want?"

The colonel sat down, carefully placing his hat on his knee.

"I can prove he did not shoot his sister, sir," he said stiffly.

"What's that got to do with it? We've never claimed he did."

The colonel flushed.

"You think that we have more than one murderer in this vicinity? That's nonsense, Floyd."

"Why more than one?"

"I'm not alone in the conviction that Gregory Spencer has

committed no crime," he said slowly. "Perhaps I should have spoken sooner, but things have been moving fast. But with Mrs. Ward having a stroke, and Nathaniel carrying a gun even last night when I distinctly saw it in his dressing gown pocket—"

Floyd was looking astonished.

"See here," he said, "you're not accusing old Mr. Ward of shooting anybody, are you?"

"Certainly not. The man who shot Elinor Hilliard was taller than Nathaniel."

"For God's sweet sake!" Floyd shouted. "Are you saying you saw him?"

"I did. Not close enough to recognize him, but I certainly saw him."

Sheer amazement kept Floyd silent. Mason's jaw had dropped. Neither one paid any attention to Dane or interrupted as the colonel told his story.

On the night Elinor had been shot, he said, he had unfortunately taken coffee after dinner, with the result that he could not sleep. He had gone downstairs about one o'clock to get a magazine, and was at the table in the center of the room when he saw a face at the window. It was raining hard. The pane was wet, and it was merely a flash, but there was no mistake about it.

He had put out the light at once and gone outside. There was no one there, but he heard someone running. He could see that it was a man, fairly tall and in a dark overcoat or raincoat, but that was all.

However, several suspicious things had been happening, the colonel explained, including Dane now in his glance, "so I thought it best to follow him. He went up the lane between Rockhill, the Ward place, and Crestview. I tried to follow him to see who it was, but I was in bedroom slippers and I'm not so young as I was. That was when I heard the shot."

"Why haven't you reported this sooner?" Floyd asked angrily.

"I would not be here at all," the colonel said simply, "but an old and dear friend passed away an hour ago. Mrs. Ward is dead. This cannot hurt her now."

"What does that mean?"

The colonel drew a long breath. His color was bad, Dane noticed.

"The fellow turned in at the Ward place," he said, and was silent.

It was a moment before Floyd spoke.

"And that's all? You didn't investigate further?"

Colonel Richardson looked at him bleakly.

"I found Elinor Hilliard," he said. "I pulled her up on the hillside, away from where some late car might run over her. She was lying in the lane. Then I ran back to my house and telephoned the doctor. His line was busy, and I was trying to get the hospital when I heard people running about and calling. I knew then she had been found. After that I—well, I just kept quiet. If she had been killed I'd have had to tell what I know, of course."

Floyd was watching him intently, his eyes hard and suspicious.

"Why are you telling it now?" he inquired.

"Because it was not Gregory Spencer. I've known Greg all his life, and this man was not so tall. I've a hard decision to make, but I can't allow an innocent man to be tried for his life."

"Who was it? You know, don't you?"

"I'm not sure, but I'm afraid it was Terry Ward." He drew a long breath. "Remember, I'm making no accusation. And I don't think the shooting was deliberate. I was after him and Mrs. Hilliard got in his way. But he's had a long, grueling experience as a fighter pilot. He may be suffering from combat fatigue. I don't know."

Dane spoke for the first time.

"Does Mrs. Hilliard know you moved her?" he asked.

"I don't think so. She was completely unconscious. Shock, of course."

"Have you any idea why she was out in the rain that night?"

The colonel stirred unhappily.

"She must have been on her way to the Wards'," he said. "That's obvious. She had followed the path to the lane and was crossing it. He may not have meant to kill her or even shoot her. He wanted to scare her, probably."

"And have you told the Wards this story?" Floyd demanded furiously.

"No. I would not have come at all, but I cannot allow Carol Spencer's brother to be crucified without a protest."

He turned quietly and went out, closing the door behind him.

TWENTY-FIVE

DANE REMAINED BEHIND when the colonel left. Floyd sat staring at the door, his mouth partly open, and Jim Mason let his chair down with a thump. Floyd's eyes slowly turned to Dane.

"What brings you here?" he inquired. "Were you in that lane too when the Hilliard woman was shot? Looks like the whole summer colony gets around in the middle of the night. Maybe you did the shooting," he added. "You are quite a shot, aren't you?"

"I haven't been camping out at Pine Hill for two weeks or so."

"And who has? We searched that place. Nothing there but the blankets."

"If you'll look again you'll find a number of fresh tin cans there, by the garage."

"And what would that mean?" Floyd roared. "What's the idea anyhow? Are you all in cahoots to try to save Greg Spencer? Some hobo camps out in an empty house, and all at once he kills a girl, shoots a woman, and scares Lucy Norton to death! The colonel says he sees him, you find where he's been staying, and there's your killer!"

Having done his duty, Dane drove slowly home. One part of the colonel's story had struck him as distinctly odd. He was still thinking it over when he saw him on the street ahead, walking slowly and dejectedly home. He stopped the car.

"Care for a lift?" he asked.

The colonel roused himself.

"Thanks. Yes, I would. I'm not as young as I like to think I am, major."

When they started again Dane reverted at once to the colonel's experience the night Elinor was shot.

"I can see you were in a difficult position," he said. "You're not sure it was Terry Ward, are you?"

"What am I to think? It was someone who knew his way around, and war does strange things to men. I know that."

"Would Mr. Ward go armed against his own grandson?"

The colonel's color rose. He looked goaded and unhappy.

"I'm afraid he's going armed against me. He hasn't been the same for some time. He may have seen me moving Elinor, you know. May have heard the shot and come out." He tried to light a cigarette with uncertain hands. "He's been different since then. We used to play a good bit of chess together. We haven't for some time."

The picture of the two elderly men, each suspecting the other, was rather pathetic. It was the old story, Dane thought, no one being entirely frank. It was the same with every crime.

"Just what do you know about Terry Ward, Colonel Richardson? Known him a long time?"

"Since he was born. Knew his father before him. Fine Boston family, you know. His grandmother's death will be a blow to the boy. Only thing is"—the colonel cleared his throat—"he'd never shoot Elinor. There may have been some reason for the other. God knows I judge nobody. But why Elinor?"

"It was raining hard. He may not have seen who it was. You yourself said something like that, sir."

The colonel looked uncertain. He even looked shaken.

"I can't help, I'm afraid," he said thickly. "Nat won't see me. He won't see anybody today. He's a broken man."

"Have you any idea where Terry is now?"

"Gone, I suppose. They move fast these days. Hop a plane and are back on some God-forsaken island before you know it. I shouldn't say that perhaps. My own son may be on just such an island. You know, I'm considered something of a crackpot around here." He smiled faintly.

"Really? About what?"

"About my son. We were very close. After my wife's death I had only the boy, and—well, let that go. Only I've always felt that I would know if anything had happened to him. Maybe you think that's foolish."

"Not at all," Dane said gravely.

"For instance, I knew when he had pneumonia in college.

I wakened out of a sound sleep, and I was so sure that I telephoned at once. He had it, you see. It's—well, I suppose it's psychic, although I don't like the word."

He got a clipping from his wallet. It was the story of a flier found after months on a Pacific island, where the natives had kept him alive. He had been badly injured, but had returned to duty. Dane read it gravely.

"Am I to understand that you think this may be your son?" he inquired.

Henry's face fell.

"That would be too much to hope, I expect. But it shows it can happen, doesn't it? There are so many islands," he added, almost wistfully, "and I've never felt that Don was gone."

"There's always hope," Dane said. "That's what keeps most of us ticking, isn't it?"

The colonel got out stiffly at his gate. He had aged even in the last day or so, and it seemed absurd that Nathaniel could suspect him of anything. Or was it? Dane pondered that on his way home. The story could be true, or it could be a cleverly concocted one, made up after all the evidence was in. The colonel had been a military man. He was used to firearms, and his story of having found Elinor in the lane was as incredible as Floyd had evidently regarded it.

He wanted badly to talk to Mr. Ward, but this was not the time for it, with Terry flying back to the blue inferno of the Pacific, with Mrs. Ward lying dead, and Nathaniel himself wandering around like an ancient distracted ghost. Time was growing short too. He still had no alibi for Greg in New York. Tim had had men working on it from his own agency, but with the plethora of army officers in the city and the definite percentage of them who drank to excess after prolonged battle strain, they had failed utterly.

In the end he decided to see Elinor again. He found her looking better, the room full of flowers, and a nurse reading a book by a window. Elinor looked frightened when she saw him. He went over to the bed.

"I would like to talk to you, Mrs. Hilliard," he said. "If you want the nurse to stay it is all right with me."

Certainly she did not want the nurse. She sent her out

quickly. Dane closed the door and went back to the bed.

"I'm wondering," he said, "if you are really willing to let your brother be found guilty of a murder you know he didn't commit?"

She looked terrified. She cowered back among her pillows, as though she feared actual bodily violence.

"I can't talk," she said wildly. "I can't say I was here that night. It would wreck my life. Howard's too, all he has built for himself."

"So that's all you are thinking of?"

She had recovered somewhat by this time.

"I told you before. I don't know who did it. I don't know anything about it. I found her on the doorstep, and I left her there."

"Will you swear to that in court? Because I'm going to see that you are called at the trial."

"I won't go to court," she said obstinately. "I'll leave the country first." She was sullen now. "Maybe Greg did it. How do I know? She was already dead, I tell you."

"Was it Greg you drove away that night, Mrs. Hilliard?"

She collapsed then. He got no more out of her. The nurse, returning, found her alone and weeping noisily, and when Dr. Harrison arrived he gave her a sedative.

"Tragic about her brother," he said as he left. "She's devoted to him."

In a way Dane had played his last card. The solution, in view of Elinor's silence, had to lie elsewhere, and he decided to fly to the Coast. He told Carol his plan that evening, sitting on the terrace in the warm darkness, with Virginia in bed and only the sleepy call of a gull now and then to break the silence.

"The story's out there," he said, "and my leave is over soon. There's no time to waste."

"But you'll be coming back here?"

Something in her voice made him reach over and take her hand, now bare of Don's ring. He touched that finger gently.

"Before I go I want to ask you something," he said. "Are you still remembering Don Richardson? Do you still think he may come back? And if he ever does will you marry him?"

"He will never cóme back, Jerry," she said positively. "I know that."

"But if he does?"

"No," she said simply.

He let go her hand.

"I've never thought of myself as a marrying man," he said soberly. "In a way I have no right to ask any girl to marry me. My work is pretty important. Don't get any false ideas about it. It's not sensational, but it cuts me off from normal living. It takes all I've got, and sometimes more."

She stirred in the dark.

"Are you proposing to me? Or are you giving me up?" she inquired.

"Both," he said promptly. "I want you to wait for me, my darling. I want you to come back to. Good God, Carol, I wonder if you know what that would mean?"

"I will wait," she said. "No matter what happens, I will always wait, Jerry."

Then and only then he took her in his arms.

He left for the Coast the next day, Sunday, and he was still there when the Grand Jury met on Wednesday. The county seat was jammed with reporters and cameramen. Carol found herself in a small hotel room, with only a bed, a dresser and a chair or two, and with a group of newspapermen next door who banged things about, talked all night, and apparently drank when they were not talking.

Evidently Campbell and Floyd had built their case carefully. There was an air of assurance about the district attorney as he made his opening speech to the twenty-three men who sat in a semicircle around the room.

"It becomes my duty, as the representative of this sovereign state," he began pompously, "to bring to your attention one of the most cruel crimes in our history. On the night of Friday, June sixteenth last, a summer night when our citizenry slept or worked to further a disastrous war, a young woman was done to death in the village of Bayside, in this county.

"Not only was she murdered by a heavy blow on the head, but an attempt was made to destroy her body. Her effects were taken to conceal her identity, and a quantity of inflammable liquid was poured over her and subsequently ignited."

He went into details here, of the discovery of the body, the failure to locate the missing clothing, and the fatal identification. "A young woman, not yet thirty, and so far as we have discovered without family, except for a child which had been born some time previously.

"This woman came from Los Angeles, where she had given her child to a family with the idea of adoption soon after its birth. She had continued to see this boy, now two years old, at intervals, and we have the statement of the foster mother that on her last visit she was in a cheerful frame of mind.

"Yet she came to Bayside, in this state, to a large summer estate known as Crestview, and there she was done to death."

He elaborated on the size of Crestview, "an establishment of so many rooms they had to be referred to by name;" that she had been assigned by the caretaker to what was known as the yellow room, and from this yellow room she had gone to meet her death.

"We know now what she told the caretaker, to obtain admission to the house. She told her that she was married, and to whom, and we will later present the certificate of this marriage discovered—along with her other effects—through the acumen of Samuel Floyd, the chief of police in Bayside.

"Unfortunately this caretaker, one Lucy Norton, is now herself dead, under circumstances which I shall not ask you to consider. But you will learn that every effort was made to conceal and destroy not only this young woman herself, but her personal effects.

"However, we now have certain facts which point to a certain individual as guilty of this heinous crime. These facts will be presented to you by various witnesses, and you will then decide whether or not to bring in a true bill against this prisoner.

"Shall we proceed, Mr. Foreman?"

Carol was the first witness. She had made her way through the curious crowd outside on her arrival with her head high, paying no attention to the cameramen as they shot her, but in the Grand Jury room she felt as though she was before a medieval inquisition. As she sat down she sensed that the men gazing at her were unfriendly; that she represented to most of them the idle rich, who lived on the bent backs of the rest of the world. Nevertheless, she told her story clearly, the finding of the house locked and Lucy gone, the discovery by Freda—now unfortunately departed into the limbo of domestic service elsewhere—and her own brief sight of the body.

She was shown the crushed white hat, the burned fur jacket, slippers, and the piece of the red negligee. But she refused to identify them. "They were brought to me later," she said. "I did not see them on the—on the body. I only saw there was someone there."

When they let her go she was relieved to find young Starr waiting for her outside, his old car at the curb and his grin as engaging as ever.

"How about a drink?" he inquired cheerfully. "Don't mind those old bozos in there. It's not a trial, you know."

"They looked as though they hated me."

"So what?" he said, pushing her through the crowd. "I wouldn't trust one of them in the dark with you. That ain't hate."

He took her to a small bar and ordered her a brandy. He took beer himself, and when they were settled at a small table he watched her color come back. When she seemed all right again he leaned forward confidentially.

"I'm in kind of a jam myself," he told her. "Haven't known whether to talk or not. You see I was around your place right after they took Mrs. Hilliard to the hospital."

"How does that put you in a jam?"

"Well, it's like this," he said, lowering his voice. "I'd been hanging around the town all day. Mrs. Norton had been found dead, and it looked queer as all hell. On the floor, with a broken leg and so on. Then when I started back about one o'clock that night I saw the ambulance coming out of your drive, and another car after it. That looked funny, so I left my car and walked up to your place.

"I was just looking around, you know. It was raining hard, but I kinda like rain. And there was a ladder under what you call the yellow room. I guess I hadn't any business to do it, but I suppose you know what I found. Somebody had been there before me. Maybe I ought to tell the police about it. I don't know. I damn near told Dane about it. I guess I funked it. He scares me, that guy."

"I don't see why. He's very kind."

He stared at her.

"Kind!" he said. "I wouldn't like to go up against him. That's all I can say. He was in the FBI before the war. I saw him kill a man myself."

Carol caught her breath.

"What sort of a man?" she asked, her voice uncertain.

"Gangster, right here in this town. Don't let that worry you. He needed killing. I guess Dane's been doing special work since the war. Secret stuff, you know. The way those fellows are trained—!" He smiled at her again. "I kind of suspected Dane of murdering that girl. Looked like spy stuff. That's out now."

Seeing that this new picture of Dane had disturbed her, he reverted to the yellow room. Had the police noticed the loose baseboard in it? Had she any idea what the girl might have hidden behind it? And who did she think had torn the room apart?

When he found she knew nothing he took her back to the hotel; to the bleak room with its bed and bureau and chair, and its silence, since the press was still waiting outside the Grand Jury room. It stood there, watching the faces of witnesses, dropping endless cigarette butts on the wooden floor, and making bets on the outcome, with the odds in favor of indictment.

TWENTY-SIX

THE SESSION WAS STILL GOING ON, in secrecy and under oaths of silence. Impressed witnesses came and went. Floyd, Dr. Harrison, Marcia Dalton, tearful and not certain now she had seen Elinor's car the night of the murder; making a bad impression too, as though she were shielding someone. The bus driver who had brought the girl, and Sam Thompson, with his story of her looking through his telephone directory.

The list of exhibits grew. It now included the ring, the marriage certificate with a sworn statement by a Mexican magistrate that he had married Marguerite Barbour and one Gregory Spencer a year before, the dead girl's clothing and bags, uncovered on the hill, and the pitiful fragments of what she had worn the night of her death.

Except for the marriage certificate her handbag had contained little of importance, a hundred-odd dollars in bills and currency, the usual powder, rouge and lipstick, some cleansing tissue, a receipt from the hotel in New York, a return railroad ticket to New York, and a check for her suitcase at Grand Central. The suitcase itself was added to the list of exhibits, with the baby's picture shown for its psychological effect on the jurors. Thereafter Campbell referred to her as "this mother," with due effect.

The table became loaded. There was even the pitcher from the attic, with a laboratory report that it had contained gasoline, and the State's contention that it had been used to prevent the discovery of the buried effects.

But the State also added one exhibit which explained what had been a mystery to Maggie. It produced the large oilcan which had disappeared from her kitchen, and Hank Williams to testify that he had sent Lucy Norton a gallon of the fluid on the morning of the murder. Maggie, brought over by Floyd under protest and put on oath, was obliged to state that it was almost empty when she had first seen it at Crestview on her arrival.

The foreman of the jury put on his glasses and inspected it.

"Is it the State's contention that the contents of this—er—holder were used in an attempt to destroy the body?"

"It is."

The oilcan had its proper effect on the jury. It was a familiar thing. They used ones like it in their own kitchens, yet here was one which had been debased to a sickening purpose. The district attorney saw this and was contented, and because Greg's attorneys knew fairly well what was going on, that—in effect—no holds were barred, they at last took an unusual step. They requested that Greg himself be allowed to appear.

Campbell stood for some time, the formal application in his hand. Then, sure of what he had, he agreed.

"The defendant has applied for permission to appear here," he said to the jury. "If it is the will of this body to hear him we will produce him."

The Grand Jury agreed, and Greg was duly warned by the foreman.

"This jury is willing to hear what you have to say. You have come here of your own free will. What you say will be at your own instance. Remember this, however. Everything you say will be recorded here, and may be used as evidence against you if we so decide."

But Campbell was not so sure when Greg appeared. He impressed them, there was no doubt about it. His size, his good looks, his uniform and the ribbons he wore. He acknowledged at once that he had married the girl, under the influence of liquor and what he now thought might have been marijuana. When shown the ring, however, he denied ever buying it. He left the country after the marriage, sending her a thousand dollars and hoping never to see her again. Asked about the child, he said he understood there was one two years old. If so, it was not his. He had never known her until the night he met her, when she was introduced to him by somebody. "But there was a crowd. I don't remember who it was."

He stated flatly that he had been in New York the night of

the murder. Unfortunately he had no alibi, but his attorneys were working on that. He had had a letter from the girl saying she was coming east to see his family. He had tried to head her off, but was too late. He had not come to Bayside at all until the Thursday after her death.

Asked if he had gone to see Lucy Norton at the hospital he denied it absolutely. As for why he had come to Crestview the night of the fire, he had come because his two sisters were alone there. No, he had not set fire to the hill. He had not known there was anything buried there.

He was pale and sweating when they finished with him. They took him back under guard to his police cell, and a kindly officer brought him some whisky.

"Understand those fellows ripped the guts right out of you," he said.

"They made me look like a fool," Greg said. "And act like a murderer," he added bitterly.

Campbell was cheerful at the end, although his face was grave.

"Remember this," he said impressively. "This woman—this mother—stood in his way. He was engaged to a young and lovely girl, of his own class. The preparations were made for this marriage, and then what happened? This woman who is now dead wrote to him. She intended to see his family, to claim what was rightfully hers. She was on her way east.

"He knew this would be fatal to his hopes. It is the State's contention that, having missed her in New York, he went to Newport and there in all probability obtained his sister's car; that in it he drove to Bayside, in some manner induced her to admit him to the house there, and there with intention and premeditation did her to death."

There was more. Campbell gave himself a free rein, and when at last he stated that he had done his duty and depended on the jury to do the same, there was not much question as to the issue. Two hours after he had finished they brought in a true bill, and the next day Gregory Spencer was taken to court and arraigned for first-degree murder. He listened to the indictment as it was read, said "Not guilty" in a clear voice, and gazed still with the hurt look in his eyes to where Carol and

Virginia were sitting in the courtroom.

Virginia gave him a brilliant smile . . .

Dane read all this in a Los Angeles paper. He had reached the Coast on Monday morning, having changed into civilian clothes on the way. Now it was Thursday, and so far he had drawn almost a complete blank. There was no chance of learning anything about the party at which Greg had met Marguerite, or who had constituted it. The town was filled with officers, coming and going.

Nor did his search for a previous marriage of the murdered girl help him any. He went to Tia Juana, without result. She could have married anyone, anywhere. Neither Arizona nor Nevada required tests or delays for licenses. And when he attempted in San Francisco to trace the telephone call which had notified the Wards that everything was okay, he found after long investigation that it had been made from a pay booth.

Two things he did get, through the Los Angeles police. The first was where Marguerite had bought her wedding ring and had it engraved. It was a small shop, and the jeweler was repairing a watch when he entered. He worked for a few minutes before he took the glass from his eye.

"Anything I can do for you?"

"I understand you sold a wedding ring to a young woman, and engraved it. The letters were 'G to M'."

The jeweler eyed him.

"Well, that's my business," he said shortly.

"I'd be glad if you could tell me any details."

"Details? There weren't any. She wanted it engraved while she waited. I don't do things that way, but she had to catch a train. I did it. She paid me. That's all."

The other information was more valuable. Again through the police he located the young woman who was caring for Marguerite's child.

On the Thursday he read that Greg had been indicted he took a taxi to an unfashionable part of town, and saw a neat white bungalow, with a small child, a boy, in a play pen in the yard. There was no one else in sight, and he walked over to the child.

"Hello, there," he said. "What's your name?"

The boy grinned, showing a partly toothless mouth, and

holding out a toy to Dane.

"All alone, are you, son? Where's your mother?"

She came out then, a pleasant-looking young woman. The police had given him her name, Mrs. Gates, and he smiled at her over the baby's play pen.

"Fine child you have here," he said pleasantly.

"Yes, isn't he? And good, too."

"You're Mrs. Gates?"

"Mrs. Jarvis Gates. Yes."

"I'd like to talk to you about—what's the boy's name?"

She stiffened.

"It's Pete," she said defiantly. "And I've been told not to talk to anybody."

"I'm working on this case, Mrs. Gates. After all, since his mother has been killed—"

"I'm not talking. I may have to go east to the trial. I didn't like her much, but all I can say is that if that man killed her I hope he gets what's coming to him."

It was some time before he could persuade her into the house. She took the boy with her and held him, as if Dane might have designs on him. The bungalow was small but neat. The front door opened into a diminutive living room, and beyond that was a bedroom. Behind he surmised was a kitchen and not much else. Evidently there was no money to waste here, he decided, and produced fifty dollars in tens and fives from his wallet.

He did not give them to her, however. He placed them on a mission oak table at his elbow.

"I want to ask you some questions, Mrs. Gates. If you don't care to answer them you don't have to, of course. And I assure you Pete is safe, so long as you want to keep him."

"I've had him for two years." Her eyes filled with sudden tears. "If they try to take him away—"

"I'm sure nobody has any such intention."

"We want to adopt him, my husband and I. We wanted to right along, but she wouldn't let us. She said he was her ace in the hole, whatever that means."

"I see," Dane said. "How did you get him in the first place?"

Either the money or his assurance that she could keep the

child loosened her tongue.

"I was in the hospital when he was born," she said. "I had just lost my own baby, and she heard about it. Maybe you know what she was like. She didn't want a baby around. She liked men and parties. She—well, she didn't want to be bothered. Anyhow she said I could have the baby. She would pay a little to help take care of him, and she promised that someday we could adopt him."

"She didn't mention the boy's father?"

"No. That's why I thought—well, I thought maybe she wasn't married. She'd used the name Barbour at the hospital, Marguerite Barbour. She didn't care for the baby, you know." She looked at Dane. "I mean, she was keeping him for some reason or other, but she didn't pay any real attention to him. She didn't even pay for him regularly.

"Then one day in the spring she came here. She was all dressed up, and she said she was going east before long. I remember what she wore, a black dress and a white hat, and a fox jacket. She said she'd paid five hundred dollars for it. And she had a bag with her initials on it, M.D.B. I asked her where she'd got all the money, but she just laughed at me.

"She said she wouldn't be gone long, and that I'd hear from her soon. She was going to New York. She didn't say why, but she owed me a lot for the baby's keep, and she promised to send it as soon as she got there. But I didn't get the money, and Jarvis had flu and was out of work. Then I saw about this murder, and the clothes and so on, so one day I just went to the police. I was afraid it might be her."

That was all. He left the fifty dollars on the table, smiled at the baby, and having got the name of the hospital concerned, took his waiting taxi and drove to it. Here at first he met with disappointment. The hospital did not disclose such information as he required. He would understand that now and then they had unmarried mothers. They had no right to disclose their names.

It required his calling the FBI before they permitted him to see their files, and the FBI in the shape of a cheerful ex-associate of his chose to be funny.

"Maternity hospital!" he said. "For God's sake, Dane, what

are you doing there? Having a baby?"

In the end he got the authority, however. The cards for two years before were placed at his disposal, and he ran rapidly through them. He found Elizabeth Gates, white, Protestant, age twenty-seven. Female infant dead on birth. And he found Marguerite Barbour, also Protestant, age twenty-six. Male child, weight seven and a half pounds.

He went back to his hotel. The day was hot, and he took a cool bath before he looked at the papers. Greg had been indicted. He even rated the first page, along with the war news. Murder Charged Against Medal Holder. Grand Jury Finds True Bill Against Spencer. War Ace Indicted. It was not unexpected, but the headlines gave him a shock.

He obtained Marguerite's former address from Mrs. Gates before he left. Now, because he felt that action—any action—was imperative, he drove there. It was a typical boardinghouse, with a pleasant little rotund woman in charge.

"Yes, she lived here," she said. "I told the police all I knew. There's no use going up to her room either. They searched it, and I have a nice schoolteacher in it now."

"I don't want to look at the room," he said, to her evident relief. "I'd like to talk about Marguerite Barbour herself."

She led him into a small neat parlor and sat down opposite him.

"I'll tell you all I know," she said. "I didn't like her. I keep a respectable house, and she—well, I had my doubts about her. But when she came she was going to have a baby. The town was crowded already. I had a room, and I couldn't turn her away. Anyhow she paid her rent regularly, which is more than I can say for some of them."

"How did she pay the rent?"

She seemed surprised.

"On the first of the month."

"How? In cash?"

"She paid by check."

"Didn't that strike you as unusual? If she was earning her living the way you think she was, she'd be likely to pay cash, wouldn't she?"

The landlady flushed delicately.

"She's dead," she said. "I'm not saying any evil about her. Anyhow she had money of her own. She said it was an allowance from an uncle, but when I think of it that's queer. No uncle has turned up since."

"I see," Dane said thoughtfully. "How did she get this allowance?"

"Every month, by mail. It was a postal money order. I know that, because she had to take her driver's license for identification to get it cashed. She had a car, you know."

"This uncle—did she ever say anything about him?"

"No. I think he came to see her once about two years ago. I wasn't here, but the maid told me. She's gone now—the maid, I mean—but she said he was a gentleman. Not the sort she mostly ran around with. Of course, I never let any of my girls take men to their rooms."

Dane considered that.

"Old or young?" he asked.

"She didn't say."

"This sum of money every month—she might have been blackmailing somebody," he suggested.

The landlady had never thought of that, although she "wouldn't put it past her." Asked as to where the letters came from she said she hadn't noticed, but the last one had arrived about the first week in June. She thought it came from Maine. There had been none since.

As Dane limped out to his waiting cab he realized that his leg was bothering him again. He wondered if excitement did not make it worse, for under his veneer of cool impassivity he realized that he was excited. The dates, the clues all fitted. He needed only one fact to complete his evidence, and he got it by long-distance that night. But he was not happy. As the cab started he was more depressed than he had thought was possible when he began to see his way through a case.

TWENTY-SEVEN

IT WAS MONDAY NIGHT when he got out of the plane and saw Alex's disapproving eye in the glare of the car's headlights. The heat even at that hour was appalling, New England going through its brief but annual hot spell. It was like being plunged into a Turkish bath, and he said so as Alex stowed away his bag.

"Better over by the sea, sir," Alex said dryly. "What you been doing to that leg?"

"The leg's all right. I'm tired, that's all."

Alex glanced at him. Dane's lean stern face looked tired and there were new lines in it, but Alex thought it best to ignore them. In answer to questions he made his usual brief replies. Nobody had been seen around Crestview. The redhead had gone home. Mrs. Hilliard was still in the hospital, but he'd heard she was up and around. Hilliard himself had gone. As for Floyd, he was strutting around so puffed up he'd had to let his belt out.

It was too late to see Carol. But Alex's statement about the heat had proved erroneous. He did not go to bed. Instead, he changed into slacks and a thin sleeveless jersey and went out of the house. For some reason he felt uneasy. He lit a cigarette, and wandering over to Crestview found Tim near the lane. He was standing there gazing up the road, and Dane's silent approach made him jump and grab for his gun. He smiled sheepishly when he saw in the starlight who it was.

"Hell!" he said disgustedly. "My nerves are about shot. How long am I to keep this up?"

"Anything new?"

"I think we've located Greg Spencer in New York the night of the murder. Not sure yet, but it looks like it."

Dane nodded.

"That's a big help," he said. "What were you watching when I came up?"

"I don't know. Where does this road go anyhow?"

"It joins a paved one up above. Why?"

"There was somebody on it a few minutes ago. Went up the hill. Anybody live up there?"

Dane was thoughtful.

"Maybe somebody who lives back in the country. Only empty summer places near. How long ago was it, Tim?"

"Ten minutes or so. I didn't see who it was. It's kind of rough walking. Heard him stumble."

"Stay here. I'll go up a bit. It's too hot to sleep anyhow."

The lane *was* rough walking. Dane had no particular reason for climbing it. There were a dozen possible reasons for someone to be out at one o'clock in the morning. But the exercise was good after his long trip in the plane, and there was a slight breeze now coming down from the hills. He went on, without any attempt at caution, cheerful because his leg responded well and his muscles had not lost their tone. When he reached the upper road he turned left, by a sort of automatism. The deserted house lay there, shielded by its overgrowing shrubbery and trees and faintly outlined in the starlight. It had no interest for him. It had served its purpose. And he had walked far enough.

It was when he turned to go back that he saw the light by the stable, low down and moving slowly. It was swinging around, forming small circles, then going on, as if searching for something on the ground. He watched it for some time before he started cautiously toward it. He was badly dressed for working his way through the underbrush. His slacks caught on briers and his slippers did little to protect his bare feet and ankles. His long training helped him, however. He was within fifty feet of the stooping figure when a branch caught his sleeve and broke with a loud snap.

He never heard the shot. Something hit him on the head and he felt himself falling. He lost consciousness at once.

Carol was awakened that night by the telephone beside her bed. Out of sheer exhaustion she was sleeping heavily. The radium dial of her clock as she fumbled for the instrument showed it was two o'clock, and her voice was thick as she answered it.

Dr. Harrison was on the wire. He sounded apologetic.

"Is that you, Carol?" he asked. "I thought I'd better call you up. We've had another accident, if you can call it that. Nothing to frighten you," he added hastily, "but Major Dane's been hurt."

The room swirled around her. By a great effort she controlled her voice.

"How badly?"

"It's not very serious. He's still out. We're taking pictures, but apparently there is no fracture. He'll do nicely, but I thought I'd better let you know."

She was trembling now.

"What happened to him, doctor? Don't tell me it's another—" Her voice broke. "Someone attacked him. That's it, isn't it?"

"He was shot. Just a crease along the head, but he's had a narrow escape. He probably fell heavily, and that didn't help things."

She was out of bed by that time, still holding the receiver.

"I'm coming down," she told him. "I'll be there in fifteen minutes."

She heard him saying urgently that she was to stay in the house, that apparently nobody was safe. But she put down the receiver while he was still talking. She dressed frantically, although some remnant of caution remained in her. She went to find Tim, but Tim was not in his room. She found him in the hospital when she got there, pacing the hall downstairs like a wild man. "Goddammit, I let him go up that hill myself! Me, Tim Murphy!" Then, seeing her face, he made an effort at control. "He'll be all right, Miss Carol. He's been through worse than this. Has more lives than a cat. Just remember that."

She sat down, because her knees would not hold her. The hospital was wide awake and active, nurses hastily roused and busy, and an intern coming out of the X-ray room with plates in his hand. He gave Carol a nod.

"Looks all right," he said reassuringly. "Had the hell of a

wallop, of course."

Tim thrust himself forward.

"We're seeing him," he said aggressively. "I want to know who shot at him. Then I'm going out and get the——" Here his language became unprintable. He used a few army words not common in polite society, and added some of his own invention.

The intern looked amused, Tim's costume and language both being on the lurid side.

"No objection to your going up, I imagine," he said genially. "Dr. Harrison's expecting Miss Spencer anyhow. Only"—he added with a grin—"I'd advise you to do your talking now. I can take it. Dane can't."

They followed him to the elevator, Tim indignant but silent, Carol beyond speech. Dr. Harrison was in an upper hall, and he examined the plates by the light of a nurse's desk lamp before he spoke to them. He looked up cheerfully.

"No fracture," he said genially. "Just a scalp wound. He'll come around pretty soon, I imagine."

Some of Tim's fury abated. As for Carol, she drew her first full breath since she had heard the news, although Tim's story did not help much. He told about Dane's appearance, his decision to walk up the lane, and then of hearing the shot. When Dane did not come back he had started up the hill. He saw nobody, heard nothing. He had a flashlight, but "all those places are grown up like nobody's business." Anyhow, he was still searching when he heard the siren of Floyd's car. It had stopped near him and Floyd and Mason got out. Floyd had pointed a gun at him.

"Like to scared the life out of me," Tim said. "Thought I'd shot somebody. Wanted to know what I was doing there, and where was the man who'd been killed. I almost burst out crying. 'I'm looking for Major Dane,' I said. 'He came up here and he hasn't come back.' He didn't trust me even then. He took my gun and saw it hadn't been fired. Then he led the way back to the stable."

Carol was trying to make a coherent pattern of all this.

"But—Floyd?" she said. "How did he know?"

"Got a telephone message. It said somebody was dead by

the stable at Pine Hill. Can you beat it? How many people were up there tonight?"

It was some little time before they were allowed in to see Dane. He was not alone. Alex was standing like an infuriated guardian angel over the bed. Nobody spoke. Dane's eyes were closed, but as Carol moved to him he looked up.

"Hello, darling," he said. Then something strange about the situation roused him. "What the hell happened?" he said. "Where am I?"

"You're all right, Jerry."

He gave her his old sardonic grin.

"That's what you say," he said, and closed his eyes again.

He was not unconscious, however. His head throbbed, but his mind was slowly clearing. When he looked up a few minutes later only Alex was in the room. Dane motioned to him, and he came over to the bed.

"Soon as it's daylight," he said cautiously, "go up to Pine Hill. Take Tim if you can. Anyhow, get there before Floyd wakes up to it." He paused. Talking was still an effort. "Whoever shot me was hunting something on the ground by the stable there. Better bring everything you find."

It was still dark when he was left alone to sleep if he could. Alex went unwillingly, leaving Dane's gun on the table beside the bed, and carefully locking the window which opened on a fire escape. But Dane did not sleep. His head ached and his mind was working overtime. He lay still, his eyes closed, and carefully put together what he knew and what he suspected.

The bandage interfered with his hearing, however, and he was not aware that his door had opened softly. Only a sort of sixth sense told him he was not alone in the room. He did not open his eyes at once. Whoever it was came nearer, and then paused beside him.

He looked up then and reaching out a muscular hand grabbed the arm poised above him. His own automatic dropped on the bed, and Elinor Hilliard gave a faint scream and would have fallen had he not held onto her. In the faint light she looked paralyzed with terror.

"Just what were you trying to do?" he said. "Kill me?"

She shook her head.

"What are you going to do with me?" she said faintly.

"Send for Floyd, I imagine." His voice was hard. "You've got away with a good bit, Mrs. Hilliard. You're not getting away with this."

He released her. She dropped into a chair, her face chalk-white and her teeth chattering.

"I wasn't going to shoot you," she said. "You said I'd have to go to court. I just thought—if you'd keep out of things until it's all over—"

"Until Greg's convicted?"

"They'll never convict him. His record's too good. It was all circumstantial evidence anyhow."

Her color was slowly coming back. He was holding the gun, and she made no attempt to escape. He could see her better now, the thin scum of cold cream still on her face, the silk negligee, but he was pitiless and scornful.

"All along," he said, "you've been playing a game to save your own skin. I'm sick of you. If you didn't know certain things I'd hand you over to Floyd at once. I may yet. Now I want the truth. Who killed Marguerite Barbour?"

"I don't know," she moaned. "That's the truth. You can arrest me if you like. I still can't tell you."

He believed her. He did not like her. He wanted to take her lovely cold-creamed throat and choke her to death, for her heartlessness and selfishness. But this was the truth and he knew it. His head was aching damnably. He lay back for a minute and closed his eyes.

"What do you know about Greg's marriage?" he asked. "Had he any enemies?"

She seemed surprised.

"I wouldn't know. I suppose so."

He looked at her.

"Could it have been a trap?"

"Of course it was a trap. That little bitch—"

"I don't mean that," he said, his voice tired. "Suppose someone wanted to get rid of the girl, and Greg was drunk. It would have been easy, wouldn't it? Greg had money. If she was told that—"

But she didn't know even that. He took her again, slowly

and painfully, through the night of the murder. She answered him as though she was sleepwalking, but at one question she roused.

"Did you see anyone in the lane when you arrived that night? At or near the lane?"

"Near it, yes," she said. "But it couldn't have been important, could it?"

It was daylight when he let her go back to her room and her bed, with a warning.

"Even money can't buy you out of some things," he told her. "And I'm not forgetting tonight. I don't forget easily. You're coming out with all you know when the time comes—unless you want your husband to learn about this."

She crept out like a whipped dog, and he managed to get up and lock the door behind her.

He was wide awake and much improved the next morning when a nurse brought him a shoe box, closely tied with string. She was curious. She stood holding it in her hands, weighing it tentatively.

"Not flowers," she said, smiling. "Not food. Maybe tobacco. You're not supposed to smoke, you know."

"I doubt very much if it's tobacco," he told her, and put it aside until she had gone.

Tim and Alex had taken him literally. He eyed with extreme distaste the collection of old horseshoe nails, dingy buttons, the eroded leather handle of a riding crop, and a rusted shoe horn. In the bottom, however, he came upon treasure. He covered the box and put it on the table beside him.

By afternoon he was sitting up in bed, resenting the skullcap bandage on his head and demanding his trousers and some food. But about the shooting he was oddly reticent. He had walked up the lane, thought he heard someone moving at Pine Hill, and had gone in to investigate. Floyd, puzzled and annoyed, looked at him shrewdly.

"You didn't only hear someone moving, Dane," he said. "You saw whoever it was, didn't you?"

"Absolutely not."

"But you've got a damned good idea who it was, haven't you?"

"What makes you say that? How much can you see of a man behind a flashlight?"

Floyd got up out of his chair, his face flushed with anger.

"I don't want to go after a man in your condition," he said, "but all along, Dane, you've been holding out on me. Either you're coming clean now or I'll arrest you as an accessory to murder. Greg Spencer wasn't alone when he killed that girl. If you know who helped him—"

"I'm sorry, Floyd," Dane said soberly. "Maybe I underestimated you at the beginning. You've done a smart job, and it isn't your fault you've been off on the wrong foot all along."

"You're crazy," Floyd shouted furiously. "I've got Spencer, and you know it. He'll go to trial, and he'll be convicted."

Dane only lay back and closed his eyes, leaving Floyd to depart in helpless rage. The chief went back to his office and sitting at his desk went over his case against Greg. It was foolproof, he thought: the motive, his engagement to marry again, his lack of any alibi in New York, the accurate knowledge by the killer of the house where the body was found, and Greg's presence in the town when Lucy Norton died. Even the child, he thought. It all fitted. Why the merry hell had Dane said he was off on the wrong foot?

After a time he called the district attorney on the phone.

"What do you make of this attack on Dane?" he said. "Fit in anywhere?"

Campbell was in a bad humor.

"Not unless he did it himself!" he snapped. "It's playing the devil with the case. The governor's been on the wire. Seen the papers?"

"Don't want to see them," Floyd said curtly, and hung up.

Late that night Dane, still nursing a bad headache and a considerable grouch, was roused by cautious footsteps on the fire escape outside his room. Alex had at last gone home, after locking the window and drawing the shade.

"Bad room to give you, sir," he said. "Don't trust that fire escape. Someone's gunning for you, and no mistake."

Dane laughed.

"Go home and go to sleep, Alex," he said. "That shot wasn't

meant to kill me. It was meant to scare somebody off. Or anybody."

Alex stalked out, but not before he had once more placed Dane's automatic on the table beside him. It was still there when, shortly after midnight, Dane heard cautious footsteps on the fire escape outside. He took the gun and sliding out of bed, stood beyond range beside the window. He was there when the steps reached the top and someone rapped carefully on the windowpane.

Whomever he had expected—and he had expected someone —it was not the young voice which answered his challenge.

"It's Starr," it said. "From the press. I have some news for you."

Dane unlocked the window, and Starr crawled in. He looked excited, and as Dane stood by he drew a piece of paper from his pocket. Dane read it without expression.

"Came through two hours ago on the teletype," he said, grinning. "See it in the paper in the morning! Queer story, isn't it?"

Dane looked tired.

"It happens, you know. It's a queer war. May I keep this?"

"Sure. I copied it for you. That's not what I came for, anyhow. I guess I'll have to plead guilty to entering and stealing. I was in the yellow room at Crestview the night the Hilliard woman was shot. I wasn't the first," he said defensively, seeing Dane's face. "I was over here late. The night telephone operator is a friend of mine." He flushed slightly. "I was on the main road when I saw the ambulance come out, and then another car. Well, I'm a newspaperman. What would you have done?"

He waited until Dane got back into bed, then he repeated the story he had told Carol in the bar. At the end, however, he grinned sheepishly. He pulled another paper out of his pocket and laid it in front of Dane.

"Found it behind the baseboard," he said. "It sort of came loose in my hand. It's the kid's birth certificate. I thought you might be interested in the name she gave him. For his father, of course."

Dane read it, then laid it down.

"I'd like to know why you held this out," he said coldly.

"You might have saved me a lot of trouble."

Starr smiled sheepishly.

"Have a heart, major. It promised to be a story. When I got around to it you were on the Coast. What was I to do? He couldn't have killed her anyhow. But that's not what brought me tonight," he said, brightening. "I know from the telephone operator who it was who called the police last night to say you'd been shot."

He looked expectant, but Dane's face did not change.

"Thanks," he said dryly, "I know that already."

Late as it was—or early in the morning—Dane made two calls as soon as Starr had gone. One was to Dr. Harrison. The doctor was naturally annoyed but alert when he heard Dane's voice.

"Sorry to disturb you at this hour," Dane said, "but it's rather important. Going back to the way the Barbour girl was killed, she was struck more than once, wasn't she?"

"Two or three times. One blow did most of the damage. The skull was pretty thin."

"You thought of a poker, didn't you?"

"Or a golf club, yes. What's it all about, Dane?"

"Just one thing more. Have you had an inquiry lately as to the exact nature of the injury which caused death?"

"Well, yes. Of course it was quite casual. I was making a professional call yesterday on—"

"Never mind," Dane said sharply. "No names, please. And thanks."

TWENTY-EIGHT

MR. WARD REACHED THE HOSPITAL early the next morning, to find a flustered nurse coming out of Dane's room carrying a washbasin and Dane's voice raised in fury.

"You get me a pair of pants," he bellowed. "If Alex took mine snatch some off one of the doctors. I'll be damned if I go around like this, draped in a blanket! Where the hell are my slacks?"

Nathaniel found him in the center of the room, his face red with indignation and a blanket held around him, over the short hospital shirt. He had the grace to look embarrassed.

"These institutions," he said as he got into bed. "Trying to wash my face for me and refusing to get me my clothes. I'm all right. It was only a graze."

He smiled, his tanned face under the white turban of bandage looking rather odd, but the old gentleman apparently did not notice. He stood inside the door as though uncertain. Then he advanced to the side of the bed and laid the morning paper on the covers.

"I take it you've seen what's here," he said. "I've come to you, major, instead of going to the police. I need some advice."

His voice was steady, the thin reedy pipe of a very old man, but he looked shaken.

"I imagine I know what it is," Dane said. "Sit down, sir, won't you?"

He glanced at the paper. Starr's story was there. He read it quickly, then he put it down.

"He has courage," he said. "The whole story is incredible, isn't it? And four Jap planes shot down!"

Mr. Ward sat very still for a moment.

"I think he wanted to die," he said finally. "Is that courage or desperation?"

"They're often the same," Dane said quietly. "At least it's no longer necessary to try an innocent man for a murder he did not commit."

Mr. Ward stiffened.

"I would never have allowed Greg Spencer to suffer, Major Dane," he said with dignity. "Since my wife's death the necessity for silence is over. I did what I could. Now of course it is out of my hands. That is why I have come to you in spite of what has happened. You're a military man. Where does justice lie, major? A quarrel, a blow, and against that the story there in the paper."

"That's what happened, is it?"

"So he told me. He was desperate. He came back to the library where I was waiting for him, and he acted like a madman. I went over to Crestview at once, hoping she was only unconscious. But she was dead, lying half in and half out the doorway, and Elinor Hilliard was bending over her body.

"I'd never seen her before. I didn't know who she was until Elinor told me she was Greg's wife. I think she thought then Greg might have done it. But she was frantic that night. She wanted time to get away, and she wouldn't let me call Lucy Norton, or anybody.

"I don't suppose I can tell you the horror I felt. It was Elinor's idea to hide the body. She didn't care where, so she herself could escape. You know Elinor," he said wryly. "She didn't care about the girl at all. Her whole idea was to gain a few hours.

"She wanted me to carry her up to the linen closet, but I'm not young. Later I did get her up in the elevator. I laid her out as decently as I could. And that's what I was doing when Lucy came along the hall. It was the worst minute of my life when she stopped at the door of the closet, major. I did the only thing I could think of, I reached out and knocked the candle out of her hand. Then in the dark I tried to get away, and I'm afraid I bumped against her and knocked her down.

"She wasn't hurt. She got up screaming and made for the stairs, and I heard her fall. When I found her in the hall below she had fainted. I didn't know she was injured, of course. My only idea at first was to get Elinor safely away. And I had to work fast. Elinor was still outside—she hadn't come in at all—and she wanted the girl's clothing. She was anxious not to have her identified, at least not for a time. We didn't expect to have more than a few minutes, until Lucy Norton came to, but even that would give her time to get away.

"Maybe I should have called the police, but look at my position. I had a half-crazy boy on my hands, and the shock might have killed someone I care for. There was Elinor to consider, too. I had got the girl's clothing from the yellow room, and she was in a hurry to go. I suppose you can guess the rest. We had to get him away and Elinor agreed to drive him to Boston, where he could get a plane. He wasn't in uniform, you know.

"Well, I am a pretty old man, and I was in bad shape when they left. Elinor didn't help me, either. At the last minute she thrust the girl's clothes at me and told me to burn them. But I couldn't burn them." He smiled thinly. "We have an oil furnace."

"So that's why you buried them?"

"Yes, I did it that night. I couldn't get into my own tool house. The gardener keeps the key. I got a spade from the one at Crestview. I didn't do a very good job, I'm afraid, but I lifted a plant or two and replaced them. It wasn't easy in the dark, and I didn't know about her fur jacket. It was in the powder room downstairs. I found it when I went back to see if Lucy was badly hurt. One of the worst things I had to do was to go back to the closet with it and try . . ."

He seemed unable to go on. Dane, watching him closely, asked him if he needed brandy. He refused.

"I'm glad to talk," he said. "It helps a little. I've carried a burden for a long time, and a sense of guilt too. When I told my wife the next night she almost lost her mind, and when later on she saw them digging up the hillside she—it killed her." He stopped again. "I have that to add to my sins," he said heavily. "After more than fifty years, major. My dear wife . . ."

He managed to go on, although it was obviously a struggle.

"It was unfortunate that I had not told her the night it happened," he said. "She had been out looking for me, and she had seen Elinor's car. It was too bad, for she mentioned it later to a caller, and as it turned out Marcia Dalton had seen the car too and recognized it as Elinor's."

He sat back in his chair, as if he had finished, and as if the telling of the story had exhausted him. Dane could not let it stop at that, however.

"How did he get to your house that night?" he asked.

"Quite openly. By plane and then taxicab. And I assure you there was no murder in him when he came. I was alone downstairs. My wife and the servants had gone to bed. I let him in. You can imagine how I felt when I saw him, in civilian clothes and with a scar on his face. He was excited, but perfectly normal. I would have said he was a happy man that night. Of course we had to take certain precautions. You understand that. To avoid shock."

"He didn't mention the girl?"

"No. I don't think he knew she was at Crestview. He was too excited to go to bed, he said, and he went out for a walk. I suppose he saw her then, at Crestview. I didn't know she was there myself, or who she was."

"He'd been fond of her?"

"Long ago. Not lately. Later on he told me he had been keeping her while he was in training, and that she had had a child by him. He said she'd been a damned nuisance ever since."

"And that night?" Dane prompted him.

"I don't know. I never asked him. She may have gone downstairs for something, a book or a cigarette, and he saw her through a window. He must have attracted her attention somehow, but she couldn't very well bring him into the house. She went outside, just as she was. Certainly she wasn't afraid of him."

"He admitted that he'd killed her?"

"He said it was an accident. He had hit her with his fist, and her head struck the stone step. Later he said he'd introduced her to Greg Spencer last year, while Greg was drinking. Said he told her to marry him. He had plenty of money. He wanted to get rid of her, of course."

There was a long silence. Dane was trying to co-ordinate the story with what he already knew. Some parts of it fitted, some did not. He stirred.

"I'm sorry, Mr. Ward," he said. "This next question will be painful, but I have to know. Did he try to burn the body? You see, I know he was staying at Pine Hill."

The old man looked sick. His face was a waxy yellow and his hands were shaking. Dane was about to ring for a nurse, but he made a gesture of protest.

"It's all right," he said unevenly. "It can do no harm now. God forgive, major. I think my wife did it."

"Your wife!"

"I had told her the story, you see. All of it, and she was a woman of strong loyalties and deep affections. She knew the body was there, and that Lucy was in the hospital. And she had a key to Crestview. We have stayed through the winter once or twice, and she would go in occasionally to see that everything was all right.

"I imagine Lucy had left some kerosene in the kitchen. There was no electric light on, and she was using a lamp there. From the first my wife was certain the dead girl would be identified and we would be involved. But also she could not endure the thought of her being where she was. She wanted me to take her back into the country and bury her. But I was not strong enough to dig a grave."

Dane had suppressed his astonishment, but he found himself rigid with pity.

"I see," he said. "After all, who can blame her? The girl was dead."

"She had been dead for two days. I think she did it on Sunday night after I had gone to church. It was a dreadful thing to do, but the weather was warm, and Carol was coming the next day. My wife never told me, of course, but I remember little things now, the tea set in the tool house and one or two other things Mrs. Spencer valued. I remember, too, that she had asked me if the house was insured."

He got out a neat handkerchief and dried the palms of his hands.

"She looked very ill that night, but she wouldn't let me call a doctor. I remember she didn't go to sleep. She sat by a window, looking out at Crestview. But of course the house didn't burn."

Dane gave him a minute or two to recover before he spoke again.

"When did you know he had come back?"

"He never went very far. Certainly not to Boston. He was afraid of what the girl might have told Lucy Norton. Elinor says he went only a few miles that night. The next thing I knew he was hiding up at Pine Hill, hoping to see Lucy and keep her quiet. Both of us—my wife and I—were nervous about him by that time, but we managed to feed him, and I took a couple of blankets to him. I suppose he did see Lucy," he added grimly, "and the shock killed her."

"What about Elinor Hilliard?" Dane inquired. "Why was she shot?"

"She was badly worried. You can understand that. I suppose she meant to see me that night. Lucy's death had frightened her. Or she may have meant to look for the clothes I'd buried. But he was not a killer, major. I hope you realize that. She may only have been in his way. Colonel Richardson was after him, you know. He may only have fired a shot to stop Henry and it struck Elinor. I don't know. I never saw him after that night. As a matter of fact I drove him to the railroad myself. But he would not talk."

Dane was thoughtful for some time. The old man was fumbling in a pocket.

"You slipped up about the blankets at Pine Hill," Dane said finally. "Why did you leave them there? You'd made a good job of the rest of it."

The old man produced a letter and laid it on his knee. He took off his pince-nez and wiped them.

"When you reach my age," he said wryly, "you forget things. When I remembered them it was too late. You'd already found them and told Floyd. And I'd lost my glasses when I was carrying out the empty cans he'd left. That is why—"

He got up, the letter in his hand.

"That is why I shot you, major," he said. "You knew I did it, of course?"

"I knew it, yes," Dane said soberly.

Nathaniel stood, looking down awkwardly at the man in the bed.

"I don't know what is proper under such circumstances," he said. "I can't apologize. I can only explain. I had missed my glasses some time before, and that night I went to look for them. When I heard you—my nerves aren't what they were. But I never meant to shoot you, only to frighten you off. I beg you to believe that."

"I'm glad you're not a better shot," Dane said cheerfully. "I thought it was like that when I was able to think at all. You see, I understand a great deal, Mr. Ward. More than you think, perhaps." He reached for the shoe box. "You'll find your glasses in here," he said, "but they're broken. Don't pay any attention to the other stuff. Just throw it away. Only"—he added with a smile—"I suggest you don't bury it."

Mr. Ward took the box awkwardly.

"What about the police?" he asked. "Should I go to them? Before he left he sent me a statement, to be opened after his death, or in case Gregory Spencer was convicted. I am keeping it at home."

"Let's wait a bit," Dane suggested. "Greg Spencer won't be tried for some time. And things sometimes work out. After all you may be wrong, you know."

The letter was on his bed when Nathaniel went out, and Dane marveled at the strength which had carried the old man through the last few weeks, and which might have to carry him even further. It was some little time when at last he picked up the letter and began to read it.

TWENTY-NINE

HE KNEW AT ONCE when Carol came in that morning she had seen the newspapers. She was very quiet, but she went to his arms at once.

"I don't want to talk about it, Jerry," she said. "Later, perhaps. Not now."

"Just so it doesn't change things between us, darling."

"Nothing is changed," she said steadily.

"Have you seen the colonel?"

"I stopped there. I didn't see him. His man said he wasn't feeling very well." She stopped, and withdrew herself from his arms. "What am I to do, Jerry? It seems so brutal somehow."

"I think that it will settle itself, Carol," he said, his steady eyes on her.

He put her in a chair—he was dressed by that time, and a small dressing had replaced the bandage—and sat down near her.

"This is not going to be easy, darling," he told her. "And I'll ask you to withhold judgment for a while. I want to read you a letter. Mr. Ward brought it in this morning."

He offered her a cigarette, but she refused, and he read the letter through to the end. Now and then he looked up, but she made no comment. She sat with her clear candid eyes on him, her face rather pale but otherwise calm.

He left off the salutation, and a following unimportant paragraph or two. He began:

"I have some news for you both, but I want you to keep it to yourselves for a while. I've found Don Richardson."

Dane glanced at Carol. She had not moved, and he went on: "I was visiting one of our fellows in a hospital, and Don was in a convalescent ward. He was playing dominoes with a sergeant, and at first he didn't see me. When he did he only looked puzzled.

" 'I think I've met you somewhere,' he said.

" 'Why you old son of a so-and-so!' I told him. 'I'll say you have. What's the matter with you?'

"Then the fellow with him said he'd lost his memory. He'd been for months on an island somewhere. The natives had looked after him, but he'd had a fractured skull. 'Got a silver plate there now,' the sergeant said. 'Been here for a good while. But things are coming back, aren't they?' he said to Don. 'You knew this guy all right.'

"Well, he didn't. Not at first anyhow. He was not in an officers' ward, for nobody knew who he was. He was just part of the flotsam and jetsam of a war, brought back and dumped. I had to hurry, but I went back the next day, and he was definitely on the up-and-up.

" 'You're Terry Ward,' he said. 'I know you now.'

"He didn't remember his crash or the island, either, but he asked about his father. He didn't want him to know until he could get back to see him. Old Richardson has a bad heart, you know. And when I'd seen him several times he said I was to write you this, that he would come to you first, and then you could all arrange how to break it to his dad so it wouldn't be a shock.

"I suppose I've been a help. They call him Jay here, because he was naked as a jay bird when they found him, and the natives had probably taken his identification tags. I agreed to keep his identity a secret until his father had learned it. To avoid shock. And I gave him a couple of hundred dollars. The reason I'm writing is that you may see him soon. He went AWOL from the hospital last week, and as I'll be leaving before long it will be up to you. Just remember this. He's changed a lot. Got a beard for one thing, although he's promised to shave it off. And they've done some plastic work on him. Not bad, but not good either. He's pretty much depressed. The boys say he talked about a Marguerite and somebody named Greg—maybe Greg Spencer—while he was delirious after the ether. And I'm sure he's got something on his mind he won't talk about.

"All I know is that he said he had some things to see to, then he was going back to the Pacific again to fly if he had to stow away to get there. He'll do it too, silver plate and all. It's the whale of a story, isn't it? Be good to him—but of course you will. He's had a rotten time. All my love to you both. Terry.

"P.S. I'll send you some sort of word if he comes back here, or manages to get back to his squadron. Just an okay."

When Dane looked up Carol was sitting with her eyes closed, as though to shut out something she could not bear. It was some time before she spoke. She was very pale.

"Marguerite!" she said. "Are you telling me that Don killed her? That Don came here and killed her? And shot Elinor? I don't believe it, Jerry. He wasn't like that."

His voice was gentle.

"I've told you this before, my darling. War changes men. They're not quite the same after it. And there are always designing women waiting around for them."

"But—murder!"

"I've asked you to withhold judgment, for a few hours anyhow. And don't forget this either, Carol darling. You've read the story in the paper. He wasn't only saved from that island. He got back to his squadron and has been fighting hard ever since."

"You think that condones what he did?" she asked. "He killed that girl because she had married Greg. And he's allowed Greg to be indicted, to sit in a cell and wait for trial. Is that courage? It's despicable, and you know it."

Dane glanced at his wrist watch. Something had to happen, and happen soon, unless he himself was crazy. Sitting on the edge of his bed—there was only one chair in the room—he began carefully to tell her Nathaniel Ward's story as he had heard it; softening nothing, making it as clear as he could. To this he added his own visit to the Coast, the Gates family, and finally the birth certificate.

Carol read it with only a slight rise of color.

"That only makes it worse," she said. "She bore him a child. She even named it for him! And then—"

She did not finish. Someone was coming along the hall. When the door opened Dr. Harrison came in. He looked grave and unhappy when he saw Carol.

"I'm afraid I have bad news for you, my dear."

She got up quickly.

"Not Greg!"

"No. Colonel Richardson died at his desk an hour ago. It was painless, of course. He was writing a letter at the time, and —well, it's understandable. He had taken bad news for two years like a man and a soldier. But good news—"

Dane drew a long breath. There were tears in Carol's eyes.

"He was one of the finest men I ever knew," she said quietly. "I'd better go there. He was all alone, except for his man. Perhaps I can do something."

Dane got Alex on the phone the moment she was out of the room. He gave him some brief instructions and hung up. His mind was already busy with what was to be done to quash the indictment against Gregory Spencer. They would reconvene the Grand Jury, he thought, and present the new evidence, and for once he was grateful for the secrecy of such proceedings. When Alex called all he said was a laconic "Okay," and Dane relaxed as though a terrific burden had been lifted from his mind.

Some time later Floyd was sitting across from him, his legs spread out and his face sulky.

"So you've made a monkey out of me," he said. "How the hell did you know?"

"I didn't. I worked on Terry Ward for some time. There had to be an X somewhere. Who was hiding out up at Pine Hill? Who got into the hospital, trying to talk to Lucy Norton, and scared her literally to death? Who ran into Elinor Hilliard at night and shot her in order to avoid recognition. Washington reported Terry was on the Coast and hadn't left there.

"Maybe I began to believe in miracles myself! But I was pretty well stymied. Washington had no record of Don's being alive. I couldn't discover anything on the Coast. Yet here were the Wards protecting somebody. Not Terry. He hadn't been east. All along they'd been in it. They—"

"Are you telling me old Nat Ward buried those clothes?" Floyd demanded.

"You'd better ask him," Dane said smoothly.

"All right. You've dug a lot of worms to get a fish," Floyd said resignedly. "So you pick on another hero for your fish! Don Richardson's guilty. How are you going to prove it?"

Dane settled back in his chair.

"I haven't said Don killed that girl, Floyd."

The chief sat forward, his face purple.

"Stop playing games with me," he bellowed. "First Don did it. He says he did. Then he didn't. Who the hell did?"

"The colonel," said Dane, lighting a cigarette. "The colonel, Floyd. And he never knew he had done it."

When Floyd said nothing, speech being beyond him, Dane went on.

"Figure it out for yourself. There was always X, you know. And X didn't behave like a guilty man. He hung around after it was over. He waited for the inquest. He tried to see Lucy Norton, to find out what she knew and hadn't told. Wouldn't a guilty man have escaped as soon as he could?"

"Pretty smart, aren't you?" Floyd said. "You got most of that from old Ward himself this morning!"

"All right," Dane said amiably. "I had two guesses, Don or the colonel. And if it was Don it didn't make sense. Why didn't he see his father? The colonel would have died to protect him. Instead of that Don took a farewell look at him through a window. The colonel didn't like the idea, so he tried to follow him. I don't think he even knew it was his own son. He really thought it was Terry Ward."

Floyd got out a bandanna handkerchief and wiped his face. He was sweating profusely.

"Go ahead," he said. "Go on and dream, Dane. So the colonel killed the girl and went home and had a good night's sleep. Go on. I can take it."

"Well, think it out for yourself," Dane said reasonably. "The colonel had been paying for the support of his grandson ever since he was born. He'd gone to the Coast and seen Marguerite—if that was really her name. I suspect she was born Margaret—and he knew her. Imagine his feelings when he saw her, the morning she arrived, on her way to Crestview. He was an early riser. He had to have seen her, to account for what happened. Maybe she saw him too.

"Anyhow he went up to the house that night, after Lucy had gone to bed. She couldn't take him into the house. She put on a negligee and went to the door to talk to him. I think she told him she had married Greg, and that she offered to bribe him. If he'd keep quiet about Don's baby he needn't pay any more hush money, or whatever you choose to call it.

"He must have been in a towering rage. Not only about the trade she suggested. Here she was, a little tramp, married to Carol's brother and capable of telling her she had been Don's mistress. Not that he thought it out, I imagine. I think he simply lost his head and attacked her. He didn't know he'd killed her, of course. He left at once, and from that Friday night until her body was found in the linen closet he must have thought she had got away. I saw him myself once, walking around the house, to be sure she had gone.

"The next thing he learned was that she was dead in the linen closet.

"He hadn't put her there. So far as he knew he hadn't killed her. I think all he felt was relief. She was out of the way, and someday he would locate the child and provide for him. The Wards believed Don Richardson had done it. Don had told them so. But his story didn't hold water. He said he'd knocked her down with his fist and she'd struck her head on the stone step. You saw that wound. It hadn't been made that way. I thought of a poker or a golf club. I didn't think of a thin skull and a heavy walking stick.

"After I found someone had been hiding out at Pine Hill I still had to do some guessing. I knew by that time it wasn't Terry Ward. I had the Wards looked up. Terry was the only relative they had. Whom were they protecting, and why? Whom were they feeding? And whom were they afraid of? They were afraid of someone. Old Nathaniel was carrying a gun. And when you dug up the clothes on the hillside Mrs. Ward had a stroke.

"But as I said before there was one thing I kept thinking about. Whoever shot Elinor Hilliard had been trying to escape from Colonel Richardson. That was out of the picture entirely. Why, in a pouring rain did X stand outside the colonel's window, peering in?

"Think that over, Floyd. Don Richardson was a happy man the night of the murder. He had got rid of the girl by marrying her to Greg Spencer while Greg was drunk. He'd always hated Greg, I imagine; the big house on the hill and the small one below, Greg's good looks, his money, even his plane. And he was on leave in Los Angeles the night of that party. I knew that from Washington.

"Then he gets here and takes a walk to quiet down. He goes over to Crestview. Why not? He's engaged to Carol, isn't he? He doesn't know the girl's there. He goes over by the path in the dark, and what he sees is his own father slashing at some-one with his cane! When his father's gone he goes over and strikes a match. It's Marguerite, and she's dead.

"Whatever his faults he was a good son. He loved his father, and his father was a sick man. What was he to do?

"Well, after all, he's presumed to be dead. What does it matter? He goes back to the Wards' with a fool tale that he's killed her, that he's knocked her down with his fist and she's hit her head on the stone doorstep. She wasn't lying on any stone doorstep when she was found. She was in the doorway of the house. That step is wood.

"My own idea is that she *had* been out that night. Remem-ber the pine needle in her slipper. She may even have gone down to the colonel's and he took her back, probably growing angrier all the way. It must have taken a lot to make him strike her. But he never knew he had killed her. The hall was dark—no electric current. He may not even have heard her fall. Nor even that Lucy Norton, seeing Don in the hospital that night, thought she was seeing a ghost and died of it.

"All along the colonel thought it was Terry Ward, and he was devoted to the Wards. He was sure it was Terry who had shot Elinor Hilliard. He did his best, got her out of the road and tried to call the doctor. But he wasn't the same after that. I saw him the next day. He put up a good show, but he was in poor shape."

Floyd stirred.

"Why was the Hilliard woman out that night anyhow?"

"I found a small hole on the hillside the next day. You see, she was covering up as well as she could. Nathaniel had told her he had buried the clothes, and she'd burned the hill. But she was still frightened. She had tried to save Don to save herself, but too much was going on. She was scared of him. So were they all, for that matter."

"She burned the hill!"

"Certainly. Who else? Carol Spencer knew it."

"Giving me the runaround again," Floyd grunted uneasily.

"As a matter of fact," Dane said, "you've got all the Spencers suspecting each other. That threw me off for a while. I suppose I've got a bias in favor of our fighting men, but I never thought Greg Spencer was guilty. I got Tim Murphy on the job—"

"Who's Murphy?"

"One of the best private operatives in New York. Got his own agency." And when Floyd relapsed into speechless fury Dane smiled.

"So," he began, "I began to believe in miracles myself. Don Richardson hadn't liked Greg, and it looked too much like co-incidence that Greg had married his girl. She *was* his girl. She'd named the boy for him. I found that out on the Coast, from his birth registration. And Terry Ward hadn't left the coast. So what? So maybe Don was alive after all.

"But, if it was Don, he wasn't acting like a man with a crime on his soul. He was hiding out at Pine Hill. Why?

"Well, I'd learned somebody else had a motive, had been paying a sort of blackmail since the boy was born. But I was still guessing until last night, when I learned that Colonel Richardson had been inquiring of the nature of the wound which killed the girl.

"Mr. Ward had mixed things up by shooting at me, and Elinor Hilliard was keeping her mouth shut. I only learned within the last few hours, for instance, that as she turned into the drive the night of the murder she saw the colonel going into his house, and he was carrying a stick."

"He always carried a stick," Floyd said belligerently. "I liked the old boy. Everybody liked him. If you're trying to say he killed that girl in cold blood—"

Dane's face looked very tired.

"Not at all," he said. "I'm saying that for the first time in his life Colonel Richardson struck a woman, and she died of it."

There was a prolonged silence. Then Floyd got up.

"I suppose you're sure of all this," he said heavily. "It's going to make a stink, Dane. That's bad for the town."

"Not necessarily. I want to say this. Don Richardson would never have allowed Spencer to suffer, or his father either. He went back to the Pacific to fight, but he left Mr. Ward a statement to be opened in case Spencer was convicted or he himself was killed."

"Saying he didn't?"

"Probably," Dane said dryly.

"Then where the hell are we?"

"Nowhere." He gave Floyd a grim smile. "Except that Greg Spencer will never go to trial."

"That's what you say," Floyd said, still truculent. "You've been doing a lot of guessing, Dane, but where's your proof? All you've done is lug in a dead man who can't defend himself. Who didn't even know he'd done it! I gave you credit for better sense."

"I think he did know it, the last day or so. Remember, he thought Mr. Ward was going armed against him. He said so. Then why? Had Nathaniel found the body and tried to dispose of it, to protect him? Did they know he had done it, and think he had lost his mind? He himself told me he was considered something of a crackpot around here.

"There's something else too, Floyd. It's just possible he thought he recognized Don at the window that rainy night. He wasn't sure, of course. That might have been the reason he followed him. In that case he must have been badly worried. Why hadn't Don come to see him? Why had he done none of the normal things? Had Don found the girl unconscious and killed her himself?"

"I'm betting on Don this minute," Floyd said. "Always was a wild kid. If that girl had two-timed him—"

"Let me go on," Dane said tiredly. "The colonel was in bad shape. He had to know. So yesterday he saw Dr. Harrison. The girl had died of one blow, by a poker or something similar. He knew then that he had killed her.

"I don't suppose he slept at all last night. Part of the time he spent writing out a confession. Then when he got the newspaper, with the news that Don was alive and fighting again, he collapsed."

Floyd's face was ugly.

"What's all this about a confession?"

"I have it here."

Floyd jerked it angrily from his hand and glanced at it. He looked apoplectic.

"How did you get hold of this?" he snarled. "Damn it all, Dane, you've been mixing in where you didn't belong ever since this case started."

"As soon as I'd heard from the doctor last night I called the colonel up and suggested it," Dane said coolly. "At its worst it was manslaughter, and he knew he hadn't long to live. Greg Spencer had to be saved somehow. You had too good a case, Floyd, and I hadn't any. The confession wasn't to be used unless Greg was found guilty. Don't blame the night telephone operator. I'm a friend of a friend of hers."

"How'd you get hold of it?"

"Oh, that! I sent Alex there this morning. Good man, Alex."

"He's a dirty snooper," Floyd bellowed, but Dane merely smiled.

"All right. Have it your own way. You'll find the colonel admits an excess of rage, during which he struck her with a heavy stick he was carrying, and seeing her fall. He admits leaving her there, but not knowing she was dead. He admits he'd been paying her what amounted to blackmail. He even admits to searching the yellow room later for the child's birth certificate and some evidence of where she had hidden him with the idea of collecting on him later. He didn't finish it, of course. His heart went back on him, or he would probably have claimed he tried to burn the body!"

"And who did?"

"Does that matter now?"

The two men stared at each other, the one shrewd and angry, the other hard and inflexible. Floyd got up.

"By God, Dane," he said, "I'm still not sure you didn't do it yourself!"

He stamped out, and Dane laughed quietly as the door slammed.

THIRTY

HE LEFT THE HOSPITAL that afternoon. Alex had stood by while he dressed, his one eye watching every movement.

"I'll bet that leg's bad again, sir," he said. "You aren't fooling me any."

"Leg! I wouldn't know I had a leg. I'll be going back soon, Alex. I have a little business to transact first. Then I'm off."

"What sort of business?" Alex inquired suspiciously. "Any more murders around?"

"This is different," Dane said, carefully knotting his tie. "Very, very different."

He was sober enough when he reached Crestview. Tim admitted him, a grinning Tim who reached for his cap with a deferential air, and spoiled it by clutching him by the arm.

"What the hell's cooking?" he said. "You're a tight-mouthed son of a so-and-so, but if you're letting me scrub pots while you have the time of your life running over the country and getting shot—"

Dane smiled.

"The pot scrubbing's over, Tim."

"Well, well! I suppose Floyd killed the girl. He's the only one I haven't suspected."

"I'll tell you later. Where's Miss Spencer?"

"Locked in her room. Maggie's been up half a dozen times with coffee. She won't let her in."

"I'll go up. She may see me."

He went up the stairs. He wasn't limping at all. In the upper hall he stopped at the door to the yellow room and looked in. It was a pretty room, he thought. The baseboard had been nailed back in place, the mulberry curtains were in neat folds, and the fragment of candle had been replaced by a fresh one, in case a storm shut off the electric current.

He glanced back along the hall. The linen closet had been repainted. It gleamed fresh and white in the light from the patio, and in the patio itself the pool had been repainted and filled. It shone like a bit of sky overhead, where a bomber was droning along, as if to remind him that there was still a war, and he had a place in it.

He moved along to Carol's door and rapped.

"It's Jerry," he said. "I have to see you."

He thought she hesitated. Then the key turned and she confronted him. She looked exhausted, but she was not crying. She stood aside to let him enter, but she made no movement toward him.

"I have to thank you for a great deal," she said quietly. "You've saved Greg, even if you had to kill Colonel Richardson to do it."

He looked puzzled.

"You told him about Don, didn't you? People don't die of joy. You called him from the hospital, and told him."

"I couldn't tell him anything he didn't know, Carol," he said gravely.

"What does that mean? If Don came here and killed that girl—"

"Listen, my dear," he said. "I'm feeling pretty low just now. I've made a mess of a lot of things, and I don't like the way the case has turned out. But remember this. I asked you today to withhold judgment. I needed something I didn't have at that time. Now I'm asking a question. Suppose Don is innocent, Carol?"

"You don't mean that Greg—"

"Not Greg. No. I'm wondering how you feel about Don, now that he is alive. You cared for him once. Now he is more than alive. He is fighting like a man. You can be proud of him. And the affair with Marguerite—can't you understand that? The hunger a man feels for a woman when he's been cut off from them for months, or years. He was young, and he'd been in training for a long time when he met her. He didn't know she was a—well, what she was."

"Are you defending him?"

"I am. He is even braver than you know, my dear. You see,

he confessed to a murder he didn't commit. That takes courage. Perhaps that changes things with you—and him."

"I'm not in love with him, if that's what you mean. But I don't understand," she said steadily. She sat down, looking lost and unhappy. "Why would he do such a thing?"

He told her then, moving around the room as he did so. Sometimes stopping in front of her, again looking out the window, where the bomber was circling lazily overhead and the empty harbor with its emerald islands lay below. Once he stopped and offered her a cigarette, but she shook her head.

"Go on," she said steadily. "I want to know it all. It's time I did, isn't it?"

When he had finished she sat very still. Nevertheless, except that she had lost color, she had taken it better than he had even hoped.

"It's hard to realize," she said, rather bleakly. "If it was anyone but the colonel. He was so kind, Jerry, so—gentle."

"He was a man," he reminded her. "Very much of a man, my dear. When that little tramp tried to bribe him he struck at her. I'm afraid I'd have done more than that."

She was trying to think things out, from this new angle.

"Then it was the colonel who scared Lucy, and shot Elinor. I—I don't believe it."

"Not the colonel, my dear. Don shot Elinor. I don't think he meant to, any more than Mr. Ward intended to hit me. It was an accident. He was trying to get away."

But he did not tell her, would never tell her, what he knew now was the real tragedy of that night; of Don, anxious for a last sight of his father, slipping down from Pine Hill in the rain to peer through a window and see the colonel, standing in full view in that lighted room. Or of the heartbreaking thing that had followed, the colonel starting up the lane after him and Don desperately trying to escape.

"What would happen if his father saw him? Can you imagine the Colonel keeping that news to himself? And what became of Don's statement to the Wards that he had killed the girl? Was he to tell his father that? The man who had done it without knowing it, and who had a bad heart anyhow? What did Elinor Hilliard matter, in a situation like that?

"He probably came across her unexpectedly," he said, "and he was pretty jumpy. Don't ask me where he got the gun, my darling. I don't know. It may have been Nathaniel Ward's. Don never meant to be taken alive. Be sure of that."

He sat down near her, watching her, wondering at the fortitude she had shown for the past month. Perhaps it was the same courage which had won Greg his decoration. Whatever it was he knew that he loved her more than he loved anything else in the world. It was no time to tell her so, however. Not so long as the bewildered look was still in her eyes.

"I still don't know why she went out at all that night, Jerry."

"I rather imagine," he said quietly, "she had decided to do away with the things on the hill. Too much was happening; Lucy's death the night before, for instance."

"Why did he come back, Jerry? It seems so strange. To hide out, up there on the hill—"

"Well, look, my dear. He was trying to protect his father. He waited for the inquest, but if Lucy knew anything she didn't tell it. Nevertheless he knew Marguerite too well to trust her. If she had told Lucy she was to see the colonel that night Lucy might break down, under pressure.

"So he saw Lucy that night at the hospital, and because she thought he meant to kill her, or perhaps because she thought he was a ghost, she—well, she died of fright. That's all I know, and it doesn't matter now. What does matter, my darling, is that it's over. All over."

She cried a little then, not for the colonel, at peace at last, not even—he realized gratefully—for Don, doing his man's work in a man's war. Some of it was relief, but there was grief, too; for the colonel, for Lucy, and for Joe now sitting alone in his empty house. For Mrs. Ward. And even, he thought wryly, for Marguerite herself, because she, too, had been young and had wanted to live. He let her alone, beyond giving her what he termed a perfectly good shoulder to weep on.

"More beautiful women than you have sobbed on it," he said. "But to hell with them. You're my girl now. Or are you?"

She smiled after a minute or two her old smile, which had so endeared her to him from the beginning.

"I'll be good to you, darling," he said gravely. "I've got a job to do, but I'll be coming back. I'd like to know I was coming back to you. Men have lived because of that, you know," he added. "Because they had someone to come back to."

"Why do I have to wait?" she asked. "I'm tired of being the spinster in the family. Or are you really asking me to marry you at last?"

He drew her into his arms, the muscular arms which had been trained to kill in many wartime ways, but which could also be gentle and protective.

"I'm asking you to marry me," he said. "Here and now. Before I go. Will you?"

"Tim gives you excellent references."

"Never mind Tim. Or Alex either. I'm not marrying them. Will you, darling?"

"Of course," she said. "I thought you'd never really say it."

There was nothing saturnine about his smile as he held her ever closer. He had forgotten his job. He had even forgotten his leg, which was fine. He put his full weight on it, and without warning it gave a jump and began to ache furiously. He released her with a grunt.

"Hell!" he said. "We may even have a little time for a honeymoon, sweetheart." And sat down abruptly on the nearest chair.